BEHIND THE FOOTLIGHTS

ALSO BY FRED SCHLOEMER

*Parenting Adult Children: Real Stories of Families
Turning Challenges into Successes*

*From a Land in Between: Prose and Poem
Tales of Alternative Lives*

Just One More Bird

BEHIND THE FOOTLIGHTS

a novel

FRED SCHLOEMER

BUTLER BOOKS

This book is a work of fiction. Names, characters, places, and incidents either are products of the author's imagination or are used fictitiously. Any resemblance to actual events or locales or persons, living or dead, is entirely coincidental.

Designed by Eric Butler

ISBN 978-1-941953-05-1

Printed in the United States of America

Published by
Butler Books
P.O. Box 7311
Louisville, KY 40257
phone: (502) 897-9393
fax: (502) 897-9797
www.butlerbooks.com

To the Trinkle family, and to every player, director, or other participant in regional theater across the nation, with deep thanks for the joy and inspiration you bring to others through your talent, hard work, and devotion to your craft.

CONTENTS

ACKNOWLEDGEMENTS

There are so many people to whom I am indebted for their help with this, my first novel.

Foremost are dear friends, Lore and Bob Trinkle, who not only gave their permission for me to draw on their inspiring love story, but also gave additional information, support, and encouragement as my work progressed.

Secondly, I want to thank another dear friend, Susie Stauffer, for her invaluable help making the many corrections suggested by my editor. It was tedious work to be sure, but a job she did willingly and wonderfully.

Additionally I want to thank lifelong friends, Ida and David Lee, for letting me use David's powerful Vietnam diary as the basis for the chapters dealing with that war. I know how hard it is for Vietnam veterans to relive any aspect of that painful journey, and I can never adequately express my gratitude to you, David, for sharing your experiences with me.

Thanks also go to my friend, Emma March, a retired pilot and aeronautics expert, for her valuable input on the history and flying record of the DC-3 prop airplane featured in Chapter 9. Your suggestions, Emma, about how a DC-3 would respond in the midst of engine failure helped me make sure that chapter was realistic and plausible.

I also want to thank dear friend and traveling companion, Tom Young, for his enthusiastic interest, as I finished final revisions and wrote additional chapters while we vacationed together. You seemed almost more excited than I, Tom, at the progress I was making, and your excitement spurred me on.

Deep thanks, too, to my editor, Susan Lindsey of Savvy Communication, for her tremendously detailed and helpful review of my work. I consider you responsible in part, Susan, for my last book winning a national award, and I take your advice very seriously.

And last but not least, deep thanks and great love to my life partner, Ernie Schnell, who always said, "Write as long as you need to," as I worked on this piece, often long after he was in bed.

Countless poems and songs have been written about the value of friends. I know that I for one certainly couldn't get by without mine, nor could I have ever completed this work without them.

Fred Schloemer
St. Pete Beach, Florida
October 2013

Five years ago, I attended a production of *The Sound of Music* at the tiny Hayswood Theater in Corydon, Indiana. The Hayswood is a community theater owned and operated by local residents who enjoy bringing live entertainment to people who normally have to go to nearby Louisville to enjoy the performing arts.

Sitting in the audience before the show, I found myself captivated by the actors' bios in the program. One after the other, the mostly amateur players enthused about this, their first experience on the stage. Most stated that they hoped that it wouldn't be their last. School children, homemakers, and retired veterans alike had all found the experience to be a life-altering event. After landing a part, some of the children aspired to a career in the arts; some of the seniors just appreciated the chance to be on a stage, doing something creative and productive.

But the best was yet to come. When the play began, I was pleasantly surprised to see that this was no half-baked production put on by a bunch of "not ready for prime time players." On the contrary, it was a highly polished production of a much-loved musical, one that has become iconic.

The producer and director of this little gem was my friend, Bob Trinkle, helped by his wife, Lore, and their family theater troupe, Bob Trinkle Productions. The Trinkles are a fun-loving

German-Irish Catholic clan, who are best-known in these parts for their murder mystery productions performed at the French Lick Resort Casino.

Watching the performers close the play by climbing up the aisles of the theater to the lobby, in lieu of "climbing every mountain" to escape Nazi-occupied Austria, I was moved by the faces of the players. Most of them were school children, wrapping up the first serious acting experience of their lives, and they were all beaming.

There's a story here, I thought at the time, about the importance of regional theater in America's vibrant arts scene. Now, after five years, here is that story at last. While it is inspired by real people I know and admire, I need to clarify that the people and events in this particular story are fictional.

I hope that readers will enjoy reading this story as much as I have enjoyed writing it. To Bob and Lore Trinkle, all I can add is, "Thanks for the memories."

Fred Schloemer

BEHIND THE FOOTLIGHTS

PART I

PALMER'S RIDGE, INDIANA

Population 2,051
Spring 1953

CHAPTER I

CATCHING HELL

Glancing at his classmates milling about on the schoolyard from his perch up in the tree, D. W. thought that they looked a lot like ants. He inched out a bit farther on the stout branch, and held his arms outstretched at his sides, like he had seen tightrope walkers do when his folks took him to Louisville for the annual Shriner's Circus.

His front foot slipped a bit as he took the next step, and he almost lost his balance, sending a shriek of alarm through the girls on the ground. The sound went through him like the pleasant warmth he got from the bourbon toddies his mother sometimes gave him at bedtime. All eyes were on him. The clear spring day was warm, and the sky above them was a deep teal blue. Even the few jeering voices calling insults up to him couldn't mar this wonderful moment.

"Come on down," an older boy ordered. "You won the dare. No sense breaking your silly neck, too!"

"Yeah, Singer, know when to quit," another boy chimed in, sounding half peremptory, half worried. "You made your point. Climb down before you fall down."

The more dulcet tones of the girls' voices couldn't mask their contempt for the boys calling up to him now. "Why don't *you* climb up and get him?" one asked with an arch tone.

"Yeah," another girl chided. "Since you're so brave and bossy, get yourself on up there and bring him down over your shoulder. You said he could never do it. Said you'd done it a dozen times before. But I don't see you scrambling up there now to prove how brave *you* are . . . like he did."

D. W. listened, taking it all in and savoring every second of the drama. At six years old, he was short and slender for his age, clearly no match for the bigger, more athletic boys in his class. They could all do things with a ball or a bat or a racquet that he found impossible and incomprehensible. He did know this for certain . . . not a one of them had an ounce more nerve than he did. Now he was proving it, much to the delight of several girls who had previously looked on him like some cute little brother.

"Don't listen to those old fuddy-duddies, D. W." one of the girls called up to him. "I think you're very brave."

Her words were like music to him. Stirred to further theatrics by the accolade, he dropped his hands to his sides, stepped off the branch and fell several feet. He was pleased to hear screams fill the air, not only from the girls this time, but from the boys as well. Just when it looked like he would fall to the ground far below, he caught a limb in his hands and arrested his descent. A pleased cry and a huge round of applause wafted up to him from the gathering below, filling his heart with pride, and sending a tingling sensation through his body.

He didn't know it at the time, but would later learn that philosophers throughout history have commented on the transcendent, life-changing experiences people often have in the midst of their mundane lives—those unexpected moments when people realize that they have encountered the sublime. So even though he didn't have the language to describe this moment, D. W. knew that something very special was going on, something that had never happened before, but that he hoped would happen again and again. It would become the moment that defined who he really was, and the memory of it would be with him all of his life.

Hanging from the branch by his thin, wiry arms, he listened to the crowd below, murmuring and worrying and conjecturing about what would happen next. The tension was both intense and exquisite.

"Maybe we should go get the fire department to bring a ladder," someone said.

"Mr. Peabody down at the drugstore has a hot air balloon," someone else offered, eliciting a chorus of groans.

D. W. knew that he didn't need these interventions. He was small, but also strong, and he was having no trouble whatsoever hanging onto the thick limb. He began crossing one hand over the other, sliding his way back to the massive tree trunk, where he could step down onto the next lowest branch, and start climbing back to the ground. He was making good progress until a wasp lit on his bare neck and stung him.

"Ow!" he cried. "Ow, ow, ow, ow, ow!"

"What's wrong, D. W.?" one of the girls called.

"Hey, Singer," one of the older boys jeered. "Havin' a problem, are you?"

He struggled to hold onto the branch, as the wasp venom shot through his central nervous system and connected with his brain stem, sending a weird, cold feeling all over him. His head started to swim and his muscles to tremble. He felt his grip begin to loosen, and watched his fingers slip from the smooth bark.

"What's Ma gonna do if I break any more bones?" he wondered.

Just as he thought of her, he heard her strident voice booming up at him.

"D. W. Singer, what in the world have you gotten yourself into now?" she shrieked. With his last bit of consciousness, he looked down to see his mother glaring up at him, her hands on her hefty hips and a huge frown on her powdered face.

"Oh, hi, Ma," he managed to say with a wan smile. "Glad you could drop by to see the show." With that, he passed out, dropping twenty feet through the air and landing squarely into her outstretched arms.

Despite the slightness of his frame, the combined weight of his body and the momentum of his fall sent them tumbling to the ground together, where they bumped heads hard enough to knock them both out. They lay there unconscious until the older kids summoned Doc Marcum.

Once there, the doctor pulled out his smelling salts and revived the mother first, then shook his head in a resigned way. "What have we got here this time?" he asked as she came to, blinking her eyes and struggling to rise.

D. W.'s mother looked at the boy lying prone beside her and back at the doctor. "This boy is going to be the death of me," she pronounced to the whole gathering. "You mark my words. He's going to be my death!"

Still stretched out beside his mother, and beginning to regain consciousness, D. W. smiled. In the dream that was starting to slip away, he was standing at the edge of a stage, behind the footlights, taking his bows before a theater filled with people who were all honoring him with wild applause. The clapping and cheering were deafening, and they went on forever. He thought it was the sweetest sound he had ever heard.

CHAPTER 2

GREAT AND SMALL
EXPECTATIONS

Everyone in the small Southern Indiana town of Palmer's Ridge knew that hometown boy D. W. Singer was destined for great things—everyone, that is, except for his parents. They had decided to call him D. W. to avoid calling him "Junior," after his father Drake Wyeth Singer, considering that appellation to be one that was far too common in these backwoods hills of Indiana. If there was anything Alexandra and Drake Singer wanted to avoid, it was being common.

As the only child of the town's sole funeral home director and general store owner, D. W. had all the advantages any young man might hope for. He was smart, handsome, talented, and popular. From first grade on, girls had batted their eyelashes at him on the school playground, laughed behind their hands, and vied for his attention, which he loved lavishing on them. He was a ladies' man from the day he was born.

Always a fun-loving boy, he had distinguished himself among his peers as the class clown. No matter what the situation, D. W. could always be counted on to play some practical joke, make a funny face behind the teacher's back, or deliver an impersonation of a pompous community leader to entertain his classmates.

That was the problem, his teacher, Betty Triplett, realized. She sat at her scratched wooden desk with his file spread out before her on the ancient marred surface. Looking over his miserable test scores and conduct grades, she sighed and shook her head. The boy and his mother were on their way for a special meeting with her that the principal had insisted on, after catching D. W. in the school cafeteria mimicking the Baptist preacher, much to the delight of the whole school.

It would all be so much easier, Betty knew, if D. W. wasn't so bright and engaging. She had lost count of the times she had been at the blackboard when the sound of ill-concealed tittering had come from behind her and she had whipped around to catch D. W. standing on his chair, pantomiming and making silly faces.

He could slip into these theatrics and be off task so rapidly, that it took all of her guile as a seasoned teacher to catch him. When she did, it was always the same. He would slip back into his seat, put his pencil to his paper, and then look up at her and smile that wonderful heart-melting D. W. Singer smile. No matter how much she hated to admit it, she had never seen anything like it.

In all her years as a teacher in the struggling, economically depressed little town, there had never been a boy with greater promise. It was the reason she always gave him another chance to make up missed work or win back her good graces. Betty Triplett was nearing retirement. She had never married and had children of her own, but she realized that if she had, she would have hoped for a son exactly like D. W., quirks and all.

Not only was he smart and talented, but he was genuinely lovable. She couldn't remember meeting anyone who didn't like him, except perhaps his mother. She couldn't really say what his father might feel for him, as the man had never come to school for a meeting or any other reason; no ball games, or fundraisers or spaghetti suppers—nothing. She could only say that the man was conspicuous in his absence, and assume that if he did care, he would have been more present in his troubled son's life.

Betty had been in Drake Singer's funeral home and store often through the years, but had seldom had more than a brief exchange of words with him. He was a handsome and elegant man, but also a cold and aloof one, with thick white hair and distant gray eyes that never made direct contact with others. Given his glacial bearing, she couldn't fathom how he had managed to pull off the string of affairs he was reputed to have had with countless local women. However, thinking of his wife, Betty couldn't say that she blamed Drake much for his infidelities.

Alexandra Singer was undoubtedly the most negative person Betty had ever met, as melancholic and pessimistic as her spirited son was cheerful. Jokes flew all across town about her legendary fatalism. When asked, "How do you do?" She invariably replied, "Doing poorly, thank you." Alexandra would then proceed to tell the inquirer exactly how poorly she was doing, detailing her numerous physical complaints, from lumbago to migraines, or her even greater emotional challenges, from coping with "that man I married who *lives* at his workplace," or "that boy Jesus sent me to teach me patience."

Betty had to admit that D. W.'s family presented a bit of the old chicken-and-egg dilemma. One couldn't be sure where the grievances began, with the wandering husband who abandoned his wife, or the whining wife who drove her husband away. All Betty knew was that D. W. had somehow come this far in his eight-year-old life with a remarkably sunny disposition, in spite of all the misery that appeared to exist under his roof at home.

As she mulled all of this, Betty heard footsteps down the hall and the sound of Alexandra's harsh voice. "Straighten your shoulders, D. W.," she barked. "And where is your comb? You didn't clean up like I told you to. Land sakes, but you're a handful!"

Betty cringed at the sound, far worse than the screech her chalk sometimes made on the blackboard. But she had to force a welcoming smile nonetheless. She was a professional after all, and owed even this difficult parent her respect. The breathless woman finally made it through the door, laboring under her considerable weight and the extra effort of dragging D. W. beside her by his elbow.

"I'm sorry we're late," Alexandra said, frowning down at D. W., and crossing her arms. "But I'll give you three guesses whose fault that was."

D. W. ignored her and looked up at Betty. "Hey, Miss Triplett." He grinned. "You sure are working late, aren't you? Bet you'll be glad to get home tonight, huh?"

Betty smiled. It was so like him—one part charm and artfulness, trying to change the subject of how he had made them late and one part genuine concern about others' comfort. She looked down at the winsome face: the tawny eyes sparkling with mirth, the ruddy complexion dusted with freckles, the riot of chestnut hair, always disheveled, that gave him his boyish air. She wondered how any mother could fail to adore this boy.

"I'm fine, thank you." She smiled at D. W. and pointed them to the two straight-backed chairs beside her desk. "I appreciate you asking about my late hours today." He smiled back at her, while his mother struggled into her seat.

"These chairs were bigger last year," she complained. "Why did you put these tiny little things in here instead?"

Betty tried to avoid making eye contact with D. W. because she knew that if she did, he would make a funny face, and she might be tempted to laugh.

"I assure you, Mrs. Singer, these are the very same chairs," she said, looking down at D. W.'s file. "No matter, let's get on to our reasons for meeting tonight."

An indignant sniff escaped Alexandra's pursed lips. "Oh, I know exactly why we're here again," she began, reaching out and pinching the boy's earlobe. "This one's gotten into some new devilment, that's for sure. What's he done this time? Tell me! I'm ready. I took my nerve pills and heart medicine right before we left the house."

"Please, Mrs. Singer," Betty murmured, nodding her head at the grip the woman held on her son's ear.

Alexandra looked irritated, but let go of the boy's ear nonetheless. "Well, that's nothing compared to what his father will give him at home if he's in trouble again."

Betty found herself wanting to make up some lie and pretend there was some whole other reason for tonight's meeting. It had never occurred to her that perhaps this boy was badly treated at home, beaten, whipped, or deprived of food. She had always assumed that the source of his antics was his fun-loving spirit, not acting out due to being abused. She knew that she had to tread carefully to avoid making things any worse for him at home than they might already be.

"I hope nothing of the kind will be necessary when we're done tonight," she said, giving D. W. a reassuring look. He relaxed his tense shoulders and smiled that radiant smile at her again. Something about his smile gave her the idea she had been seeking.

"On the contrary," Betty began, "we're here to praise D. W., not to bury him." She knew the Shakespearean allusion would be lost on Mrs. Singer, but she also never expected an eight-year-old boy to get it. However, the words were no sooner out of her mouth than he burst into appreciative laughter.

"That's a good one, Miss Triplett. Whatever made you think of that?"

Betty looked anew at this remarkable boy sitting across from her. Where in the world, she wondered, had he ever run across Anthony's speech from *Julius Caesar* in this tiny town without a library or movie theater? Maybe there was more to this boy than even she had imagined.

Alexandra narrowed her eyes, seeing the knowing glance pass between teacher and student.

"What are you two talking about?" she asked with a suspicious face. "Praising and burying and such—I never heard of such a thing."

Betty realized that she had better be cautious. Difficult though this woman might be, she was still the wife of the richest and most prominent man in town, and she could make herself even more difficult if she chose to.

"Forgive me, Mrs. Singer. D. W. and I have been engaging in a little word play. Something from class, you know . . . a play we've been studying." She glanced at D. W. and saw the awareness of her little white lie dawn in his eyes.

Alexandra seemed to buy the ruse, though, and settled back in her creaking chair a bit. "So what do we have to 'praise' D. W. for? Did he make all Ds instead of all Fs this grading period?" She cackled at her own joke.

Betty fought to restrain the anger welling up in her at this insensitive woman who didn't appreciate what a gift she had in her son. It wouldn't do D. W. any good to tell off this unlikable mother. No, she would have to play her hand more artfully.

"Actually, D. W.'s grades are fine this period," she lied once more. Out of the corner of her eye, she saw the boy look up at her again with a quizzical face. She realized that he knew how disingenuous she was being, and she hoped this gamble paid off, for she didn't like setting a poor example for a student by lying.

"What's more important," she said, hurrying on, "is that we've realized your son is a gifted performer, Mrs. Singer."

Alexandra stared at her as if she were an alien. "The devil you say. You don't mean all those voices he's always making and characters he's always playing, do you? Because if you do, I think you're plumb crazy. We've been trying to get the boy to leave all that playacting alone and pay attention to the real world since he was two years old."

Betty set her jaw. This was going to be harder than she had hoped.

"Indeed," she said, trying for a compromise. "Children need to be realistic, to be sure, but they also have to have creative outlets . . . art, music, drama, and make-believe. Think of *Peter Pan*, Mrs. Singer, of *Alice in Wonderland*, and *Winnie the Pooh*. All of these stories feature children who were caught somewhere between fantasy and reality, and whose lives were enriched by their encounters with the imaginary. What would our world be like without *The Velveteen Rabbit* or *The Nutcracker?*"

Alexandra stared again at Betty. "The *what* kind of rabbit?"

Betty threw up her hands in exasperation. "What can I do to get you to hear me, Mrs. Singer? Your son has a gift, a rare talent I've never seen before. He can turn himself into any character on a moment's notice, capture the exact sound of another person's voice and mimic it perfectly. He can make others laugh, or cry I'd also imagine, with merely a small shift in that funny face. Your son needs more than our poor school can offer him. He needs some special program somewhere that prepares children for a career in the arts. Not a life in this depressed little town that doesn't know what to do with him except to laugh at his antics and encourage his worst behaviors."

Betty stopped short, out of breath and surprised to see how strongly she had been speaking. She was also surprised to see how mesmerized both Alexandra and D. W. were by her passion. In the pregnant silence that followed, she could have heard the proverbial pin drop. Finally, Alexandra seemed to come to herself. She leaned across Betty's desk and tapped her finger on D. W.'s file.

"Let me make sure that I'm hearing all of this right. You're telling me that I need to encourage this boy to make up stories and act a fool while he neglects his real studies, and slips further and further behind his classmates in his grades. How will he ever take over his father's business that way? What kind of life will he have when he grows up and all he can do is make faces and get laughs mimicking folks?"

Betty wished she could reach across the battered desktop and shake her. She struggled to remind herself that she was in a very small town in the foothills of Southern Indiana. Drawing a deep breath, she looked up at Alexandra's implacable stare and gave her measure for measure.

"Mrs. Singer," she said, in the most reasonable tone she could muster. "Surely you can't have helped but notice there's a whole wide world outside of Palmer's Ridge, filled with all kinds of people and places and things we don't have any notion of here . . . orchestras and art museums and ballet troupes and actors. You go to the movies over in Corydon sometimes, surely?"

Alexandra grunted a grudging assent, and Betty took that as a good sign.

"So who do you think makes those motion pictures? Who produces them and acts in them and pays for them, if there isn't some sort of reward for all of them at the day's end? The arts are a business in this world, Mrs. Singer. As surely as your husband makes a prosperous living at his funeral parlor and store, many people make an equally prosperous living in the arts."

Betty stopped and tried to gauge whether she was reaching the thick-headed woman or not. Alexandra stared back at her with a face that registered mainly confusion and doubt, but Betty also thought that maybe she saw some curiosity there, so she pressed her advantage.

She glanced over at D. W. and wasn't sure quite what she saw in his face—amazement, surely, but also something more that she couldn't quite define. Then she realized what it was. For the first time in his young life, D. W. had *hope*; hope for something better than the alienation and differentness he felt in this rigid, conservative world he inhabited. Emboldened by his wistful face, yet surprised at her own bravado, Betty put her last card down on the table, a card that she hadn't even known she held.

15

"Mrs. Singer, I'd like to share a dream I have with you. I want to start a theater program here at school that will help D. W. develop his God-given talent. We'll have plays and recitals and all kind of offerings for gifted children like D. W., plus we'll offer a whole new world to other children who may not be as talented as he is, but who still enjoy performing." She stopped, a little confused by how well-developed her proposal sounded when she had only now thought of it.

Alexandra burst out laughing, a haughty sneer on her face. "You mean to tell me you want to start a whole new program around this boy who can't even make good in the classes he's already attending? Why, he's barely squeaked by every year as it is, and I'm not so sure that he hasn't been passed on each year only because you people don't want to admit you failed as his teachers."

Betty tried hard to quell the angry flush she felt rising in her face. "That's the point. D. W. isn't doing well in our school because it doesn't meet his needs. He's bored with our traditional teaching methods and he's actually far too bright for them. His behavior problems are his way of expressing his frustration."

Alexandra was hearing none of it. "There's an old saying in business that Mr. Singer likes: 'No sense throwing good money after bad.' That's what you'd be doing if you spend one minute of your time or one penny of school funds doing anything special for this boy. He needs to learn to follow directions, knuckle down, and do what he's supposed to do for a change, not get out of work with make-believe games. You mark my words, if you encourage my boy in this foolishness, I'll have your job." She stabbed Betty's desktop with a crimson-polished nail several times for emphasis.

Betty Triplett had been at the Palmer's Ridge Primary

School since she graduated from teacher's college almost forty years before, watching and helping it grow from a one-room schoolhouse to its present eight-room, two-storied brick building. She was a dedicated career educator who had faced and overcome countless challenges. There had been inadequate supplies and textbooks, unruly and unresponsive students, and damages to school property by fires and a tornado. To all the small community, she appeared a demure, aging spinster, well-bred to the point of timidity, and certainly no powerhouse of any kind.

What no one knew about her was her upbringing in an alcoholic home, where she had parented three younger siblings after her mother's death in the Spanish flu epidemic of 1918. She had also managed to keep her drunken father from beating her siblings during his nightly rages, until his own death from liver failure a few years later. That was when she went to work teaching and supported the others up to their eighteenth birthdays.

Listening to Alexandra Singer, and remembering all of that, Betty realized that she had developed a deep antipathy for bullying over the years, and she would do anything she could to combat it. She would *not* let Alexandra bully her or this gifted child any longer.

However, Betty had also learned that there were many creative ways for a person to fight, some far more effective in certain circumstances than direct confrontation. She knew that despite Alexandra's short-sightedness, the woman was probably one of the most powerful people in town, if only through her marriage to a wealthy community leader. Betty decided that strategy rather than honesty would have to be her chief weapon in the ensuing battle with D. W.'s mother.

"Well, then, that settles it," she said, placing her palms on

D. W.'s file, and looking up at Alexandra with a resigned look. "I suppose there's nothing else to talk about here."

Alexandra almost crowed. "It certainly does settle things. Except for this . . . you need to do your job and somehow get this boy through the rest of the school year without calling me to come in here and listen to any more foolishness about how wonderful he is. I expect you to treat him like anybody else, only *more* firmly, not less. Do you hear me?"

Betty smiled a tight smile. "I think we understand each other perfectly. Now I suppose we all have other things to do the rest of the evening." She closed D. W.'s file and stood up, gesturing toward the door. She might have to take this troublesome woman's harangue in stride, for now anyway, but it was still her classroom, and she had the authority to decide when a conference in it was over.

To Betty's surprise, Alexandra took being dismissed without further resistance. She stood up, threw her expensive fox fur across her shoulder, and stormed toward the door. "You'd better be right behind me, young man, or there'll be trouble when I get you home."

D. W. stood up and trotted quickly after his mother, but before he left the room, he turned to give Betty a long, penetrating look, and for once, the impish face was somber. What was his fertile mind thinking, she wondered. Then he seemed to rally as he was going out the door, and waved goodbye to her with a cheeky wink. In spite of his impertinence, she had to stifle a laugh as she waved back at him and pointed him out into the hall.

Once they were gone, a deepening gloom overtook her. She collapsed onto her desk chair and reopened the thick file in front of her. There the damning evidence lay: three solid years' worth of misconduct reports, failing grades, and various disciplinary actions. Looking through it all with a dismal heart, Betty finally had to admit to the total dilemma she faced as a teacher.

How was she ever going to get through to this boy? How would she ever help him get the kind of education he really needed? And how would she ever find a way to get around this veritable Medusa who was his mother?

She sat ruminating over these questions until the elderly janitor, Mr. Guthrie, came to check her room and raised a ruckus that she was still there. When he fussed at her that it was way past time for her to be home, she finally let him escort her out of the building.

CHAPTER 3

REVELATIONS

Feeling like a king with a grand new carriage or limousine, twelve-year-old D. W. Singer pedaled his way through the streets of Palmer's Ridge, delivering newspapers on his shiny red Schwinn bicycle. The bike was a recent birthday present from his parents, and his ticket to this, his first real job.

He had helped out in his father's store and funeral home for years now, doing a variety of odd jobs. However, in those settings, he had always known that everyone saw him as the boss's son and that, as a result, nobody really expected any worthwhile work from him or felt any genuine respect for whatever efforts he did make. So he had decided to branch out, find his own job, and make some spending money, so that he didn't have to always be beholden to his dad for handouts.

He had been on this paper route for a week and hadn't been paid by the newspaper yet, but he was already getting all kinds of other compensation. After the first few days on the job, old man Carmichael, the meanest man in town, was standing on his front steps, waiting for him to come by with his evening paper.

When D. W. saw him waiting there, looking like a vampire ready to swoop down on him, all he could think was, "What I have done wrong now?" He was pleasantly surprised when he reached Mr. Carmichael's side, and the old curmudgeon tossed him a quarter.

"Gosh, thanks a lot, Mr. Carmichael," he said, catching the coin. "But what's this for?"

The old man grunted and turned to go back into his empty house. "You're the first paper boy in over twenty years to get my paper on the front stoop instead of under the shrubs." Then he closed the front door behind him with a bang.

At another house a few more stops along his route, a harried single mother had a plateful of fresh-baked Toll House cookies for him. "I really need those grocery coupons in the paper to make ends meet," she said. "The last couple of boys missed our house more often than they made it. You take a big handful of these cookies."

And so it was, almost everywhere he went. As the week wore on, and he continued to win praise from all of his customers, he realized what a nice fit this job was for him; what a glimpse into the goodness of people it gave him. He also realized how much he'd needed that reassurance lately, because he certainly wasn't getting any of it at home. In fact, it sometimes seemed to him that his home was the unhappiest place on earth.

When and if they spoke to each other at all, his parents had nothing but unkind, even cruel things to say. True, they never raised their voices; that would have been considered ill-bred and vulgar for people of their status. They didn't need to, for they had mastered the far more satisfying art of assaulting one another through inflection and innuendo. In the absence of talking to one another, they often communicated through D. W. instead, in a rich repertoire of hostile messages.

"D. W.," his father would say to him as he left for work in the morning, "would you please tell your mother—if she ever gets out of bed today, that is—that I'll be at a town council meeting until late tonight? Tell her to not hold dinner for me—that is, if she decides to make dinner at all for a change."

"D. W., please!" his mother would implore him when he brought her morning coffee to her room and tried to cajole her to get out of bed, "I have a terrible migraine. Please call down to your father's store and tell him to have some aspirin delivered immediately. Not that he'll listen, of course. I'm the last person on the planet he cares about. How it must break your heart, knowing you have such a cold, unfeeling father."

As a younger child, D. W. had fallen prey to their practice of using him as a pawn to hurt each other. He had even tried to arbitrate matters and set things right between them.

Now though, beginning to feel the first restive rumblings of adolescence, he had come to a sobering, liberating revelation; his parents were full of crap. He was sick to death of both of them, and ready to set himself free of them somehow. That was the question for him now . . . how?

This paper route was a start. Certainly, he knew that it would never set him on the road to complete independence, but it was a beginning. For the first time in his life, he had something to do that wasn't dictated by his parents' convoluted whims and moods, and that felt very, very good.

As he continued on his route, waving at all the passersby, he couldn't help but notice and take some pleasure in the admiring looks of the other kids. The boys clearly envied him the shiny new bike. The girls, on the other hand, did what girls always did. He wasn't quite sure how to describe it; he just knew that, for as long as he could remember, any time a human being of the female persuasion came into his presence, she started doing all kinds of strange things with her hands and hair and eyes. They would giggle, look away, look back, look down, giggle again, and then flash him a big smile, usually wriggling, twirling their skirts, and tossing their curls. It wasn't only little girls who engaged in this strange behavior. Sometimes he found that even teenaged girls and the occasional adult woman fell into it.

Frankly, he found the whole business totally mystifying, but he had also come to accept it as a fact of life. Even now, as his face was beginning to break out and his voice to do weird, unsettling things, changing octaves in mid-sentence, he still always felt some strange, unexplainable, yet powerful resonance with women.

He continued pedaling down the streets of the little town, delivering his papers on the route that he had already memorized, greeting his customers, and feeling quite the man of the hour . . . until he reached the town's outer limits. There he encountered a sorry enclave of sagging trailers, run-down bungalows, and outright hovels, tarpaper shacks where mongrel dogs roamed the lots, alongside scrawny chickens and mangy cats.

He knew that most of these customers didn't even pay for their papers, and seldom answered their doors. What was he to do? Go on and drop off their papers anyway, or pedal away from these residences without making a delivery?

Feeling increasingly uncomfortable, he was on the verge of leaving the whole area when something caught his eye. It was his father's brand-new silver 1959 Cadillac Coupe de Ville, parked behind some shrubs in the front yard of one of the most squalid trailers on the street. Its exaggerated back-fender fins poked up a good foot above the car's body, and D. W. thought they looked totally ridiculous.

He knew it was his father's car, not only because there was no one else in the county who had the money to buy a late-model Cadillac, but also because he recognized the special license plate his father always had on every car he'd ever owned—merely his name, "Drake."

At first sight of the vehicle, D. W. wanted to escape the whole sordid scene as soon as possible. He had no desire to know what his father's expensive car was doing in this derelict neighborhood, but assumed it signaled nothing good. Tossing his last paper onto the rickety stoop of the rusted trailer, he turned his bike and started to pedal away with fast, furious strides.

As he was exiting the driveway, a sound reached his ears that proved an irresistible siren song and caused him to stop. It was somewhere between a high-pitched squeal and a scream. In there, alongside it, was a male voice, shouting in a lower timbre, which D. W. recognized as his father's.

"Almost there, baby . . . almost there!" he shouted. "Here it comes now! I'm coming now!"

D. W. stood riveted in the trailer's weedy front yard, listening to the ugly sounds of his father having sex with some woman other than his mother, probably a prostitute. He was only twelve, but he already knew enough about the sex act to know when he was hearing it occur.

He was paralyzed for several moments, standing there in the seedy setting, his brand-new, sparkling red bike beneath him—the bike that the rutting man inside the trailer had recently bought him. He considered his limited options: he could continue running from the scene, with some cost to his sense of self-respect; he could go back to the trailer, knock on the door and confront his father; he could go get his mother and bring her back to confront his dad; or, what? None of these options appealed to him, and he found himself standing there, chewing on his lip.

Suddenly, he knew what to do. He got off the bike, picked it up, went to his father's beautiful new Cadillac, and threw the bike with all his might into the windshield of the magnificent car. The glass crumpled beneath it, falling in a million shards onto the Moroccan leather seats. The bike stuck out into the air over the dashboard like some bizarre, modern sculpture.

"What was that?" he heard two voices shout in unison from the trailer, and he took off running. He knew his father would realize he had been there; that was the whole point of his putting his unmistakable "signature" on the car. But he didn't want to have to confront his father personally. He also knew that the proud man would never acknowledge having had his car vandalized by his own son while he was having sex inside a filthy trailer. His father would simply get it fixed and never say a word to anyone.

At the same time, D. W. realized that it was highly unlikely he would ever get another bike or any other gifts of importance from his father, either, but he had already resigned himself to that. He could do his paper route on foot, after all. It would be worth every footstep to him, remembering the sight of that shattered windshield with his bike sticking out of it, and imagining the incredulous look on his father's face when he came out of the trailer and saw it.

* * *

Drake stood in the doorway of the trailer clad only in his boxers, his muscular chest heaving with the exertion of his recent orgasm, as well as the shock of what he saw outside. He surveyed the damage to his Cadillac and watched his son high-tailing it down the road. Soon, to his surprise, he found himself smiling.

Got to hand it to the guy: he's sure got guts. Imagine telling your old man off that way.

He thought about all the times he had watched D. W. through the years, almost as if watching a suspenseful movie, trying to figure out the boy and the plot unfolding around him. Like most parents of his generation, he had been raised to think of children as unfinished human beings, not fully deserving of true personhood yet, whose primary role in life was to mind adults. However, D. W. had challenged those notions from the day he was born.

He had always had such a strong life force in him—never a fragile, simpering baby, but one with a strong lusty spirit and a bold voice to match it, right from the start. Sometimes Drake took malicious satisfaction in watching the boy test his mother's patience. He would never forgive her for spurning his love, and it served her right for his child to give her hell—just as it served her right for him to have sex with any woman he pleased.

So many times through the years he wanted to divorce her, but the laws of the land dictated she would get custody of their son, and he felt sure she would move far away, solely to hurt him further. Despite the emotional distance he felt from D. W., he wasn't prepared to give him up. He still harbored a dream that they might grow closer one day, and he might be able to entice the boy to take over the family business. He knew it was a long shot, as he had trouble being close to anyone. It was part of his legacy from his own distant father. In addition, the boy clearly had his sights set on some more artistic career, and had recently quit his job with Drake because he wanted to be more independent.

Remembering that day, Drake had to smile again. *Yes, the boy has guts, all right. But what is he going to do with them?*

A plaintive voice called out to him from the bedroom. "You comin' back to bed, honey?"

He returned to the bed, but only to get his clothes, and chuck the girl under the chin. "That's a mighty tempting invitation, my dear, but I have a little job to do."

He dressed, called his store manager, Doogie, to come pick him up, and went out onto the stoop to smoke a fat cigar.

*　*　*

It was long before dawn, and D. W. was heading out to do his paper route—on foot, as he had been doing for several weeks. Because his mother didn't like him leaving the porch light on, he tiptoed in the dark out the back door of the house.

As he'd predicted, his father had never said a word about the damage to his car, nor had he shown any anger toward D. W. He was his usual dignified, detached self, leaving D. W. more perplexed than ever about what made the man tick.

In the darkness, D. W. bumped into something on the porch and stumbled back a few steps. Regaining his balance, he peered into the gloom and saw a faint sparkle. He inched closer, and smelled fresh paint and new rubber. Reaching out, he felt through the air and his hands landed on something familiar—the padded leather seat of his bike.

He went back into the house to switch on the outdoor light, then returned to the porch. The Schwinn was completely restored to its original glory, with shiny new chrome fenders, wheels and handlebars. There was even a flashy rearview mirror on those bars that hadn't been there before.

What in the world? His mind raced, and he was nonplussed for several moments, until he realized it could only be one thing . . . his father had the bike repaired. Still, he couldn't quite absorb the idea.

What was Dad thinking? Why would he fix the bike I used to damage his favorite thing, his Cadillac? After mulling it all over for a while, he finally understood. As the awareness dawned on him, he broke into a huge grin. *Got to hand it to the old man. I would have never seen this one coming. I think he kind of liked what I did.*

Nonetheless, he knew that the two of them would never speak of these matters. His vindictiveness and his father's unexpected grace would merely become additional items on a long list of things that they couldn't discuss.

However, afterward, in the midst of going about their usual business of pretending not to notice each other, D. W. sometimes thought he caught his father eyeing him with a newfound respect.

CHAPTER 4

NIGHT MOVES

It was three o'clock in the morning in the rambling, dark Singer house. Alexandra had just heard the chimes from the grandfather clock in the foyer. It had been there for generations, Drake's mother told her on their wedding day. Sometimes, though, she wanted to take an axe to it, relentless marker that it was of how slow, sad, and small her world had become.

The previous day had been an especially difficult one for her, and yet, she didn't quite understand why. On the face of it, it should have been a happy day. D. W. was graduating from middle school. He was fifteen and already six feet tall, eating them out of house and home. She couldn't keep enough milk and bread and peanut butter in the house to sate him.

More than that, he had finally seemed to come into another, even more satisfying kind of growth spurt. He had started getting better grades in school, and Alexandra had to credit Miss Triplett's ongoing tutoring of him over the years. How that old woman had ever found the patience to put up with him all this time, Alexandra would never know.

What's more, D. W. had starred in the school's talent show, held right before graduation ceremonies. He had sung the beautiful ballad "Moon River" solo, danced in a number from the popular musical *Oliver*, and, more importantly, served as the emcee for the whole affair, doing an admirable job of it all, she had to admit.

Sitting there in the audience, watching her son become a local celebrity in tiny, albeit growing, Palmer's Ridge, Alexandra had mixed emotions. She was so very proud of him on the one hand, but on the other hand (and she had a hard time admitting this to herself) she was also incredibly jealous of him, and more than a little bit puzzled.

Where did he get his talent, she wondered? She knew of no one on either side of the family who had ever shown any kind of musical or theatrical abilities. The only time she herself had spent in the spotlight had been when she was named homecoming queen her senior year in her hometown, nearby Lanesville. If she hadn't birthed the boy herself, she would have thought he was a foundling. Then a sobering thought came to her; what if his talent was some special gift from God?

She had always written off his childhood playacting as a behavior problem, needing firmer discipline, not encouragement. Miss Triplett had tried to convince her otherwise, and she had refused to hear her. Now it appeared that maybe the aging teacher had been right. Once D. W. was no longer in her class, the wily woman had indeed started the theater program she'd outlined to Alexandra long ago, and he had excelled in it from his first performance.

Now thinking of this new possibility, that God had blessed her son somehow, Alexandra felt guilty for the way she had greeted him after the show. He had looked so proud and puffed up, that she had felt the need to take him down a peg or two. She didn't want him to get too full of himself.

"Well, aren't you 'Mr. Too Big for His Britches' tonight,"

she had said with a little smirk, and watched his face fall in an instant. He had been walking toward her, beaming, to see how she liked the show, but after her comment, had smiled sadly and walked away.

She had regretted her comment immediately, but also tried to justify it to herself. A mother had an obligation to rein in a child's pride, didn't she? The Bible had all kinds of scripture warning against the sin. However, now that it had occurred to her that maybe God had blessed her child, it also occurred to her that *she* may be the one who had sinned, by spurning one of God's gifts, and negating her son's talent. Her face grew hot with shame, and she wished she could somehow retract her hurtful words.

She had already been tossing in her bed, unable to sleep. This last thought was a final straw, though, and she knew now she would never be able to get any rest tonight. She dragged herself out of bed, shrugged into her silk robe, and wandered out into the second floor hallway. Nightlights sent a golden glow onto the polished hardwood floors there, guiding her way to the stairs. When she reached them, she had to make a choice.

Upstairs on the third floor was D. W.'s room, still in the old nursery where he had slept all his life; downstairs were the living quarters and kitchen, where half of a chocolate layer cake lay uneaten on the kitchen counter. She glanced down at her frame and knew she didn't need to be eating any more of that cake in the middle of the night, but, when she considered going up to apologize to D. W., her heart leapt to her throat.

She thought and thought, trying to remember the last time she had apologized to him for something, and eventually realized that she never had. How would she go about it? What would she say? What if he didn't accept her apology? Wouldn't that give him some kind of advantage over her? He was such a scamp that would never do at all. It was more risk than she was willing to take at the moment. She turned toward the downstairs steps and soon stood at the kitchen counter, cutting herself a big piece of the gooey cake.

Somehow food always helped her think things through. Moreover, it was her one steadfast friend, always there to keep her company and cheer her up when nobody else would. It was the only thing that she really looked forward to, the only thing that gave her any real pleasure. She could never put this thought into words, and could barely even let herself think it now, but sometimes she felt an almost erotic pleasure eating, especially eating rich, sticky sweets, like this chocolate cake. As this realization tiptoed on the edge of her consciousness, she felt another wave of shame, and sliced herself an even bigger piece of cake to assuage it.

Licking the buttery icing from her fingers after that slice, she resumed pondering whether and how to apologize to D. W., but her thoughts were no more comfortable now than they had been earlier. She eyed the remaining cake, and was surprised to see that it was almost gone. Could she really have eaten all of that cake so fast? Well, no matter, she decided; having eaten that much, she might as well go on and finish it off. It had taken her mind off her worries, after all. Maybe eating the rest of it would completely ease her conscience.

As she was stuffing the last big bite in her mouth, she heard the squeak of the backdoor hinges, saw the overhead lights go on, and turned to see her errant husband enter the room. His clothes were rumpled and his tie askew, but he still looked as composed and haughty as he always did. He took one look at the empty cake plate, then leveled a long, piercing look at her, and his lip curled in a sneer.

"Well, why doesn't this surprise me?" he said in an airy voice, and quickly walked past her. "Merely coming to get a change of clothes. I won't trouble you with my presence for long."

A furious blush burned her cheeks and neck. "God sees your whoring ways," she hissed. "He sees them and he'll punish you one day. You'll burn in hell, that's for sure!"

He turned in the doorway. "Oh, no, my dear," he said softly, with another curl of his lip. "I've already been in hell, living with you all these years." He spun and left the room before she could make a retort.

She stewed with impotent rage, wanting to take the crystal cake stand and dash it onto the floor, or better yet, run after him and club him over the head with it. But she realized it was no use trying to fight him anymore. He was too good at it, so he always won, largely, she realized, because he didn't feel anything for anyone. He had nothing to lose; his apathy gave him a powerful advantage.

She went to the refrigerator and pulled the door open with such force that it set the jars inside rattling. What else was there to eat in this house, she wondered. Wasn't there some apple pie in there somewhere? Or had that ravenous boy eaten that, too? She rummaged through the Tupperware containers for so long that she lost track of time, until she heard Drake's snide laughter behind her. She whipped around to see him, all spruced up and straightening his tie.

"I'll treasure this picture until the day I die," he said and breezed past her to the back door.

"I hope that day comes soon!" she spat after him. "Real, real soon! You hear me, whoremonger? I hope you die soon!"

Still, once he was gone, she felt sick and deflated. Why did it always have to be this way with him? Where had they gone so terribly wrong? She remembered the good times. They had seemed such a likely match at first, both from well-to-do families in their neighboring small, Southern Indiana towns, and both considered the handsomest, most eligible catches among their classmates.

It had started off so well between them. They had traveled widely, and enjoyed canoeing, horseback-riding, or walking near one of the many lakes and rivers that graced this hilly region. Oh, sure, there was always what she liked to call "that sex thing," between them. She could never comprehend, nor had any desire to try to understand, the strange motivations that compelled men to want to mount their wives like stallions, ramming their manhood into them to a sticky, disgusting conclusion. It was totally beyond her.

After the first few months of marriage, enduring the unspeakable things he put her through nightly between the sheets, she had begun to rein in all of that. She was a lady, after all, and no true lady put up with such nonsense from her husband. In her world, it was a wife's job to civilize and control her husband's worst self. So feeling morally superior to him on the matter, she had never felt any doubts about denying him the marital bed.

D. W. had been the product of their last violent coupling, an event she would always consider rape, despite being married to the man who perpetrated it on her. So unwelcome were his advances by then, and so painful that last union with him, that she had never been able to look her son in the face without remembering and resenting both the act, and the boy who resulted from it.

Now, though, looking back over their years together, she had to admit that denying her husband sex had probably been the beginning of the end. Here she was again, for the second time that night, looking back over her behavior and questioning the rightness of it. This kind of self-examination was a new and deeply uncomfortable thing for her, and she literally squirmed as she engaged in it. She resumed her quest in the fridge, muttering, "Where in the world is that last bit of pie?"

Frustrated when she couldn't find it, she finally gave up the search and settled for a huge cheese sandwich loaded with pickles and mayonnaise. By then, it was nearing dawn, and she realized that she should probably go back to bed and get some sleep. She hauled herself up the stairs to the second floor, and paused to catch her breath. As she did, she felt that the flight of stairs going up to the third floor beckoned her. "Go up and speak to your son," they seemed to whisper, and once more, she felt her heart in her throat.

Then, for some reason, she began to get angry. Why should she be so daunted by the simple thought of talking to her son? What was so bad about that, after all? How hard could it be? It was only a few words: "I'm sorry, son. Can you please forgive me?"

She squared her shoulders, and started up the stairs with resolute steps. Arriving at his door, she had another moment of doubt, but again, grew angry at her paralysis, and that impelled her into his room. Once there, she realized she probably should have knocked, because he was sound asleep, oblivious to her entry. Seeing him lying there on his back, she realized with a start that she hadn't watched him sleeping since he was a very small child. There had never been any reason to.

Now that she was here, she had a bittersweet moment of déjà vu. He had always looked like a little angel when he slept, and now, tonight, he did again. Oh, certainly, he was way too big to look like a "little" anything, but his serene face in the pale light of dawn still looked like an angel to her.

He was becoming quite a handsome young man, she realized. Funny that she had never noticed that before. She was always so much more focused on whether his clothes were pressed and his hair was combed. Gazing down on him now, she saw how his face had cleared of acne, his unruly chestnut hair was beginning to settle into gentle waves, and the hint of a beard was beginning to emerge on his full lips and chiseled jaw.

Alexandra was no connoisseur of art, but she and Drake had been to Europe on their whirlwind honeymoon in 1947, where they had dutifully visited all the great museums. She couldn't remember which artist painted it, but she knew that she had seen a portrait somewhere of a beautiful sleeping youth who looked just like her son did now. Remembering that image, her heart swelled with pride.

How she wanted to tell him that. How she wanted to nudge him awake, and kneel beside his bed to tell him how well he had done in the show, and how glad she was that he was making better grades. She leaned forward and started to do that. Then something stopped her. She didn't quite understand what it was. Not self-respect, certainly, as Drake had thoroughly robbed her of that. No, it was something else, but what?

Digging down deep into her heart, she had to face a side of herself that she had always successfully avoided before. *I am simply not a very giving person*, she realized.

There was the troubling truth. She didn't find it easy to trust or give to others because she was always working so hard to make sure they didn't harm her in some way. The charm had kept her from being hurt many times through the years, but it had also kept her from getting close to anyone. A childhood of emotional abuse by her wealthy but unfeeling parents' was the obvious explanation, but knowing that didn't make the problem any better.

D. W. stirred in his sleep and mumbled something unintelligible. She became aware that he was probably close to waking, and decided she had best leave the room before he did. Going to the door, she put her hand on the knob, and turned to take one last look at him. As she did, her heart melted at the sight—such a beautiful young man, and such a force of nature, all sprung from her loins and a miserable marriage with no other redeeming feature but him. In that instant, all the hurt and anger about how he had been conceived evaporated. It would come back to haunt her again over the years ahead, but for now it was gone, and she could look at him for the first time without rancor.

"You did really fine in the show tonight, son," she whispered. "It made me proud to be your mother." She exited the room, returned to her own bed, and found that she was finally able to sleep.

CHAPTER 5

TIGER, TIGER, BURNING BRIGHT...

Toby Schumann craned his neck to see out the window of the bus carrying him to summer camp for what he intended to be the last time. The driver had just announced over the crackly intercom system that they were approaching the little mountain town of Frazier, Arkansas, and that they would be disembarking there within minutes. Staff and vans from Camp Osage would be waiting to transport all of the boys on board to the nearby camp.

As luck would have it, Toby couldn't see a thing from his view out the bus window. Maybe that was best though, he thought, realizing anew with a sinking heart how angry and sad he was to be going to camp this year.

He had argued valiantly with his parents that he was way too old for this sort of juvenile summer sortie, but they had won out in the end. Wallowing in self-pity, Toby thought how his parents always seemed to win, forgetting how often he was able to parlay being an only child, and a male one at that, into some advantage when dealing with his folks. They had held sway this time, though, and that was all that really mattered to him presently. For he was stuck for the next several weeks in his own private idea of hell, thrown together with a horde of athletic, acne-rid-dled adolescent males in the boondocks of northern Arkansas, with no way out except through his own lively imagination.

Camp Osage lay in the Ozark Mountains on the shores of a man-made lake created by the Army Corps of Engineers during the New Deal. Before the lake was created, the impoverished rural town of Frazier had existed there for 150 years. Hundreds of residents had given birth, eked out an existence on its hard-scrabble soil and unforgiving landscape, and died where they had lived. Now most of their former homesteads, and even their grave sites, rested fathoms below the surface of a freshwater lake that was rapidly becoming one of the most popular vacation sites in the region.

Only Frazier's downtrodden business district had survived, hugging the long, undulating shoreline of the new lake. It was on its last legs, though, waiting for the wrecker's ball, and new city planners to come in with their reconstruction plans. Someday soon, trendy bars, bistros, and boutiques would line the main street that had once been a sleepy frontier town. For now, Frazier was a pale ghost of its former self, just waiting for a second coming.

Toby knew nothing of this history, however, as he wriggled against the prickly upholstered seats of the lumbering bus taking him and his fellow campers to their destination at Camp Osage. He was dreading the ultimate debarkation, and the subsequent, predictable, testosterone-laden male-bonding experiences he had come to expect from summer camps through painful past experiences.

His parents were prosperous Jewish merchants with a chain of popular clothing stores in New York City. He was their sole surviving child, and had come to be that only through the grace of God. As a weak, asthmatic baby, he had been near death more times than his worried mother cared to remember. Yet somehow, he had always held on to life and made it through, partly through her ministrations, and partly through his own tenacity. Both his mother and Toby would readily agree that he was a very determined, even stubborn, young man.

That stubborn side of self was the spirit that infused his whole being as he dug himself into the seat of the bus carrying him to camp. He was almost fifteen, and way past the age for summer camp, as far as he was concerned. However, his mother and far more passive father had somehow determined, in their infinite, though often questionable wisdom, that he was ripe for one more summer camp experience. So they had packed him off, one last time to yet another miserable mountain town to endure the indignities, and worse yet, abuses, of a final summer camp experience.

Through the years, he had often asked his parents why, when they felt the need to send him to camp, they chose to send him to some fundamentalist Christian one in the South or Midwest, rather than the countless Jewish camps that crowded the Catskill Mountains much closer to home. They claimed it gave him a broadening, cross-cultural experience. To him, it felt almost as if they had researched carefully to find some particularly alien and toxic destination to send him. That was certainly what he was expecting from Camp Osage in rural, mountainous Arkansas. He felt the bus lurch toward its final stop in Frazier and prepare to spew its passengers onto the pavement outside the tiny bus stop.

As the smelly diesel vehicle screeched to a clumsy halt, the driver pulled on the hydraulic door handle, and Toby heard it open with an ominous hiss. Reaching in the rack above his seat for his backpack, he tried to see what lay outside the parked vehicle, but it wasn't a particularly reassuring first impression.

Frazier appeared to be yet another one of a thousand somnolent little towns he had already viewed on his way here through the green-tinted glass of the aged bus. Through the spotted window pane, he saw a single main street, lined with shops and other businesses in varying states of disrepair. A hand-painted sign next to the bus station touted pink lettering reading, "Gerry's Beauty & Nail Salon," the words intertwined with crude daisies and twisting ivy tendrils. However, the dusty storefront promised little of beauty or grace inside. Cheap curtains hung limply in the dirty windows of the shop, and a dim fluorescent light hung in the center of its single room, casting a disheartening pall over the whole establishment.

Toby thought of the upscale salon where his mom went every Thursday to have her hair and nails done before Friday night temple, and realized with a glum outlook how far he was from New York. He glanced across the aisle of the bus at the storefronts on the other side of the street and saw an equally dismal lineup. Reuben's Tax Service, Patsy's Pet Grooming, and Stan's Fresh Produce all looked as if few patrons ever crossed their thresholds. He slung his backpack across his thin shoulders and sighed. It was going to be a rough summer if bustling downtown Frazier was any predictor of what he might expect in the weeks ahead at nearby Camp Osage.

Stumbling down the narrow rubber-padded steps of the bus, he lost his footing and found himself struggling to keep his balance. The oversized mass and weight of the backpack on his slender frame threw him hopelessly off-kilter. He hit the ground outside the bus with a graceless thud, sending the contents of his backpack spilling across the weed-grown sidewalk in front of the sorry bus station. There under the pitiless glare of the noonday sun, he saw his stack of Marvel comic books, his underwear, and worst of all, his favorite GI Joe doll, outfitted in his best dress officer uniform, all tumbling across the cracked concrete.

Like many boys his age, Toby was a contradictory mixture of little boy and near-adult. On the one hand, he felt himself to be terribly urbane and sophisticated, chaffing at the times his mother babied him. On the other, he still slept with stuffed animals and couldn't quite bring himself to dispose of much-loved objects such as the lantern-jawed, manly GI Joe doll. It had been the source of so many hours of pleasure to him, in solitary play at his family's urban apartment.

He also knew that there was another, darker element to his affection for Joe. For some time now, Toby had found men attractive, especially muscular, hyper-masculine men like the dauntless Joe. This attraction brought him tremendous angst and shame, yet he couldn't deny it. All he could hope to do was suppress and conceal it for the rest of his life.

He had to get up and retrieve his things before someone saw them and figured out that he wasn't like the other boys tumbling out of the bus all around him. There was no way in the world he was going to be known in this new Christian camp community as the skinny Jewish kid from New York who read comic books about super heroes and played with male dolls.

Still, he had to fight to overcome the strong urge to faint that filled his swimming head. Trying with all his might to regain his lost footing, and not having very much success, he felt a strong hand grab and support his left arm. He looked up and could see nothing but the black silhouette of a curly head, backlit by the glaring noon sun behind it; that and a tiger-eye amulet dangling from a leather strap around the neck of the phantom visage. A powerful male lifted him to his feet, giving him both his balance and his dignity back in an instant. The experience felt very good to him . . . wonderful, in fact.

Back on his feet, Toby scrambled to collect his belongings, but he quickly became lightheaded. His rescuer knelt to help. From his vantage point standing above the young man, Toby saw a riot of chestnut curls, broad shoulders, and what appeared to be a tall, trim body, but he still couldn't see the face of the fellow who had helped him up and was now helping him again.

"Please don't bother," Toby stammered, seeing the young man reaching for his shorts. He couldn't bear the thought of someone other than his mom or himself handling his underwear.

"No bother," the young man said with a deep, baritone voice. "We all wear these things and you just took quite a dive here. I'd take it easy for a while if I were you. At least until you know you don't have a concussion."

Toby had to admit it made sense and he stood by helplessly as the young man gathered all of his things in his broad arms, even the embarrassing doll. Holding the load to his chest, the older boy stood, turned to Toby, and began handing items over to him. Toby crammed them into the depths of the pack, trying to fight back the hot flush that was rising to his cheeks.

Finally the young man had returned everything but the doll. He held it in his hand for a long moment, eyeing it closely, and

Toby braced for the inevitable, hostile teasing he knew must be coming. However, his young rescuer surprised him.

"Hey, Joe, long time no see," the young man said. He held the doll out at arm's length to admire it, and then broke into a big grin. He looked up at Toby with nostalgia in his eyes.

"I know this guy myself. We used to spend a lot of time together . . . fighting off the bad guys." He handed the doll over to Toby with an almost reluctant air.

Toby took the doll and shoved it deep into his backpack, glad to have this source of shame concealed. Reassured his secret was safely stored away, he looked up and saw his new friend extending his right hand.

"Sorry," Toby mumbled, embarrassed yet again. He grabbed and shook the older boy's hand firmly. "Tobias Schumann, from Manhattan, New York. Everyone calls me Toby."

"D. W. Singer," the older boy said, adding with a laugh. "From Nowheresville, Indiana."

Toby laugh backed, finally getting a good look at his new acquaintance. What he saw made him forget the virile GI Joe doll in an instant, for D. W. Singer was possibly the handsomest young man Toby had ever met. A high, clear forehead and thick chestnut eyebrows framed riveting brown eyes that danced with a tawny light, much like that of the tiger-eye amulet he wore. The remnants of boyhood freckles dusted his strong nose and high, wide cheekbones. A dazzling white smile and firm jaw with a deep cleft in the dimpled chin finished off the face that Toby realized could have been in the movies. That was only from the neck up. Toby tried hard not to look down and check out his new friend's strong, lithe body too obviously, but it was hard not to notice that D. W. was a very fit young man. Letting himself at least glance down at D. W.'s chest, Toby saw that the older boy was wearing a uniform from Camp Osage and that his shirt said "Counselor" above the left breast pocket.

"You're from Camp Osage?" Toby asked.

D. W. glanced down at the title on his shirt. "Oh that," he said in a non-committal way. "Yeah, I guess so. I've been coming to this damned camp since I was eight years old. They finally had to make me a counselor because I caused so much trouble as a camper. Guess they figured this was the best way to tame me."

Toby knit his eyebrows. "What do you mean?"

D. W. motioned for him to step aside in order to let the others boys who were exiting the bus get past them. The two new acquaintances fell into an ambling walk away from the bus station as they continued to get to know each other.

D. W. shoved his big hands in his short's pockets. "I'm what folks call a problem child." He looked over at Toby's face and saw the puzzled expression there. "You know, too smart for his own good, mouthy, and defiant, reckless, and impulsive . . . always testing the limits, but also too smart to kick out of school, or church, or, in this case, camp. So they've always had to figure out some way to deal with me, usually by making me a leader of some sort . . . you know, to get me to go along with them and cooperate, one way or another."

Toby nodded. "I think I know what you mean. I was reading and chanting Hebrew by the time I was four. Something about it just made sense and clicked for me. You can imagine how that went over at Hebrew School when I got older and everyone else there was struggling so hard to get it. I might as well have had a tattoo printed on my forehead: *I'm an egghead. Beat up on me.*"

D. W. chuckled. "That's good. You're a funny guy. It'll come in handy over the next couple of weeks because there's not a whole lot of fun that this batch of Christians approve of." He said the word *Christians* with a dour, sourpuss face that made Toby laugh again.

Suddenly D. W. seemed to take notice of their surroundings and realized that they had strayed a good distance from the bus. He looked over his shoulder. "We better get back to the group. After all, I'm supposed to be on duty here. Good to know you, man. We'll get you through the next couple of weeks, one way or another, okay?"

D. W. saluted, and then took off in an easy lope back to the bus station, where Toby saw him begin helping other campers extract their luggage from the bowels of the bus. Toby headed back himself, where he knew he had a steamer trunk full of unnecessary things his mother had insisted he bring. Trudging back in the hot summer air, he tried hard to forget the sight of D. W.'s muscular buttocks straining against the taut twill fabric of his khaki shorts as he jogged back to the station. However, it was an image Toby found impossible to erase from his mind.

He knew then, even more clearly than he had before, that it was going to be a very difficult couple of weeks ahead.

*   *   *

The pandemonium in the mess hall at Camp Osage couldn't have been more chaotic if the devil himself had planned it. Toby sidled his way through the crowd of campers, trying to keep his backpack from bumping into others as best he could. Despite his efforts, he jarred several boys who turned on him without a moment's hesitation and whacked him firmly on the head.

"Watch what you're doing!" one sneered.

49

"Do that again and I'll knock the shit out of you!" another young camper promised him.

He was trying to wend his way to the corner in the camp mess hall where a hand-painted sign beckoned campers with last names beginning with the letters S through Z. Similar signs were posted throughout the crowded hall and everyone else was trying to accomplish the same thankless mission, but somehow he seemed to arouse more ire than anyone else in the gathering. Acutely sensitive to his different ethnicity, he could only assume he had already been pegged as an outlier, and that the inevitable hazing he was doomed to undergo was beginning. He wondered suddenly how long he could survive in the mountains of Arkansas on his own if he immediately ran away from this hateful, prejudiced crowd.

Making his way through the mass of male, adolescent humanity, he at last found himself at the right table in the mess hall. Then he received the first of many unexpected blessings he would encounter in his summer camp experience. Maybe there was a God after all, he thought to himself, as he saw that the counselor greeting campers was the same strong, handsome young man he had met at the bus station earlier. He fought the silly urge to cry as he watched the older boy welcome the other campers, shake hands, clap fellows on their shoulders, and tell them how to find their cabins on the expansive campgrounds. Toby knew in that moment that he was already beginning to fall in love a little bit.

Pushing that thought to the back of his mind, he sidled up to the table and threw his backpack down on the floor in front of it. Straightening his back and affecting a military air, he looked D. W. in the eye and gave him a smart salute.

"Camper First Class Tobias Schumann, reporting for duty . . . sir!" With that, he clicked his heels together as loudly as was possible in light of the fact that he was wearing sneakers.

D. W. looked back at him for a moment with a deadpan face, then he doubled up with hearty laughter. "You are one gutsy guy," he said, clapping Toby on the back. "I think the next couple of weeks are going to be a lot more interesting than the last session was."

Toby felt his heart swell with pride at already being accepted and affirmed by such an influential young man at the camp. He let himself indulge in the brief fantasy that maybe he might actually enjoy camp this year. Within a few moments, however, his excitement and great expectations evaporated.

Other campers had noticed his display, but were less favorably impressed. A group of blond, blue-eyed, athletic-looking boys sidled up to him and looked him up and down. Toby glanced over at D. W. and felt his heart sink to see that the older boy was helping another younger camper sign in.

One of the three boys finally looked him square in the eye. "Schumann . . . that's a Jew name, isn't it? Guess you think you're pretty smart?" he asked in a slow Southern drawl.

Aw shit, here it comes, Toby thought. It was earlier than usual this year. Normally this stuff didn't come down on him until at least the third or fourth day of camp. Well, he would deal with it this time as he had in the past, with a protocol he had developed long ago, part bravado, part strategy.

He looked at his interrogator with clear disinterest. "Not that it's any of your business, but since you've been rude enough to intrude into a conversation that doesn't involve you, no, I don't think I'm smart."

51

He watched the bigger boy take this in and try to figure out how to respond to it. The boy's friends gathered closer to him with expectant looks on their faces. They wanted to see where this encounter went, and watching them, it occurred to Toby that probably no one had ever stood up to their bullying friend before. He took the opportunity to swiftly level the next parry.

"I don't *think* I'm smart. I *know* I'm smart. Now, excuse me, but I've got more important things to do than stand here and answer stupid questions."

He hefted the heavy backpack over his shoulder and walked off as slowly as possible, signifying to the others that he was totally unafraid, all the while feeling his heart pounding wildly. Based on past experience, he knew that the next few seconds would be the most telling. If the others came after him now, they would be after him all session. If they accepted the boundary he had set for them and left him alone, he could probably expect some peace of mind and safety for the next two weeks.

This particular group of gnats surprised him by doing neither. They didn't come after him or back down from him. Instead, one of them called after him with a light, almost humorous tone. "We'll see, funny Jew boy, just how smart you are. Only, remember, two weeks is an awfully long time."

Toby fought the urge to turn and see who had levied the anti-Semitic threat, knowing that it would only give them the satisfaction of having hit their mark. Instead, he continued walking away slowly, looking about the meeting hall, feigning great interest in the log ceiling beams overhead and the large trophy case, pretending he hadn't heard anything.

His heart continued beating rapidly until he was well away from the hall. It wouldn't stop beating that way for several days, and it would get worse before it got better. For, after finding his cabin and unpacking his things into the musty footlocker at the end of his bed, he heard his roommates shuffle in the door behind him. He turned to them with a smile of greeting, but it faded instantly when he saw who they were.

It was the three blond tormentors he had met in the mess hall. Was it some awful coincidence, he wondered, that they had been assigned to room with him? Or could they have actually asked to bunk with him to be able to get to him?

Toby realized then that he was going to have to spend the next two weeks with a band of budding Klan members. Judging from the grim smiles on their faces as they threw their packs onto their beds and circled him where he knelt on the floor, he wondered if he would ever see Manhattan again.

*   *   *

Over the next few days, events unfolded for Toby in a seamless series of disasters he would always remember as "the reign of terror." He had landed the roommates from hell, who detested him and everything he stood for, without even knowing him. By his mere existence as a wealthy, articulate, rather effete New York Jew, he was an affront to them and their way of life. Sometimes he truly believed they might smother him in his sleep.

They started with indirect insults, disparaging remarks about the pushy habits of "Hebes" and "Kikes," always made in an offhand manner barely within earshot of him. From there, they escalated to the tried-and-true maneuver beloved by boys living in community since the dawn of time—appearing to bump into him accidentally while he was carrying his tray in the cafeteria and spilling his food. His meal would spray across the mess hall floor, where he would then have to clean it up amidst the laughter of the other boys, and sometimes even forfeit his meal for a peanut butter sandwich if the food was all gone. At night, he would wake up to find spiders and cockroaches crawling across his face, then burn with rage when he heard their chuckles as he jumped up, shrieking, swatting the odious pests.

So far, that was it. They had given him their best hazing, but still hadn't come up with anything he hadn't already experienced at some other camp in some other backward region many times before. Sitting by the lake one afternoon, he mused that they were probably the most persistent and mean-spirited persecutors he had encountered thus far and therefore a force to be reckoned with. However, he also realized that they were some of the stupidest and least creative oppressors he had ever encountered, and he took comfort and hope in that realization. He may be a full head shorter and at least twenty-five pounds smaller than they were, but he felt pretty certain that he was also about fifty points higher on the intelligence quotient, and that this intellectual advantage could come in handy if things ever turned really nasty. Toby also found sustenance in the awareness that D. W. was counselor to the whole lot of them.

To Toby, camp seemed to be mainly about male bonding and initiation rites, with the requisite strutting, competing, and beating of chests that went along with these collective rituals. However this year, from the beginning, he had noticed something very different here. The program at Camp Osage also included a fine arts component, something he had never experienced at previous camps.

The first night, they had gathered around the campfire to mark the end of their orientation day. Mr. Biggs, their jovial, middle-aged camp director, had made all the usual welcoming remarks, lame jokes, and ingratiating platitudes about how this two-week experience would "create lasting friendships, and moreover, change the very course of young lives."

Yeah, yeah, yeah, Toby had thought as he stifled a yawn and tried hard not to look as bored and cynical as he felt. Then the director had turned the program over to the six senior counselors, including D. W. Toby sat up. The counselors never said a word, but lined up in the center of the gathering with their various wind pipes, drums, and gourd rattles, and began chanting a Native American prayer that Toby had never heard before, but that nonetheless moved him to goose bumps. Something in the combination of sibilant consonant sounds, guttural glottal endings, and jubilant, plaintive voices made his heart melt and his spirits soar. "Tunkashila! Wa ma yanka, yo he!"

The singers and drummers repeated the lines several times and then began circling the campers, weaving in and out among them, continuing the chorus and refrain, urging the boys to join them, drumming and shaking rattles in the young campers' startled faces.

At first the boys were clearly confused and uncertain how to respond. Here was a foreign song and language they had never heard before and didn't understand. How could they possibly sing along?

Toby watched them glance uncomfortably at each other and knew exactly what they were thinking; also exactly what they needed. Taking a deep breath, he stood up and found D. W.'s eyes, taking courage in the welcome and affirmation he saw there.

"Tunkashila!" Toby sang. "Wa ma yanka, yo he! Tunkashila! Wa ma yanka, yo he!"

He didn't know what the words meant. He only knew that they rang sweetly in his ears. Best of all, it felt good to see the smile in D. W.'s eyes as he danced closer to Toby and joined his rich baritone with the younger boy's frail tenor.

D. W. stood next to Toby, continuing to sing the prayer, and put his arm around the younger boy's shoulders, as he turned to face the crowd and waved his left arm in the air, summoning the rest of them to rise up and sing along. At first, they seemed hesitant, but one by one, they eventually all succumbed to D. W.'s persuasive call to action. Ultimately every boy present rose up, looked into the fire, and waving mosquitoes away from their faces with their hands, sang the Lakota prayer at the top of his lungs.

Toby watched it all unfold as if mesmerized. He felt the unknown Lakota words falling from his lips, and looked about him, watching the strange, surreal impact of the experience on his fellow campers. It wasn't only for him that the indecipherable foreign words and music hit some deep primal chord. It was obvious from the others' reactions that they too were transported in some way to an undisclosed, indescribable spiritual place. He felt the heavy, muscled arm resting on his shoulder and looked up to see D. W. gazing down at him, still singing the prayer at the peak of his strong voice with a big, beaming smile.

At his age, Toby had only the vaguest notion of what sex between two human beings must be like. He knew men put their penises into women's vaginas and moved them back and forth somehow to reach an orgasm. He had no idea if, when, and how men or women might have sex with their own gender. When he looked up into D. W.'s smiling eyes, though, he knew what it felt like to join souls with another person, whatever their gender might be. For there in the tawny eyes looking down at him and the handsome, ruddy face sending its heat to him, he thought that he saw the countenance of a young god.

If this was going to be the way of things at Camp Osage, Toby decided maybe he could enjoy the next two weeks after all, no matter what his cabin-mates might do to try to spoil things for him. Later he would regret the naivete of that thought.

*   *   *

Down in the depths of the green lake water beneath the camp's swimming dock, dark forces were at work. Minnows pursued and swallowed smaller minnows; largemouth bass swallowed up even the largest of the minnows; finally, pimple-faced adolescent boys dipped fishing lines into the emerald depths and pulled even the biggest of the bass out of their ancestral homes.

Toby watched it all from the sidelines, as usual, cradling a book in his lap. He hoped no one would notice him, and he longed for sundown to arrive. It was his second week at camp and anything that could go wrong had gone wrong.

He had thought that he was prepared for whatever his three roommates might throw at him, but they had managed to surprise him with some unexpected twists. Coming back to the cabin after swimming one afternoon, Toby had already wriggled out of his wet swimsuit and thrown it on the floor when he looked down at the clothes the other boys had left strewn there earlier that day. It took him a moment to recognize the evil symbol, and a moment more before he fully comprehended that it had been planted there intentionally. He saw the clear outline of a swastika in the apparently random way the others had thrown their discarded clothes on the floor. Worse yet, Toby realized that the beauty of this particular scare tactic was that they could always claim it had been unintentional, and that he was paranoid, imagining things because he was a Jew. He knew then in an instant that he had underestimated their creativity.

They continued to alarm and unsettle him with comparable hate tactics as the seemingly endless two weeks of summer camp unfolded. Sorting wooden beads and shells together in crafts class, preparing to string them into native-style necklaces and bracelets, Toby looked over at the others boys' beads and saw that they spelled *Auschwitz*. When the crafts instructor turned to oversee their work, the boys artfully ran their fingers through the beads, sending them rolling across the table and erasing the hateful message, but not before Toby had seen it and fully registered its import. These boys meant him serious harm.

He wrestled with what to do. With the exception of D. W., there wasn't a single soul he could trust here, and, though D. W. was kind and compassionate, Toby surmised that even he would dismiss his fears as paranoid ruminations. He assumed that as counselor to all of them, D. W. would probably try to reassure him that these boys posed him no real harm.

Toby considered the question over in his mind and answered it for himself . . . *wrong!* These boys were truly dangerous. He knew that beyond a doubt, but how could he prove it to anyone else? That was the problem.

Sorting through all of this in his head, he set about preparing himself for the closing ceremonies that night. By long tradition, the leaders at Camp Osage had observed a ritual of reenacting the settling of Frazier by its founding fathers on the final night of camp. Afterward, the camp director, with great pomp and circumstance, gave the campers all the awards and medals they had earned over the previous two weeks, and everyone closed the evening in the mess hall with punch, cookies, and the obligatory Duck Dance and Bunny Hop.

As one of the swarthiest residents of the camp, Toby had been the logical choice to play the Native American chief who had given the land that Frazier was situated on to the settlers. The story went that the tired and hungry settlers came down the river on canoes and rafts, and were welcomed by a benevolent Native American chieftain who invited them to make their home there. Though Toby suspected this tale was probably revisionist history at its worst, he had no way to fact-check it.

Tonight's reenactment of these events had Toby in a canoe on the lake, welcoming the settlers, played by his three blond roommates in another canoe. The four boys had practiced this scenario under Mr. Biggs's tutelage every afternoon for the last three days until he had finally exclaimed "Perfect!" that very afternoon. Despite the director's affirmation, somehow Toby didn't feel it was all quite so perfect.

His three roommates had all behaved respectfully the whole time they had rehearsed together. Maybe that was what worried Toby the most; they had never been more polite to him than they were during the preparations for this final camp experience.

He had nothing to hang his suspicions on other than intuition, and he knew that he could probably never get anyone to validate such fears. So he shrugged on the cheesy native costume that Mr. Biggs had provided for tonight's show, a full simulated eagle feather headdress that Toby knew was worn only by Plains Indians, not Woodlands tribes such as those that had lived in this region. He was surprised to find how heavy it was for a bunch of feathers lashed together, but looking at the craftsmanship, he saw that the feathers had been carefully interwoven with ceramic beads and metal wiring, making the whole thing unexpectedly cumbersome. In addition, the clasp on the leather chin strap tended to stick. Toby found the whole thing ridiculous and maddening.

Finally suited up, he trudged down to the lakeside. It was going to be a long night, but thankfully his last one at Camp Osage. Tomorrow, with any luck, he would be on his way home, without any further incidents.

Stumbling through the camp in his ungainly ersatz Indian garb, trying hard not to react to the other campers giggling and pointing at him, Toby looked around him at what had been the scene of so much misery for the previous two weeks. On the face of it, it looked like such a benign and welcoming place. Picturesque log cabins clustered beneath blue-green white pines and tall, graceful ash trees, resplendent with the verdant foliage of full summer. A sweet, sticky haze hung over the little valley that cradled the campgrounds as the afternoon sun began to head toward the horizon. The massive mess hall stood at the center of it all, the towering flag pole before it sporting both an American flag and a pennant with what was reputed to be the symbol of the Osage tribe (though Toby wasn't buying that, knowing that he was wearing Lakota Sioux instead of Osage garb).

He realized sadly that he could have really had some fun here these last two weeks, especially considering how excited he had been to meet and become friends with D. W. But his cabin-mates had ruined it all. They had made his life a living hell; he was constantly waiting for the other shoe to drop, or the next subtle, yet exquisitely disturbing threat to emerge. He had never been able to relax for a minute, never take a deep breath or enjoy a truly restful night's sleep. The only consolation was that he was definitely going to have a very long talk with his parents after this year's camp experience, and he was going to use everything he had ever learned from his mother about guilt trips. Oh, he was going to make them pay alright for this one. They were going to pay and pay for years to come, if he had his way.

Arriving at the lakefront where the closing ceremony was to occur, Toby realized he was going to have to put aside such thoughts. He looked about the gathering and saw that it was true madness. Younger campers were wandering about in costumes even more ludicrous and ungainly than his, if that was possible. Winged wood fairies, chartreuse green tree frogs, rangy coyotes, and red-faced elves tripped over their garments, stumbling, falling, and cussing. It was as if some mad theme park employee, high on drugs, had infiltrated their ranks and set them up to self-destruct.

He wandered through the teeming activity, trying to help younger campers with tangled costumes and other wardrobe dilemmas wherever he could. However, for the most part, there wasn't a whole lot he could do. The evening seemed to have taken on a surreal energy of its own. Looking about him at the motley crew of boys from different age groups, struggling into various improbable costumes, animal and vegetable, Native American and colonial, Toby finally threw in the towel. This particular little world was not a rational place where cause-and-effect laws held sway. It was time to acknowledge the laws of chaos and submit to them. Hearing Doris Day's voice in his head, he surrendered to the idea that whatever will be, will be.

In the midst of the confusion, Mr. Biggs spotted him and

came puffing to his side, clutching a cluttered clipboard and an old megaphone. "Camper Schumann, I'm so glad to see you. The program is supposed to be starting now, but we can't get the younger campers suited up and the crowd is becoming restless. You have some theater experience, right?"

Toby realized that he probably needed to lie and say no, that he knew nothing about performing, but the truth slipped out of his mouth before he knew it. "Yes, sir, I've been in children's theater since I was six."

"Good," Mr. Biggs said. "Here are the program notes and the megaphone. Get up there on the stage and improvise something while we pull the rest of the boys together. I'm counting on you, Schumann. Make this thing happen!"

"But I'm in the show myself, remember?" Toby protested. "I'm in the final act, the reenactment of the founding."

"No problem," Mr. Biggs said. "Just announce your departure when it's time for the last act and I'll take charge from there." With that he waddled off, leaning down now and then to assist a smaller boy with a costume or headdress.

Toby struggled to hold the hefty clipboard and ungainly megaphone in his thin arms. *What have I gotten myself into now?* As he listened to the rumblings of the crowd gathered around the makeshift plywood stage that had been erected on the lakefront, he had to admit that the natives were definitely getting restless, and someone needed to do something about it soon.

Hundreds of boys from all age groups milled about the open forum. Everyone present was due to be in some sort of song or skit or other performance shortly. But for now, they were all at loose ends. They were suited up for their various roles and tableaux, but no one was directing them. Toby knew from his experiences at other camps that a lack of structure in a group of young males was a recipe for disaster.

He could feel the tension mounting in the air, as boys began shoving and jostling each other. "Get off my tail!" a pre-teen dressed as a wolf shouted at another boy. The offender was stumbling about, bumping into others because he couldn't see through the ill-fitting medicine man's mask he was wearing. Toby scanned the crowd and saw that similar incidents were erupting all through it.

It was time for somebody to do something. Darting toward the stage as best he could in his own silly, trailing headdress, he jumped onto it as if he knew exactly what he was doing. No one watching would have ever guessed how uncertain and almost panicky he felt. That was where his early theater training came in handy, as he remembered platitudes from long-ago drama coaches about how "the show must go on," and how "you should never let them see you sweat." Reciting these axioms in his head like a mantra, he went to front center stage and put the megaphone to his lips.

"Hey, hey, hey, what do you say?" he shouted, doing his best imitation of the toothsome game show hosts he loved to watch on idle summer mornings at home. "It's time for the game America loves to play, *Tomorrow's Stars!*" He hoped to redirect the rising havoc by giving the boys something on which to focus all their unbridled energy and attention. Over the edge of the megaphone, he was pleased to see heads turning toward him, eyebrows raised, wondering what the heck he was up to, but he could also tell that he had their attention.

"Here's the way it works. You all know this is talent night at Camp Osage, an annual tradition here, but what you didn't know is that *tonight* a secret panel of distinguished judges will be watching all of our performers and deciding who will be the stars of tomorrow. At the end of the evening, the judges will announce their decisions and a first, second, and third place winner will be announced. All three will win a special prize!"

Toby had mixed emotions of relief and doubt as he watched the boys light up with the excitement of knowing that the boring talent show, an event that they had dreaded, actually had some payoff. He could feel the electricity take hold of the crowd as they began talking animatedly, bragging about who would win, but he also saw Mr. Biggs staring at him with clear disapproval from the midst of the throng. Biggs knew there was no secret judge's panel, or specially selected prizes. Realizing he was busted, Toby gave the camp director a big smile, shrugged, and mouthed the words, Oh, well!

He was blowing all of this out of his ass, of course, having made the whole thing up on the spur of the moment, but somehow he sensed that it was the right thing to do, and he hoped Mr. Biggs would eventually also see the rightness of it. He figured he could always talk his folks into sending the winners some mail-order gift certificates to their stores.

In the midst of his musings, while he was watching the other boys gear up for the evening ahead with a whole new spirit, Toby looked out and saw a face staring at him. D. W. stood at the far edge of the crowd, and looked straight into Toby's eyes. The older boy smiled approvingly, put his right hand to his temple in a small salute, and then turned to tend to some younger campers. In that brief moment, watching D. W. send him a sign of affirmation, Toby felt the happiest he had ever been in his whole life.

The evening unfolded more smoothly than Toby would have ever dreamed possible. Infused with a new motivation for their various performances, the boys jumped into them with true relish. Toby watched campers who had merely plodded through rehearsals shine in their roles, some even hamming it up. In between each act, he took center stage and played the adrenalin-charged emcee to the hilt.

"How about that last performance?" he'd ask the audience with enthusiasm. "Who'd have ever thought that a guy dressed in a raccoon costume could juggle so many oranges at once? It's truly amazing! Yes sir, that's what it is, truly amazing!"

Hokey as this performance seemed to Toby, the crowd loved it. With each performance, they seemed to become more excited by the question of who would win the prizes that night, fanned to a near frenzy by his between-act histrionics.

On some level, Toby knew that he was in his element. He had never felt like one of these boys, never felt that he belonged among them, nor shared in their particular brand of humanity. They were universally Christian, while he was a Jew. They were all from the South or Midwest, while he was a New Yorker. They were all clearly budding heterosexuals, while he was pretty sure he was gay.

However, tonight he was doing what he knew best, and, more than that, he was succeeding. He was putting on a show, using his imagination, and making things happen. When the last act before his own finished, he came to the podium for the final time and looked out at the audience. He wasn't prepared for what he saw, but it would change his life forever.

There was the assembly of boys, dressed in strange costumes, watching the stage intently. Bright smiles and eager eyes followed his every move, awaiting his next pronouncements. Looking out at them, Toby felt an unexpected surge of affection. He might be nothing like them. He might be something they would abhor and abominate if they knew his true self. However tonight, standing before them on this makeshift stage, wearing this ridiculous misplaced Sioux headdress that was choking and weighing him down, Toby knew that he had a special bond with them. It was the strange, tentative, yet curiously strong bond of the performer with his audience. How he savored that connection.

Relishing the moment, he realized nonetheless that it was time to move on, so he stepped to the edge of the stage and lifted the megaphone to his mouth one last time.

"Let's hear it," he shouted to the crowd. "How about a big round of applause for *all* of our performers tonight, since they've all done a marvelous job."

In response, clapping hands, Rebel yells, and piercing whistles almost drowned him out before the last words were out of his mouth. Urging the crowd to continue their applause with his right hand, he scanned the back rows for Mr. Biggs and finally found the portly man looking on, appearing to be more than a little discomfited by all the uproar.

"Mr. Biggs," he said into the megaphone, "if you'll take over for me now, it's time for our finale." He left the megaphone at the edge of the stage and started to exit to prepare for his own act, but then something magical happened that he would never have predicted. As he started to clamber down the shaky steps, he heard a chorus of voices rising up all around him in a thunderous war cry, chanting in unison, "Toby! Toby! Toby! Toby!"

For a moment, he was puzzled, unable to assimilate what was happening. Then it sank in; they were acknowledging him for his role as emcee. He stopped and turned to the crowd, stepped back onto the stage slowly, and with that, the gathering went wild, coming to their feet and clapping even more loudly in a standing ovation.

Hearing and watching this experience unfold, he thought about all the children's theater he had done in New York through the years. He remembered all the Grimm's fairy tales and Louisa May Alcott stories that had been forced upon him and his fellow youth performers, and realized that this was the first time he had ever had the opportunity to relate to an audience as *himself*, albeit ill-dressed in a numbskull Native American headdress. The applause he was reaping was different than any applause he had ever experienced. This applause was for *him*, for Toby Schumann, emcee and master crowd-control manager, not some simpering fairy tale character or one-dimensional male bit-part player in a melodrama about girls.

Recognizing he needed to do something to acknowledge this accolade, he took a deep breath and strutted to front stage again. He tried to get the chinstrap to his headdress loose so that he could take the thing off and make a proper bow, but he found the strap as hard to unclasp as it had been to fasten. He gave up on that idea and decided on another plan. Raising both arms and then lowering them to encourage the noise to die down, he thanked the boys for their applause.

"Enough," he said humbly. "Thank you. Just remember, tonight our main job is to find Tomorrow's Stars!" With that, seeing Mr. Biggs lumbering up the steps to take charge of the proceedings, he bounded from the stage. He ducked out the back and hopped to the ground, then darted for the lake where he and his cabin mates were supposed to rendezvous.

The plan was for the four boys to launch two separate canoes—Toby alone in one, playing the role of Chief Joseph Locust Longtree, and the other three boys dressed in frontier garb, playing the settlers who had founded Frazier. They were to paddle quickly to two predetermined spots about a hundred yards offshore and begin paddling toward each other, while Mr. Biggs read the narrative of how the benevolent native chief had given the land to the settlers. At the end of Mr. Biggs's reading, Toby was to paddle off in a slow, solemn way, while the settlers waved their goodbyes. Thinking about how horrible his three roomies had been to him over the previous two weeks, Toby couldn't help but think that playing this amicable meeting was going to be the greatest acting challenge of his life. He took comfort, though, in the knowledge that after it was over, he would have only one night left in their toxic company, and then he would head for home.

When they arrived where the canoes were tied, Toby and his fellow players scarcely acknowledged each other. He was determined to avoid being intimidated by them in any way, so he simply shoved his canoe into the water. Jumping into its rear seat as he did, he had to take care to avoid getting entangled in the heavy headdress he had been fighting all night. He would be glad to be rid of it shortly. He somehow managed to guide his canoe out of the little harbor into deeper waters.

"Nice job tonight playing the big shot," a sarcastic voice called after him as he paddled away. "Guess you're feeling pretty good about yourself right now, huh, Jew boy?"

No matter how hard he tried to prevent it from impacting him, Toby had to admit they got to him every time they uttered that hateful phrase. He never let on, as that would be the ultimate surrender. He kept paddling and looked all around him at the shoreline and the emerging stars and anything else he could find to signal to them that he didn't give a damn about their nasty remarks.

Night was coming on fast, and it was time to wrap up the evening's program, so that all the campers could get back to their bunks and bed down in time to rise early the next day for departure. As he paddled farther out onto the lake, Toby could hear the paddles of his cabin-mates dipping into the water behind him, and the other boys trooping down to the lakeside. Once they were all there, Mr. Biggs began his narrative about the founding of Frazier.

"It was a time of exploration and expansion unequaled in history," Mr. Biggs read from his notes in a stentorian voice. "The American West constantly urged settlers onward, driving them forward to their Manifest Destiny, the taming of a wild frontier and the birthing of a new nation."

Toby tried not to think too much about readings he had done in the New York City Library about the "American Holocaust," the systematic annihilation of the indigenous people who had inhabited the continent before white people ever arrived on it.

"Just hold tight and get home," he kept repeating to himself. "One more night and you're out of here."

He arrived at the spot they had designated in rehearsals to begin their tableau about the founding of Frazier. Turning and working his paddle in the water to stop and reverse his canoe, he waited for Mr. Biggs's cues to begin the final act of the evening's entertainment. Looking out across the placid lake in the fading light, he saw the other canoe and his cabin mates dressed in pioneer garb about twenty feet away. They leered at him, winked, and mouthed obscenities while Mr. Biggs read from his script about the benevolent gesture that had occurred between a long-ago Indian chief and the hungry settlers. Watching them work the miasma of hate they carried about them to a new and even more poisonous level, Toby loathed them with all his heart.

At last he heard the line that would send him paddling forward to his co-players and eventually free him from the night's tortures.

"Recognizing the inevitability and rightness of the white man's entitlement to their lands," Mr. Biggs read from his notes, "the wisest leaders of the Indian nations gave their land to the settlers."

That was Toby's cue to paddle toward the settlers' canoe, and he did so with all the expected pomp and circumstance required for such a moment. All the while, he watched the boys whose canoe he was approaching grin and chuckle and trying to egg him into an open conflict.

"Just a few more minutes," he silently repeated to himself. "A few more hours, and I'm back in civilization again."

Mr. Biggs's pompous voice intruded into his thoughts. "Thus it was," he intoned, "that Chief Joseph resolved to turn over his people's lands to the hardworking and resolute pioneers. History tells us that on a mid-summer day, much like this one we are enjoying, he paddled into the midst of the settlers on the river that once ran here, and welcomed them to make their home here."

Right on cue, though thoroughly doubting the revisionist history he was enacting, Toby paddled up to the others boys' canoe and raised his right hand in a gesture of greeting. He refused, however, to say the "How!" that Mr. Biggs had scripted for him. Instead, he chose to pantomime the act of turning over his homeland to the invaders.

To his surprise, Toby found that the other boys played their parts with a dignity he would never have expected of them. Sitting in their canoe, they all saluted him with respect and made their rehearsed hand gestures to signal that they accepted his gift gratefully, moving their hands to their hearts and holding them there with smiles of thanks, while Mr. Biggs finished his monologue.

"With that," he declared, "the chief bade the settlers a fond farewell, and paddled off into the dusk, never to be seen again."

With that line, Toby turned his canoe again and began paddling away, exactly as they had rehearsed numerous times. However, this time, as he did so, he found the paddling harder than it had been before. Looking down in the bottom of the canoe, he saw that there was more than the usual inch or two of water accumulated there. In fact, it appeared that his craft was rapidly taking on water. He turned and looked over his shoulder at the other boys and saw their looks of malicious glee.

The realization hit him in an instant. They had scuttled his canoe, punching tiny holes in it that wouldn't be apparent or do their damage for a while. Then they had sat back, going on with the performance as if nothing were wrong, waiting for the craft to founder, probably hoping to ruin the tableau and embarrass Toby in the process.

Well, he thought, grimly, they had missed that opportunity at least, but now he wondered whether he could make it back to the shore. There was no alternative but to give it his best shot. So he turned the canoe toward shore and began paddling for all he was worth.

Heading toward land, Toby saw that the assembly were milling about, clapping at the end of the final act. He presumed they would also be waiting for his announcement of the three winners from tonight's "competition," and he wondered fleetingly how he was going to pull off that feat. Glancing down, he realized he may not have to worry about that, for the water in the canoe was rising even faster.

With a sinking heart, he felt the tipping point occur where the volume of water in the canoe reached a level sufficient to sink the little craft. The canoe slipped out from under him and disappeared into the depths, leaving behind only a whisper of air bubbles. He was adrift in the water, still a good sixty yards from the beach, without a life vest or other flotation device other than the flimsy wooden paddle he clutched tightly in his hands.

He heard laughter and tried to turn to see his cabin mates back in their canoe, pointing at his distress, and chuckling happily. But the heavy headdress was taking on water rapidly, and sinking, pulling his head back so that he could barely move it.

What's happening? Feathers are supposed to float, aren't they? Then he remembered that the feathers had been tied together with wire and embedded with heavy glass beads. The crazy thing was being dragged down by the weight of all that metal and beadwork.

Frantic, he let go of the paddle and tried using both hands to unfasten the leather chin strap, but he couldn't get it undone, especially now that the strap was wet. He was beginning to panic, and found that his fingers fumbled at the clasp, scratching at it uselessly and getting nowhere fast. Meanwhile, he watched the little paddle, the only flotation assistance he'd had, drift silently away from him.

The headdress was completely sodden and pulled his head all the way back into the water. Trying to keep his mouth and chin above the surface, he continued struggling with the clasp. All he could see was the darkening water around him and the evening sky overheard, the stars beginning to show in the gathering dusk. He heard the water lapping at his ears, and an additional sound, the roar of a crowd, not clapping and cheering this time, but crying out in alarm.

"He's in trouble!"

"Toby's going under!"

"Somebody do something!"

Then even that sound became muted as his ears filled with water. The waves lapped over his nose and he smelled the dank, algae scent of the water. It made him cough and gasp for air through his mouth, still barely above the surface, but he was rapidly losing the battle for breath.

Finally, the relentless tug of the sinking headdress pulled his head completely under the water. He fought to hold his breath as he flailed his arms at the surface, grabbing big handfuls of the water and trying to pull himself back to the top with all his strength. At last, he felt his lungs explode, and he opened his mouth.

The first intake of water surprised him. He didn't know what he had expected, but he was startled to find that it burned, filling his mouth and throat and lungs with a searing fire. The pain was excruciating and he tried to cry out, but no sound could emerge from his constricted throat. He was drowning and he knew it, and his only remaining prayer was that he would somehow lose consciousness soon, so that he could escape this unimaginable torture.

Just then, thank God, his prayer was answered. He felt himself slip away from the pain in an instant, his last sensation being one of flying. His arms and legs were suddenly weightless and his body went soaring through space as if he had wings.

Toby realized almost right away that he was dead, because he couldn't feel his body anymore. The first thought that occurred to him was, *Why does everyone fear this thing so much when it feels so wonderful?* He was in a place like nowhere he had ever experienced on earth. There were no walls or structures, no up or down, nor directions of any kind, only a warm, white atmosphere filled with swirling mist, almost like the inside of a cloud he had once glimpsed through an airplane window.

He floated through this other world like a beam of light, darting here and there, exploring the groundless terrain, finding only nothingness, but enjoying the novelty of the sensation. Something came to him from a distant memory, a word uttered once by someone he could scarcely recall. *Nowheresville. That's where I am*, his spirit self thought with an inner chuckle. *I'm in Nowheresville.*

But with that recollection, a startling thing happened. He felt his body again, and in particular, he felt his lips. More than that, he felt his lips being kissed, and the sensation was exquisite. A delicious tingling feeling went rushing through his body, the body he felt rapidly being restored to him.

He felt strong hands cradling his face, as the mouth joined to his kept kissing it lovingly. Toby wondered for a moment if this was what heaven was, for he had never felt such complete and total happiness. He became aware that his heart was thumping thunderously, so hard that he thought it might burst at any moment. He became further aware of his eyes, of how they were fluttering rapidly, and in between the fluttering he saw vague colors and shapes taking form—dark blues and greens, warm flesh and earth tones swimming around in the air with a dizzying kaleidoscope effect.

Eventually he was able to open his eyes completely and something recognizable finally came into view. When it did, he decided he must surely be in heaven, because the first thing he saw as he came to was the beautiful brown eyes of D. W. Singer looking deep into his. He realized then that it was D. W. who had been kissing him and he thought anew that his heart must surely burst, but with happiness.

Then, suddenly, things took a dreadful turn for the worse. His delight evaporated in an instant and a racking pain washed over his body. His head began to spin and his stomach to roll. He didn't know what was happening anymore. D. W. was still kissing him and he was trying to kiss him back, trying to hold onto the incredible pleasure he had felt at knowing that the older boy whom he had pined for, also wanted him in return.

It was no use. His spinning head and churning stomach overcame all other emotions and sensations. He pulled his face away from D. W.'s and hurled a long plume of algae-flavored water across the ground beside him. To his utter amazement, as he continued to vomit, a loud cheer went up all around him. Shaking his head, he blinked and focused his eyes, to find himself surrounded by the whole population of the camp. They were all laughing and shouting and clapping for him again, though in a different way now.

"Nice going, Toby. You really know how to steal the show, don't you?"

"Yeah, Schumann, you didn't have to drown to get our attention. We already gave you a standing ovation."

Struggling to sit up, Toby felt strong hands restraining him and looked up to see D. W. kneeling over him, pressing him gently but firmly on the shoulders. "We've been here before," he said. "Remember?"

Toby knew exactly what the older boy was talking about, recalling that first day at the bus station, when he had fallen onto the sidewalk and nearly split his head open. He tried to agree, but found that he still couldn't talk, so he simply nodded and acquiesced to D. W.'s orders, letting himself lie back and close his eyes.

Lying there inert, listening to the other boys chatter, Toby was surprised to find himself drifting off to sleep. He would have thought that he might never sleep again for fear of not waking up, but listening to the drone of the boys' voices against the backdrop of crickets and cicadas singing in the nearby woods, he was lulled into slumber.

* * *

He awoke next morning in the camp infirmary with a nurse hovering over him, eyeing him closely. Much of the night before was a blur, but one powerful memory remained. The strong, clean scent of D. W.'s big athletic body still hung over him, and the reassuring touch of the older boy's hands still rested on his shoulders.

Later, standing beside his luggage in the hot August sun, Toby looked around at the swarm of campers that spilled over the tiny loading dock by the bus. In the midst of the commotion, he felt more than a little overwhelmed, not fully himself after his near demise less than twenty-four hours earlier. The bus station and downtown Frazier hadn't improved since his first introduction to them. The dusty storefronts still sported their sorry, dejected faces, and the same weeds sprouted in healthy profusion from the cracked sidewalks in front of the store facades.

He saw D. W. in the crowd, walking his way, scrutinizing him with concern. Toby felt the little leap that always grabbed his heart whenever he laid eyes on the older boy, but this time it was heightened by the fresh memory of the feel of beard stubble and warm lips against his. For the rest of his life, Toby would never be able to kiss another man without thinking for a fleeting instant about the taste and feel and smell of the beautiful young man he had known at his final summer camp.

D. W. arrived in front of Toby, and circled him twice, looking him up and down, as if he were inspecting a horse or cow at an auction. "You seem to be alive and kicking," he said at last. "How do you feel?"

Toby took a deep breath and felt the painful pressure in his sternum and residual tightness in his lungs. "I'm okay, thanks. Not *good*, but okay."

D. W. motioned Toby to come with him and together the two boys strolled side by side, down the sidewalk, away from the crowd. Toby breathed in the humid mountain air, hot enough already to sting his nose, even early in the morning. He also inhaled the sweet familiar fragrance of his older companion. A sudden shyness seemed to come over both boys, for neither of them said anything for several minutes. Then D. W. broke the awkwardness.

"Something happened here this last couple of weeks," he said. Toby thought he heard a certain cautious, cryptic message in the older boy's tone and wording.

"Something special . . . something important. You feel it too, don't you?"

Toby's mind reeled. He wanted to shout, *Yes, something important happened here, you big lug. I found out for sure that I'm gay because I'm in love with you!* Of course, he could never say that. "I think so," he said instead. "It's hard to put into words."

"Exactly," D. W. nodded. "That's exactly it." They walked on in silence again for a while, until D. W. stopped and chuckled. "You gave us quite a scare. I don't think I've ever been more frightened in my life."

Toby found it hard to believe. He didn't think D. W. was ever scared of anything; he always seemed so confident and decisive. "No kidding? It sure didn't show."

D. W. smiled a slow smile and gave him a little wink. *"Acting!* We're a couple of actors, the two of us. Right?"

Toby's heart melted, hearing D. W.'s words pairing the two of them, putting them together in some way. He had never thought of himself as anything even remotely like D. W. Yet here was his idol, describing the two of them as comrades.

"Maybe so," Toby replied.

"No 'maybe' about it," D. W. said and put his arm around Toby's shoulders as they started to walk back to the bus station.

Toby wanted to lean into the bigger boy and snuggle close to his muscled body, but he knew better than to risk any touch so intimate. Instead, he tried to savor the brotherly embrace and keep his fantasies from getting the better of him. Still, he felt he had to say something to try to convey his thanks to the older boy.

"Hey, listen, thanks a lot . . . for . . . for saving me last night. I was a goner for sure. I don't know how you ever found me down there in the water so quickly."

D. W. took his arm off Toby's shoulder and turned to face him. "Oh, that part wasn't me. That was your bunk mates' doing."

Toby tried to take it in, but couldn't quite believe his ears. *"What?"*

D. W. nodded. "That's right. I could have never swum out there, much less found you that fast from the shore. Those guys were in the water, swimming your way the minute you went under. They dove down after you and pulled you back up to the surface within seconds."

Toby was dumbfounded. He shook his head over and over again.

"It's true," D. W. said. "I could never have revived you if they hadn't gotten you to shore so fast." He seemed to have an afterthought that tickled him. "Now talk about scared . . . you should've seen those guys' faces while I was working on you. I'm pretty sure all three pissed their pants, but I can't prove it since they were already wet."

Toby had to laugh at that, but he continued shaking his head in disbelief as the two finished their stroll back to the bus station. Then, as they were about to rejoin the group, he had an idea about a better way he could thank D. W. for all the older boy had done for him.

"Hold on a sec. There's something I want you to have."

Shrugging off his backpack, he kneeled, unzipped it, and began rummaging through its contents. Finally he found what he was looking for and pulled it out, a little reluctantly.

His old friend, GI Joe, lay in his clammy hand, the hawk-like nose and steely eyes looking up at him, one last time. They had been through a lot together, he and Joe. Now they had been through the best thing of all in their adventures together, meeting D. W. Singer in this miserable little town in the middle of nowhere, at a camp that he hoped he would never see again.

In spite of his loathing for Arkansas, and his eagerness to leave it, Toby would always have fond memories of at least one aspect of this time in his life.

Standing and facing D. W., he flushed as he silently took the older boy's big right hand in his and placed the doll in its palm. He was embarrassed to find himself fighting back tears as he ventured a shy glance at his hero.

D. W.'s eyes were shining, too. "I can't," he said thickly. "Not your Joe."

Toby found that all he could do was nod his head, but he did it adamantly, making clear, even without words that he wouldn't take no for an answer.

"Well, all right then," D. W. said. "If you insist, but only if you take this in return."

He pulled the amulet from around his neck and put it over Toby's head, patting it into place on his chest. Toby looked down and saw the piece of polished tiger-eye that he had seen D. W. wear everywhere, every day, for the last two weeks. He put his hand around it and could still feel the warmth of the other boy's body in it.

"Thanks," Toby said simply, not trusting himself to say more. As he looked up into D. W.'s eyes, he knew no further words were needed. He sensed the older boy had intuited all of the things he couldn't express in words, and even seemed to be okay with all of it. Toby also sensed that D. W. didn't feel the same way about him, that D. W. wasn't a boy who loved other boys the way he did, but that he didn't hold this difference against Toby. It was the first time in his life that Toby had ever been able to imagine coming out to the world as his true self and possibly finding acceptance from others. Merely imagining the possibility made his heart leap with hope.

The crowd at the bus station had swelled and surrounded them while they exchanged gifts, and the two friends became aware that they were the object of curious stares. So giving each other one long last smile, they shook hands in their best manly way, and parted company without another word. Toby turned to find his luggage in the confusion at the loading platform, but was soon interrupted by a rising hue and cry.

"Hey, Schumann, what about the winners from last night?"

"Yeah, you never announced them, or the prizes they won either!"

Soon a chorus of voices assailed him and he found himself at the center of a small storm. Time to think fast, he told himself, and he searched his memory for the best performances last night.

"Good question, boys," he began. "Well, here are the judges' decisions. The third prize goes to Jeffrey Tobin for his recital of the *Song of Hiawatha*." Jeffrey, a portly seven-year-old stepped forward, his barrel chest puffing up with pride.

"Second prize goes to Art Daley for his juggling act," Toby said next. Art strutted forward and took a little bow, drawing good-natured jeers and catcalls from the crowd.

Toby hit a wall, wondering who to name as the first-prize winner. There had been over a dozen acts that were equally amateurish and mediocre, with nary a star performance from the lot of them. His mind went blank as he tried to come up with something quickly, and he felt the crowd beginning to grow restless waiting for his next pronouncement.

"Come *on*, Schumann," they began to grouse. "Who's the big winner?"

His eyes scanned the crowd and landed on three blond heads barely visible at the back of the gathering. For once, they were keeping a low profile and looking humble. D. W. appeared to have been right, Toby thought. They all looked damned scared, still. He had his final choice.

"The first and grand prize is a *shared* one," he announced in a low, provocative voice. "It goes to three boys actually . . . Eric Smith, John Sullivan, and Mickey Jones."

A buzz went through the crowd and voices began to rise in query.

"What did *they* do that was so special?"

"Right, they just sat out there in their canoe!"

Toby enjoyed watching the three boys squirm under the discomfiting glares and mounting ire of their peers. They weren't used to being on the receiving end of judgment. He savored the scene for as long as he thought he could get away with it, and then eventually decided it was time to let them off the hook.

"These boys' special achievement last night wasn't for a talent or performance on the *stage*," he said, looking around at the expectant faces and letting himself indulge in a small smile. "It was for life-saving skills."

A brief silence greeted this news, but soon a little wave of affirming grunts and nods rippled through the crowd. Toby could see that they got his point and were satisfied with the decision.

"So what do we win?" Jeffrey Tobin asked brightly.

Stuck again for a moment, Toby fell back on family resources. "Gift certificates to Schumann's Department Store mail-order catalog," he announced, lapsing back into his gushing emcee persona of the previous night. Turning to his three cabin-mates and making sure he had eye contact with all of them, he added in a steely voice, "A fine *Jewish* establishment in the heart of New York City. All you winners come up here and give me your addresses and I'll make sure you get your gift certificates soon."

The crowd clapped politely, but quickly lost interest, and went back to the business of loading their luggage into the bus. As the throng cleared a little, Toby found himself locked in a tense staring game with the three boys who had made his life pure hell for the last two weeks, but who had also saved it. He saw them struggling to reclaim some of their old malice and bravado . . . saw too how hard it was for them to be beholden to him.

As he continued to stare them down, Toby thought maybe he saw something shift within them. The angry tension seemed to drain from their rigid necks and shoulders, and they seemed to breathe more easily.

In response, Toby let himself do the same. He let his guard down a little and took a number of long, deep breaths, exhaling completely after each one, feeling his lungs begin to heal. As he was about to break the standoff and turn away, Toby thought he saw a smile of grudging respect beginning at the corners of Eric's mouth. When he glanced at the other boys' faces one last time, he knew it for sure. They were all looking at him with a new, albeit reluctant, appreciation.

In spite of that, Toby reminded himself that these boys would never be his friends. It was unlikely that they would ever be friends with anyone Jewish, or African American, or any other ethnic group but their own. Toby also knew that for the rest of their lives, they would struggle with a paradox. They had saved the life of a Jew, and been terrified when they almost ended it. They hadn't found it quite as easy as they had thought it would be to really harm someone different from themselves.

For some reason, Toby took great comfort from this awareness. He would carry it with him always, as one of the greatest gifts he had ever received—that and a tiger-eye amulet he would always have with him.

CHAPTER 6

OUR FATHER WHO
ART IN HEAVEN

On the hot summer day Drake Singer's funeral was held, the little rural church he'd attended all of his life was packed with mourners. It wasn't that Drake had been such a popular man. Most people who knew him, including his wife and son, felt that they didn't really know him at all. He had been an important man in town, however, and his passing deserved special attention, especially considering how sudden and unexpected it had been.

Rumor had it that he died of a heart attack after one of his many trysts with a young woman, this one a cocktail waitress in the next county. No one would ever be able to prove anything of the kind, however. The local sheriff and county police had done their best to whitewash the real story. The official report noted only that his body had been found one morning, slumped over the steering wheel of his car outside Hardesty's Roadhouse, where he had reportedly eaten "a huge steak dinner." The report failed to note that the pretty little waitress who lived in the apartment over Hardesty's was the last person to see him alive the night before, and that she was beside herself with guilt and grief to find him dead below her window the next morning.

"He seemed so . . . so . . . so *healthy* last night," she had sobbed into the sheriff's lapel when he broke the news to her that morning. Her remark never made it into any official documents, and the sheriff was soon dating the little cocktail waitress himself, despite having a wife and child at home.

Standing by the front door of the church, greeting mourners as they arrived, D. W. tried hard to ignore the whispers about the lurid circumstances of his father's death. However, at age seventeen, he was experiencing the terrible pressure all adolescents feel to be accepted by others. It was impossible for him to completely shrug off the amused grins and pointed stares of the townspeople crowding the church today.

He eyed the gathering and found his mother in a front pew, surrounded by a gaggle of church ladies making sympathetic noises and patting her with gloved hands. Though he could hear her blubbering all the way at the back of the church, he felt comforted by the knowledge that she was having the time of her life. Both he and everyone else in town knew that Alexandra Singer was never happier than when she was dealing with some catastrophe, and this was probably the biggest one of her life.

He glanced out at the little gravel parking lot outside the white frame church and saw that it was filled with cars. Most of the drivers seemed to have come inside. A last straggler bounded up the steps, and gave D. W. a sad smile and quick handshake before sliding into an overflowing back pew. Pastor McHugh went to the pulpit and nodded to D. W. to indicate that the service was about to begin.

D. W. looked out at the lush, late summer landscape. At that moment, he wanted nothing more than to run into the thick, surrounding woods, going deep into their dark, embracing arms where he would hide for as long as he could, maybe even until his adulthood, when he could finally quit this stifling community. Even as he entertained the seductive fantasy, he knew that nothing of the kind would ever really happen.

He was startled back to reality by an usher shutting the paneled wood double doors with a soft thud. D. W. wished he could stay in the back and watch the service from a point of relative peace and safety, but it wouldn't do to leave his mother in her front pew all alone. So he forced himself up the narrow aisle with reluctant steps and squeezed into the pew beside her. She threw both arms around him and began wailing even louder than she had before, although he wouldn't have thought that possible.

"What are we going to do without your wonderful father?" she sobbed. D. W. wondered for a moment who she was talking about. He certainly didn't remember the austere man lying in the casket at the front of the church as a "wonderful father." Then he realized that Alexandra's performance was for effect, so he played along, patting her shoulder tenderly and forcing a sympathetic smile.

The pastor cued the pianist to start the opening hymn and the congregation launched into the plaintive opening bars of "In the Garden." For some reason D. W. couldn't quite explain, he had always hated the wistful song. There had always seemed to be something dishonest about it. The lyrics promised comfort and peace, merely through a walk in the garden with Jesus. He also knew from considerable personal experience that much of what went on in church in Jesus's name was negative. He thought about all the years he had listened to parishioners judging each other, gossiping behind each other's backs, while the minister threatened hell and damnation from the pulpit for all kinds of behavior that D. W. considered simple human nature.

Still, he knew that he needed to at least appear to participate fully in his own father's funeral, so he gave the song his best effort and soon his full, newly ripened baritone rang from the wooden rafters. He was glad when he reached the last lines of the hymn and heard the pianist close with a little flourish. The congregation settled back into the sticky, shellacked pews, and Pastor McHugh proceeded with the opening lines of the funeral service. D. W. soon found himself daydreaming, totally absent emotionally from the proceedings, thinking lusty thoughts about a pretty girl from school sitting in the next row over with her mother and younger sister. Something about attending church always seemed to bring out the worst in him.

The pastor warmed to his role of honoring the most affluent church member he'd ever had. "We come together today to say our last goodbyes to Drake Singer, valued member of our community—father, husband, town councilman . . . *friend*."

D. W. looked around the gathering and didn't see a single head nod. He knew it was because no one in their small world would have ever characterized his father as a friend. No one had the temerity to challenge the preacher during a funeral, though, especially when he seemed to be on a roll.

"And so, while we note the rich life and many accomplishments of Drake Singer, we also know, that in the eyes of God, we are all mere mortal flesh, 'dust to dust and ashes to ashes,' meant to do our small time on this earth, doing our best to live a righteous, God-fearing life, until the time we are called to our Maker for His judgment."

The preacher smiled an obsequious smile and looked down at Alexandra and D. W. "Fortunately, we all know in our hearts what a good and righteous man Drake Singer was." He said it with a sincerity that D. W. found admirable, from a theatrical standpoint anyway. How did the preacher manage it, he wondered, considering the details of his father's death?

"We can rest assured in his everlasting life and peace with Jesus," Pastor McHugh continued. "As we gather here to mourn him, I hear a choir of angels welcoming our beloved friend, this good man and community leader, this devoted husband and father, into the land of milk and honey, into the peace that passes all understanding, into the gates of Heaven, where he will rest everlastingly with our Father, Son, and the Holy Ghost. Amen!"

With that, he nodded to the elderly pianist, and took his seat with a studied air that somehow conveyed both exhaustion and complacency. Startled into action, the woman at the rickety old upright attacked the keys with a sudden fervor that brought the gathering to its feet, scrambling for the right page in the hymnal. They mouthed the words to the first part of "Amazing Grace" on their own, but most knew they would need the hymnal to navigate their way through the less well-known second and third verses.

D. W. sang along, but winced inside at yet another familiar hymn that he disliked heartily. He had grown up hearing and singing this one, *ad nauseam*, it sometimes seemed to him. Recently, he had learned the historical background of the tune as a rallying cry against the British slave trade, and he knew that most of the people who were singing it beside him were inveterate bigots. He also knew that they considered themselves vastly superior to African American people, and that they would never have embraced the song if they had understood the true meaning of its lyrics or its historical origins.

He sang along only halfheartedly as the song progressed from first to final verses, and was relieved when it was over. It had always seemed to him so slow and plodding.

Breathing a sigh of relief to have the pedantic tune out of the way at last, he resumed his seat along with the rest of the congregation and waited for the next chapter to unfold. Pastor McHugh went to the lectern again and gazed for several moments at his congregation, letting the drama of the moment mount. Finally he spoke.

"Brothers and sisters," he began with a benevolent tone. "We have lost one of our own here today, a good man who lies before us now, waiting to meet his Creator. Let us send him off with some memories of his time here on earth. Who will come to the pulpit today and share remembrances of our brother, Drake Singer? Anyone? Just come up here to the altar."

The minister scanned the packed church with a beseeching look in his eyes, while D. W. noted the paradox unfolding before him. At his father's funeral, the pastor had to acknowledge the dead man's position in the community and at least appear to give honor to it. But D. W. sensed that even the pastor didn't much like or respect his father—that in fact, the pastor only tolerated him in his church because he was such a generous contributor. For despite his many idiosyncrasies, Drake Singer had believed in tithing. No matter what his other shortcomings might be, he had always given to the church.

Listening to the pastor's invitation to the community to remember his father, D. W. was struck by the total lack of response from the assembly. A deafening silence greeted the pastor's last words. D. W. felt his mother stir beside him and saw her glance over her shoulder a time or two to see who might be rising from their seats to eulogize her husband. She looked down again at her folded hands in her lap, waiting for someone to stand up and speak for the man with whom she had spent most of her life.

Finally, after a painfully long interval, D. W. was relieved to hear footsteps shuffling down the aisle between the pews. At last, someone was going to stand up and speak for his father. However, when the limping figure eventually came into view, his heart sank to see who it was. The first to stand up and speak for his father was Doogie Jacobs, the crippled, mildly retarded handyman who had worked in his father's store and funeral parlor for thirty years. Doogie went to the pulpit with dignity and grabbing its sides, addressed the gathering with true gravitas.

"Mornin', brothers and sisters," he began, and to D. W.'s surprise, the whole congregation answered back, "Mornin'!" Doogie seemed to take that as a good sign and warmed to his task.

"Guess everybody around here knows I'm Doogie, the cripple, who ain't got all his ducks in a row upstairs." A little laugh went through the gathering, and D. W. found himself admiring the way the man smiled and took it all with grace.

"Yeah, that's me." He laughed along with them. "But what most smart people don't realize is how much *they* don't know."

The congregation burst into laughter again, and then stopped suddenly as the ambiguous message sunk in. A woman whispered to her husband, "What do you suppose he meant by *that?*" Doogie took the opportunity to forge on.

"Way I figure it, none of us knows much of anything, really. An' that's why I never minded people callin' me dumb, so much. But this much I do know."

He turned and looked long and hard at D. W. and Alexandra.

"This man we're buryin' here today never done me a bad turn in over thirty years of me workin' for him. He always called me 'Mr. Jacobs' and he always paid me regular, even when I knew he hadn't had no cash come in all week."

Doogie stopped there, his voice thickening. He seemed to have trouble with some of his memories. "An' he also never let anyone else treat me bad, neither. Not no customer, nor salesman, nor supplier . . . nobody!"

He stopped and looked out over the packed church pews with a sudden shy, startled look, as if it had only now occurred to him what a large gathering he was addressing. Trying to collect himself, he took a deep breath.

"So I say 'thank you' to him. Yes sir, thank you, Mr. Drake, for my job and everything else you done for me. Oh, I know there's folks in this town, folks here today, in fact, that think you were a pretty hard-hearted son of a gun, but you and I know different . . . don't we?"

Doogie turned to D. W. and Alexandra again and smiled, bowing slightly before leaving the lectern. He shuffled back to his seat and settled into it with a sigh of relief.

Silence hung over the gathering as everyone wondered who would have the nerve to follow up on Doogie's performance. D. W. found himself trying to digest what he had just heard from Doogie, trying to come to terms with this whole other view of the man he had known as his father, but had never really known at all. The possibility that the cold, detached man he knew might have had unrecognized depths of kindness in him was almost more than he could absorb.

As he sifted through all this, he lost track of time, until suddenly he realized that once again, it had been several minutes and no one was rising from their seat to speak. D. W. felt the tension almost humming in the air. He looked over at his mother and saw the color rising in her neck, despite her best efforts to appear immersed in her own grief and loss. He felt a rare stab of compassion for her. With all her pretenses about how important her husband had been in this pitiful little community, it must have been difficult for her to have no one but a disabled man she thought little of speak up at this critical moment.

D. W. reached over and put a comforting hand on his mother's arm, but was startled when she drew away from him, using the ruse of drying her eyes with her handkerchief to cover the rebuff. He felt the color rise to his own cheeks at her rejection, and resolved he would leave her to her own devices for the rest of the day.

Snubbed and wounded, he tried hard to keep breathing evenly as he continued to ruminate on his mother's angry repudiation. What in the world had he ever done, he wondered, to cause her to hate him so? Was it simply because he was his father's son? Was it merely because, as such, he represented to her all the things about her own miserable life that she couldn't control or bend to her will? Because, whatever anyone might say about his father, pro or con, no one could ever say that Drake Singer was a man who let his wife control him. God alone knew, D. W. thought, why they had ever married in the first place. He liked to believe that maybe there had been some love and attraction between them somewhere along the line, at least a little bit, maybe once upon a time.

Please God, D. W. found himself praying, even though he hadn't been much of a believer recently. *Please God, don't let Dad go to his grave without someone in this miserable town beside his*

*employee giving him a proper eulogy. Let at least one other person
remember something really special and nice about him.*

The embarrassing silence continued for several moments
more and D. W. was beginning to wonder why the minister
let the awkward lapse go on so long. Just when he thought he
couldn't stand another second of the tension, he heard the sound
of high-heeled shoes on the hardwood floor, clicking down the
aisle. As soon as he heard it, D. W. wished he had never made his
earlier prayer. Someone was coming up to the lectern to say some
further words about his father, and that someone was obviously
female. *This can't be good*, he thought.

When he caught sight of her at last, D. W.'s worst fears were
confirmed, and his heart sank again. It was Tiara Bliss, the
front register clerk from the local five-and-dime store, a twenty-
something high school dropout, whose basic prettiness and
youthful bloom were obscured by the thick makeup and cheap
clothes she always wore. D. W. tried to hide his blush as Tiara
looked down at him with a sympathetic pout as she passed. She
reached out and tenderly touched his shoulder with fingertips
painted with flame red nail polish.

Tiara reached the podium, gazed out over the gathering,
and looked like she wanted to reconsider speaking. A look of
sheer panic crossed her countenance and even her heavy makeup
couldn't hide the abject fear. She appeared to consider running,
glancing over her left shoulder as if to check for a nearby exit.
Finding none, she turned to face the audience again, squared her
shoulders with a plucky air, and forced a tight smile.

"Well, now, I didn't see this one comin.' I haven't had to get
up and talk before a group since high school, and I forgot till I

got up here just now how bad I am at it." She laughed at herself and something about her remark encouraged the gathering to join in. There were probably lots of others who hadn't spoken to a group since high school and who hated it as much as Tiara did.

Clearly soothed by the audience response to her confession of nerves, Tiara took the pulpit in her hands and leaned into it a bit. She scanned the packed church and let out a little whistle.

"Huh!" She laughed again. "Mr. Drake sure would be pleased to see all of y'all here now, wouldn't he?" Another little ripple of laughter rolled through the crowd.

Tiara glanced down at her clenched hands on the corners of the lectern and let them go suddenly, stretching and flexing her fingers. She continued to eye the audience with a gaze that was half scared and overwhelmed, half emboldened and energized.

"Ain't life the funniest thing? Here I am up at the pulpit of a Baptist church. Me, who hasn't been to church in years, trying to think of something kind to say about Mr. Drake, because nobody else besides Doogie come up here to do the same thing, and I got to feeling so bad and embarrassed and all for him and his kin, sittin' back there in the back, waitin' for somebody to come up and say somethin' nice about him." She seemed to lose track of her thoughts, and looked for a moment like she wanted to run again. Then she squared her chin and gazed out at the crowd with some measure of growing confidence.

"Well, I think he was just fine," she said simply. D. W. glanced over at his mom to see what her reaction was, but she was looking down at her folded hands with a detached, disinterested air. He reminded himself that he had decided to let her be the rest of the day, so he settled back into his seat and looked forward to hearing the rest of whatever Tiara had to say about his father. He wondered what the real nature of his father's relationship with this woman might have been.

"I mean, what a *gentleman*, right?" She looked out at the group with a beseeching face, and several women finally seemed to take pity on her and the dead man, nodding in agreement. Tiara smiled at them with relief and dove back in.

"Plus, no man ever filled out a suit like Drake Singer." She giggled and a little rustle of shocked uncertainty rippled through the group. Eventually some fellow in the back got tickled by the comment and burst out laughing, and soon the whole crowd was laughing along with him.

Tiara beamed. "That's right now. Let's admit it, girls, this was one fine lookin' man here. Come on, ladies, 'fess up." At that, a roar of laughter went through the crowd, and D. W. was secretly pleased to see both his mother and the minister squirm.

Tiara took a deep breath and pushed a stray strand of dyed blonde hair out of her face. "Thing is," she said with a sad smile, "that's not what matters most about Mr. Drake."

D. W. felt a little knot rise in his gut and wondered what about his father might matter more to Tiara, and what else she might disclose to this edgy little crowd in the midst of a very strange Southern Baptist funeral in the backwoods of Southern Indiana. Apparently some of the others had the same question, because as soon as the words were out of Tiara's mouth, the whole assembly leaned forward in their seats, hanging on her next utterance as if it were some prophecy.

The moment wasn't lost on Tiara. She may have hated public speaking in high school, but something about it had clearly gotten under her skin today, for she was suddenly a five-and-dime gal gone wild. She was ready to say and do almost anything, just to speak her truth and have her fifteen seconds in the spotlight.

"What I really need to say is this," she said at last, measuring her words carefully and looking out at the congregation with true sincerity. "Drake Singer never came into my store that I didn't feel glad to see him." She stopped and looked out at the group with a question mark on her face. "Do you know what I'm saying here?" she asked, and several people nodded. "What I mean is this—this man could walk into a room, or a store, or I guess just about anywhere, and people would stop what they were doin' and turn around and take notice of him. That was Mr. Drake. And I don't know what that means, but I know that it's pretty darn special. And so I say, let's all put our hands together here today and say 'thank you Lord, for our time with Drake Singer.' He was a hard man to know, but he was a fine man to look at."

Tiara caught herself and looked out at the assembly with a diffident air. "Thank you very much," she whispered. Looking down demurely, she departed the pulpit, quickly clacking her way back to her seat at the rear of the church.

D. W. was partly relieved and partly disappointed to find the odd display over. He continued to ponder the numerous questions he had about who his father was, and what the man really stood for, if anything. Clearly, this was a man he hadn't known, but had anyone else here today known him any better?

Suddenly D. W. found himself standing up and walking to the altar. He turned and faced the congregation and looked out over the crowded pews, scanning the assembly for kind eyes *somewhere* . . . for a face that signaled some sense of true sympathy or compassion for the man being buried. It took him a while, but eventually he found what he was seeking.

There at the back of the church, he saw Sarah Sue Kramer, the fry cook from the local cafeteria, sitting at the end of a pew and sobbing with true sadness, into a huge wad of tissues. He wondered what history between Sarah Sue and his father made the poor girl cry so hard, but put the question out of his head. There was something he needed to do and he'd better keep his mind on that task or he would never be able to get through it.

He turned to the audience, took a deep breath through his nose, and closed his eyes. Then he opened his mouth and sang *a capella*. He drew out the opening words, "Our Father, which art in heaven," giving them the right sweetness and softness, then followed them with a richer, fuller shading, and smiled as he delivered the words, "Hallowed be Thy name."

It was a hard song to sing, one that he had only heard once in the past. He had slept over at a Catholic classmate's home in Corydon and gone to mass with him and his family the following Sunday morning. He had been surprised to hear how different the music they sang was from the folksy Baptist hymns he was used to. When a young male tenor got up and sang the piece during the offertory, he had been totally enthralled by it. He had committed every word, every note, and every nuance of the complex piece to memory right away. So now, standing before this strange assembly, on this strangest day of his life, it was as if he had practiced the challenging piece a thousand times.

D. W. thought, as he sang, of fathers . . . not of his own largely inadequate and absent one, but of all the loving, loyal men whom he had seen throughout his life, walking beside their sons after ball games and school recitals. These fathers would drape a loving arm across their boys' shoulders and give them a good side hug, praising them for their performance, and making them feel good about themselves—the kind of parenting he had never experienced.

Now, totally captured by the power of the melody and lyrics, he proceeded into the body of the work with tenderness and passion. Something about the words and melody lifted him out of himself to a place he had never been before, a place he had only imagined might exist, one that was beautiful, clean and sacred, where everyone was always safe. He let go of any effort to understand what he was singing, giving himself up to the incredible, poignant beauty of the melody and its intricate colorations.

"Thy kingdom come, thy will be done, on earth, as it is in heaven."

He drew out the notes, just as he had heard it sung years ago, took another deep breath, and gathered himself for what lay ahead. The next segment called for a series of almost staccato phrasings, but at the end of those, he would be challenged to deliver some of the hardest, highest, and longest notes in the piece. "Give us this day our daily bread. And forgive us our trespasses, as we forgive our trespassers."

He got through the light, tripping lyrics there, and having done so, finally allowed himself to open his eyes and look out at the gathering before him. He almost wished that he hadn't, for what he saw was a sea of familiar faces, looking up at him, their eyes and mouths open wide with surprise.

It was too late to turn back. He was committed to completing the piece and he only hoped he could make all the high notes and sustain his breathing so that he didn't faint and make a fool of himself. He closed his eyes, and forged on into the final bars, climbing as they did into a crescendo from which there was no escape, and no mercy for the timid. He would either finish the piece in triumph, or he would never be able to hold his head up in this judgmental little town again. "And lead us not into temptation, but deliver us from evil."

He breathed deeply through his nose, struggling to take in every ounce of air he could so that he could deliver the long, sustained notes and climbing energy required for the final, powerful lyrics. "For Thine is the Kingdom, and the Power, and the Glory, forever . . . Amen."

Funny, he thought to himself, as he was measuring out the seven syllables and notes required for the "amen" that such a short, simple word could be conflated into such a long and challenging, yet engaging singing experience.

He finished the piece and closed his mouth abruptly, hearing the last notes ringing off the wooden rafters and coming back at him in a faint echo. Eyes still closed, he wondered what he would see when he finally opened them. He had never sung this piece before, never even practiced or walked through its notes on paper. What had he been thinking, getting up here and singing it, *a capella* at that, without a moment's hesitation? He had needed to say or do something that honored fathers, though, even if his own mortal father had been totally lacking.

The silence in the little church was deafening. He dared to pry a single eyelid open and look out at the crowded pews before him. When he did, he wished he had done so sooner. For there, in the stifling heat of the musty walls, he saw a performer's dream come true. There wasn't a dry eye in the house. Everyone, from the minister, to Doogie, to Tiara, to his own mother, was weeping openly, some more vocally than others. He opened his other eye and scanned the crowd more fully. There in the back row, he saw a familiar, loving face, beaming at him and nodding her affirmation. Miss Triplett waved and blew him a little kiss, something he never expected from the toughest teacher he ever had.

Despite his relief to see his performance so well received, he figured he'd better step down and let the minister get on with burying his father. When he resumed his seat by his mother, he was startled when she grabbed his hand and squeezed it tightly, still without speaking to him or looking him in the eye. He squeezed back hard, and put his arm around her shoulder, pulling her body into his and holding it tightly. Something in his gesture seemed to melt some of the bitterness and steel in her heart, and she leaned into him, letting go of all artifice, giving herself up for the first time in her life to her true feelings. The tsunami of grief and rage that emerged was almost more than he could bear. As Pastor McHugh closed the funeral service with a few last words, and the heat-withered congregation played along with the farce, D. W. and his mother had the first real moment of closeness in their lives.

Not a word was spoken, but countless, complex thoughts and feelings flitted between them as they held each other tightly in the front pew, crying and shaking, and rocking back and forth together. Somewhere in the back of his mind, D. W. questioned whether this was even happening, whether it wasn't some strange, surreal dream. For here he was, in the presence of his whole community, exchanging a true, heartfelt hug with his mother, a woman he would have bet his life didn't have the capacity to experience genuine feelings of any sort, except perhaps anger.

Time to shut off all thought, he told himself, and just surrender to the moment. He knew from past experience that she could turn at any minute and cast him aside without a word of explanation, but he was tired of always guarding himself against the hurt she was capable of inflicting. Maybe, it suddenly occurred to him, he drew some of that hurt upon himself by expecting it, dreading it, and trying so hard to avoid it.

He forced himself to let go of his fears of rejection, his anger, and his distrust, and leaned into his mother's shaking body, holding her close to him without reservations. And in that moment, immeasurable healing occurred in their troubled connection. Oh, he knew for a certainty, even in the midst of this first, unexpected moment of grace, that she would turn on him again and wound him to the quick once more, one way or another. But he was so tired of constantly scanning his world and trying to predict where the next assault would occur, that he forced himself to let go of his fears.

Soon he realized that the pallbearers were lifting his father's expensive mahogany casket and carrying it down the aisle of the church. As they did, the pianist launched into "Abide With Me," and the congregation rose one final time. Stumbling to his feet while still trying to stay connected to his mother in a fierce side hug, D. W. breathed a sigh of relief. At last, a hymn he loved was being sung at his father's funeral. He launched into the bittersweet words with full heart and voice. "Abide with me; fast falls the eventide. The darkness deepens; Lord, with me abide. When other helpers fail and comforts flee, help of the helpless, O abide with me."

Again, he was aware of the surprising strength of his own voice. It was almost as if he had gone to the garage to tackle some household repair job and discovered a shiny new tool there, perfectly designed to do everything he would ever need. He had always loved singing, but knew it mainly as a diversion or pastime, something to while away the hours when he was bored or blue. Today, for the first time, he realized that his voice was a powerful vehicle that could take him places he needed to go. He would never have been able to put all of this into words. Yet he knew it in his heart, as surely as he knew his own name . . . D. W. *Singer.*

As he finished the poignant words, "in life, in death, O Lord, abide with me," just right for a funeral, he noticed his mother looking at him, as if she were seeing him for the first time. For some reason, he suddenly felt self-conscious. Looking for a distraction, he glanced to the back of the church and saw through the open front doors that the pallbearers were carrying his father's casket to the little burial ground across the way from the chapel.

"Come on, Ma," he said, turning back to her and letting go of her shoulder at last. "Looks like it's time."

He got the surprise of his life when she grabbed his hand and put it to her lips, kissing his knuckles, and then holding his hand to her heart.

"Thank you, son," she whispered, looking up at him with an almost adoring look in her teary eyes.

For some reason, D. W. recoiled inside, though he managed to avoid pulling away from her physically. They had just crossed miles of emotional distance, and he was excited and pleased to have taken that journey, but there was something confusing about the present moment, something that he wasn't comfortable with, that warned him to be careful.

"You're welcome, Ma," he said cautiously. "I'm so glad to have been able to help you in some way today."

She clutched their joined hands to her heart and closed her eyes, nodding her head wearily. "I'm so glad to still have you, son. As long as we have each other, I know we can get through anything."

Something about her touch made D. W. squirm inside, and he gently extricated his hands from her grasp. Moments ago, he would have never dreamed he would rebuff his mother. He had secretly longed all of his life for her to love him. But now, only seconds into a new intimacy with her, he was already beginning to have doubts. How well did he really know this woman? She had always kept him at arm's length with her endless criticisms. How much did he really know about why his father had fled from her?

It occurred to him that maybe his father had good reasons for his philandering. He had a sudden new compassion for the man they were presently burying. Perhaps he had tried to be close to his wife but had found her inaccessible, as D. W. himself always had. Or perhaps, he realized, she had frightened his father off with her needy, clinging behavior.

It was more than he could figure out now. He looked to the wooden cross hanging over the altar at the front of the church, and in a rare moment of religiosity, prayed for help dealing with whatever lay ahead for him and this troubled woman who was his mother, but also an enigma.

He looked all around and realized the congregation was waiting for his mom and him to exit so that they could follow them to the cemetery.

"Come on, Ma. We're holding things up here."

She opened her eyes and seemed to come to herself, taking in the crowd waiting for her lead. That was all it took for her worst theatrics to kick into full gear. She threw her forearm across her forehead and collapsed into D. W.'s arms, literally keening with grief.

"Help me walk, son. I know I'll never make it without you!" With that she leaned hard into his side, almost sending them both tumbling to the floor, until D. W. somehow managed to leverage his lesser weight against hers and keep them both upright. Struggling with all his strength, he steered her out of the pew, down the narrow aisle to the front steps of the church, and eventually across the gravel parking lot to the burial plot.

Oh yeah, we can get through anything as long as we have each other, he thought. He knew now exactly what that meant; they could get through anything as long as he was ready to carry his mother. In response to that awareness, he forged a little oath in his heart.

I will never give up my life or happiness for this woman. She may be my kin and I may need to do what I can to help her get by. But I will never let her suck the life out of me.

They made it to the crowded little churchyard, filled with tottering, moss-covered stones. Someone had given the neglected plot a quick mowing that morning, and the ground was strewn with clots of new-cut grass that threatened to trip the mourners as they picked their way to the grave site.

There D. W. relinquished his mom's arm to one of her church lady friends and straightened his sore shoulders, shaking his head and blinking his eyes to clear them. The minister was standing at the head of his father's casket. He opened his Bible and began the final words of the burial service, and then the casket was lowered into the grave.

As D. W. listened, he was only half present. He looked across the gathering at the pretty little classmate standing by her mother, wondering what it would feel like to kiss her pink lips. He struggled again to contain the energy gathering in his loins and jutting against the fabric of his trousers. Fortunately Pastor McHugh gave him a welcome distraction when he turned to him and offered him the shovel to deliver the first clods of earth onto the top of his father's casket.

D. W. took the shaft of the shovel, glanced around at the assembly and walked up to the edge of the burial pit. Looking down to where his father's expensive coffin lay glistening, waiting to be buried, he thought to himself what a silly and self-defeating thing this ritual was. A man had died. His family and community had spent a small fortune and a whole lot of needless drama and trouble putting him into a suitably gaudy box to get rid of him. Now he, the man's son, was supposed to begin the last act in the drama, the burial. The whole hypocritical lot of them would put the man to rest, telling themselves they had done their best to show their respect, and move on, probably with little further thought for him.

Some difficult, defiant side of him balked at the assignment. He didn't quite know what was going on inside of him. He did know this though; no matter how much he loved acting and performing, he wasn't prepared to sell himself out to anyone, for any reason. He could play a role or sing a song on demand anytime anyone asked it of him, but he would never play a part that didn't feel honest to him.

Instead of bending to gather a scoop of dirt with the shovel, he turned to the crowd and held the tool up before him like a scepter. He turned in a complete circle, looking everyone present deep in the eyes and smiling slightly. As he did so, he thought to himself how Alexandra wasn't the only one who could engage in theatrics. He knew, watching the crowd in front of him that all eyes were on him. They were more than a little uncomfortable with what he was doing, and wondering what in the hell he was going to do next.

"Good friends!" he barked, enjoying the startled response that rippled through the group at the volume and abruptness of his words. "Good friends," he said more softly. "Thank you for joining Ma and me today to pay our respects to my Pa, and send him off well."

He still held the shovel in front of him as he talked and turned from side to side, addressing the crowd, making eye contact with as many as he could. He noticed as he did so that a lot of the people seemed to be growing more and more uncomfortable by the moment. Folks in this fundamentalist Christian part of the world liked their religious ceremonies predictable. They didn't know what to do with ambiguity. Something about that awareness gave D. W. a sense of power, accompanied by a little surge of adrenalin.

Screw what these people want to hear, he thought. *Let's see how a little dose of honesty goes down.*

"Ma and I thank you again for coming here today. It's an awful thing to lose a husband and a father, but it's a little bit easier to bear, knowing people who really care about you want to come and give support. Doogie and Tiara said some kind words here today that I'll always remember."

He looked out at the crowd and saw the mourners begin to exchange an uncertain look or two. *Good*, he thought. That was exactly what he was hoping for.

"On the other hand," he continued, "I know there are also a

lot of folks here today who are only to see what happens at the funeral of a man who died under questionable circumstances."

He looked over at his mother and saw the tentative closeness they had just developed evaporate in an instant. She shot him an angry glare, pulled away from the church lady patting her arm, and sent him the clear, nonverbal question, *What in the world are you doing?*

That was okay with him, though. Why should their brief, recent truce change any aspect of their relationship? They would soon be back to business as usual.

He turned again to the crowd and stared at each of them. "So for all of those people here today, here's an invitation."

Turning the shaft of the shovel, he offered the handle to the crowd. "Let he, or she, who is without sin, throw the first shovel of dirt."

A sibilant, indignant whisper rippled through the gathering, as people turned to one another. He glanced over at Pastor McHugh and saw the minister struggling with the dilemma of what to do. D. W. fought back laughter as he watched the pastor wrestle with how to respond. Fortunately, the pastor did nothing. Neither did anyone else. No one had the nerve to take on D. W. The adolescent boy, rapidly becoming a man, watched the change occur in the emotional tenor of the group. Indignation gave way to shame, and people began looking down and shuffling their feet, trying to appear unaffected. He let himself indulge in a little moment of triumph before he turned back to the dirt piled beside his father's grave and drove the shovel deep into it. Raising a big load of the red Indiana clay in it, he lifted the shovel and dropped its contents onto the top of his father's casket below.

The heavy, clotted soil made a loud thud as it hit the coffin lid.

His role was over now. Stabbing the shovel into the ground, he sent another round of level stares into the crowd and stepped back.

First, his mother approached the grave, gathered a scant cup of soil in the shovel, and deposited it gingerly on her husband's casket. After she completed the task, she gave D. W. a triumphant glower and walked past him with a sniff.

Next Doogie took the shovel and paid his respects to the man who had treated him better than anyone else on the planet. Next was a neighbor, a fellow member of the local Moose Lodge, followed by a string of other mourners who all secretly counted themselves lucky to have been in on this, the greatest show that had ever occurred in their small, sleepy town.

D. W. stood back and watched them with narrowed eyes. They made sympathetic comments to his mother, and then stumbled out of the sorry little graveyard through its clotted, mole-tracked lawn. Few passersby made eye contact with him, and he realized he would be *persona non grata* for a long while. But that was okay, too. The good, clean feeling he had in his heart right now, the first time he had experienced that particular feeling in a very long time, made it all worthwhile.

Only one mourner broke the mold that afternoon. Miss Triplett approached D. W. as the crowd began to thin and put her elbow out for him to take her arm. Following her cue, he offered her his support for a stroll through the tilting headstones around them. She was silent for a time, but eventually indulged in a soft chuckle.

"That was quite a performance," she said. "Probably the best you will ever do, even if you live a hundred years."

D. W. looked into her eyes, concerned by her words, but saw the affection and approval there and relaxed.

"You really think so?" he asked. "I wondered if maybe I could have put a little more punch into that speech at the grave side."

She glanced at him with a puzzled face, until she saw the twinkle in his eyes and laughed softly.

"Oh, *you*," she chided gently. "Can't keep from joking, even at a funeral."

Taking her thin arm even more firmly in his, he led them both to a distant corner of the cemetery where they took seats on the top of the layered stone wall.

Breathing in the rich summer scents all around them, D. W. wondered how a person could be so happy after a burial. The sweet, new-mown grass underfoot, the flowering red crepe myrtles nearby, and the fragrant resin from white pines overhead, all filled his heart with peace. This was a very good day, he realized, even if it was the day he had buried his father. Another thought came to him: maybe that was why it was such a good day. Maybe putting his father into the earth was something he had secretly wanted to do for years.

As always, Miss Triplett seemed to intuit his thoughts and feelings. She patted his arm and turned his face to hers with a bony hand.

"You comported yourself admirably today, D. W." she said firmly. "Admirably and *honorably*, I should say. I don't think there's ever been another teenaged boy, er, *young man* who could have done such a fine job of standing down a bunch of vultures as you did today."

D. W. had to smile, hearing her describe his behavior as "comportment," as if she were still his teacher, checking off the boxes on a report card. He looked deep into her rheumy eyes, saw the sincerity there, and then surprised them both greatly

110

by breaking into tears. She reached into her pocketbook for a lavender-scented hanky, and put it to his eyes.

"You go right on and cry, young man," she said. "It's about time you got to have some normal feelings for a change."

He put his head down on her frail shoulder and let the torrent flow, still fighting to keep his grieving silent. He didn't want to cause a scene like his mother had; in fact, he had a true horror of public displays of strong emotion, unless, of course, they were in the context of some theatrical role. But something about Miss Triplett's arthritic hand patting his shoulder and the sweet scent of the hanky she pressed gently to his eyes brought him deeper and deeper into his sadness. Before he knew what was happening, he was sobbing loudly into her slight shoulder. Miss Triplett knew better than to try to stop him.

"Go on and cry," she murmured, time and again, brushing her handkerchief across his eyes now and then. "You've got the right, so you go on and cry."

About the time it seemed to him he would never be able to get his tears in check, he found that they suddenly stopped. Raising his head, he looked around the churchyard and saw that he and his former teacher were the last people there. Everyone else had gone; he didn't know where—presumably to the traditional open house that was being held at his home following the funeral. Free sandwiches, cake, and coffee were hard to refuse, after all, even if they were meted out by stingy Alexandra Singer.

Running his forearm across his nose in an inelegant gesture, D. W. looked up at Miss Triplett. "You really think I did okay?" he asked.

"No!" she declared firmly. "I think you did far more than okay. I think you were *magnificent*."

111

He tried to absorb the compliment from his toughest critic ever. "It was a tough crowd, for sure," he said with a smile.

She took his face in her hands. "Probably the toughest you'll ever know. Remember this day, son. Think of it as the worst crowd you've ever had to play to. And when you do, no matter where you go, or what you face, you'll always know you can get through it somehow, because you've already been through the toughest thing you'll ever do. Once you think of that, everything else will seem easy."

He saw the wisdom of what she said and nodded. "It's not over yet. Did you see the way Ma looked at me? Did you see the way people avoided me afterward? If looks could kill . . ."

Miss Triplett sniffed. "Who needs them? Not you, that's for sure. You don't ever need anyone's approval for doing the right thing. Merely knowing you did it is something to be proud of."

D. W. took in her sage words and nodded again. Then a devilish thought occurred to him and he couldn't restrain the impulse to act on it. "Miss Triplett, do you realize that you just ended a sentence with a preposition?"

She stared at him for a moment, as if he had slapped her, and then burst out laughing. "I declare, D. W. Singer! It appears I've taught you a thing or two, after all, despite your best efforts to the contrary."

He stood up and held out his elbow with a small, courtly flourish. "Miss Triplett, you taught me more than a thing or two."

She rose, taking his extended arm in hers, and patted his hand as they walked slowly from the graveyard. While they strolled, he was surprised when he looked over at her to see tears trickling from her eyes. Stopping, he turned to her.

"I'm sorry, ma'am. I didn't mean any offense. I was only playing with you."

She shook her head and put the hanky he had already soaked to her own eyes. "No, it's not that at all. It's that . . ."

D. W. had never known Miss Triplett to be inarticulate, so he watched her struggle for words as if he were watching some strange, mysterious event unfold. Finally she stopped and seemed to decide to spit something out for once, rather than struggle to be proper.

"I think you're old enough now to realize that teachers work long, hard hours, and that sometimes we wonder why in the world we do it. The schools don't have enough money to give us the salaries and supplies we need to make ends meet, and the students and parents seem to hate us sometimes."

D. W. nodded again, thinking about how often he had silently cursed her under his breath for catching him in some prank.

"Fortunately, teaching isn't really about any of that. All that really matters is our knowing that we made a difference, somehow, somewhere . . . with someone."

She drew in a deep breath, smiled, and then poked him gently in the chest with a bony finger. "So tease me all you want, Mr. D. W. Singer, for making a grammatical error. It's music to my ears, because I know exactly where you learned it."

With that, she gave him a proud smile and turned to leave the cemetery, unassisted. Watching her go, D. W. had to hand it to her. She may be old and fragile, a mere shadow of her former self. Forced retirement hadn't agreed with her—he could see it in her face—but she was still the same indomitable spirit who had inspired him to make more of himself than the aimless schoolboy he once was.

113

Trailing behind her, a little humbled, he called out, "Can I help you to your car, Miss Triplett?"

Without stopping, she waved him away. "I taught you that too," she called over her shoulder. "You had the manners of a Neanderthal when I first laid eyes on you."

He hurried to catch up with her. "Aw, Miss Triplett. I was just joking around. I'm sorry."

She kept walking, ignoring him as if he were a fly. "And I taught you that, too. How to make a sincere and gracious apology."

Continuing this banter, they made it to her old Plymouth roadster in the church parking lot. D. W. rushed to open the door for her, and had to laugh when she said, "I taught you that, too, how to open a door for a lady."

"All right, all right," he pleaded. "Have mercy. I admit it all. I have you to thank for everything."

She smiled before climbing into the driver's seat and tapped him again on the chest. "Not for everything. Only for some very important things. I hope, that among them, is the belief in yourself. Now, would you like a ride to your house, or would you rather walk?"

He closed the door behind her and raced to the passenger side before she could change her mind. He jumped in as she started the engine and gave him another surprise.

"Sing the 'Our Father' for me again on the way to your house, will you, please? I have never heard it done better, and it's a very difficult piece."

He sat back in his seat, closed his eyes, and took a deep breath. It was going to be a lot easier this time because he really knew his audience.

CHAPTER 7

ANOTHER *OUR TOWN*

D. W. watched the love of his life, Breanna Banet, read the notice about today's senior play auditions on the bulletin board outside the principal's office at Palmer's Ridge High. It was late February and way past time, in the opinion of English teacher, Baxter Phillips, for senior play rehearsals to begin, if the class ever hoped to get a decent production together before graduation day.

This year, Mr. Phillips had decided on Thornton Wilder's *Our Town*. D. W. prayed fervently to be cast in the role of George, the young neighbor and eventual husband of the central character, Emily, because he knew that Breanna was sure to win the role of Emily. After all, she was the most beautiful, poised, and accomplished young woman he had ever met. How could she fail to land the lead in her high school's senior play, even though she had only recently moved there and was up against a bevy of local girls.

Over the previous eight weeks, since Breanna had moved to Palmer's Ridge from Saint Louis, D. W. had watched her from afar. He secretly studied everything she did, from powdering her patrician nose, to reaching down in an elegant curtsy to retrieve her book satchel from the bottom of her locker. She had the willowy grace and mystery of a Tolkien fairy princess, and the erect carriage and elegance of European aristocracy. She also had the staggering intelligence of those new mechanical minds, the new-fangled computer things that people in Palmer's Ridge were beginning to hear about in *Time* magazine, those who read it anyway.

Within days of arriving at the school, Breanna had effortlessly won the senior spelling bee, solved logarithms in advanced math class that even the teacher couldn't fathom, and recited the entire text of *The Lady of Shallot* without glancing at a note. She also made every other girl at the school furiously jealous by capturing the heart of every boy at school.

It was almost as if she were some superhuman being, D. W. mused, watching her as she scrutinized the audition notice. Her gray Athena eyes squinted slightly, looking a little myopic, he realized suddenly. The idea that she might be nearsighted sent a strange little tug of empathy and excitement to his gut. For his empress to have a small flaw was both charming and challenging to him. On the one hand, he worshipped at the font of her beauty, grace, and achievement; on the other, he wanted to be able to protect her and provide some form of service to her. What better way to do that than to ascertain her few flaws and rush to her aid, helping her to overcome them?

He was savoring a rich fantasy about Breanna thanking him profusely for his help when he came to with a rude jolt. He looked up to find her staring at him with a deep, disdainful glare, her cool gray eyes registering their clear disapproval of him. His heart sank as he walked up to her, hating the plaintive tone in his voice as he addressed her.

"Hey, Breanna. Anything wrong?"

"Your fly is undone," she said, looking away as she delivered this damaging salvo and returned to her scrutiny of the bulletin board.

D. W. fumbled to correct the problem, and then tried his best to regain some measure of dignity.

"You're trying out for the lead, of course?" he asked.

She turned to him and delivered another of her patrician stares. "Well, I can't exactly do that, can I? The stage manager is a *male* part. I seriously doubt that even Mr. Phillips, confused though he may be about his own sexuality, would assign that role to a female."

D. W. collapsed into helpless laughter. He had never heard anything as original and forthright as her assessment of Mr. Phillips. Every word she uttered, every move she made, was totally enthralling.

"That's good, *really* good. How do you come up with this stuff, Breanna?" But even as he spoke, he hated the obsequious tone in his voice. An awful memory came to him of Uriah Heep in Dickens's *Great Expectations*, and he felt then every bit as toadying as the villainous clerk.

Breanna turned to him again and, ignoring his question, startled him with a question of her own. "Will you read with me in the auditions?"

D. W. was taken aback, but struggled to conceal his excitement. He found that he had to consciously restrain himself from jumping up and down and clapping his hands.

"Huh . . . me, read with you?" he asked, trying to capture a noncommittal tone. "Yeah, sure, Breanna. I guess so. Why not?"

"Then we're ready," she pronounced with an imperious air, and handing him her book bag, began to glide down the halls toward the gym. Once more, D. W. had to fight to control the impulse to let out a rebel yell. As she led him down the hall to the auditorium, Breanna outlined her plans for their upcoming readings, while D. W. did his best to keep himself from hyperventilating.

"If Mr. Phillips will let us, we should do a number of scenes. That way he can get a sense of our range and versatility."

D. W. hung on her every word, enraptured by a combination of his closeness to her, (the closest he had ever been), her overpowering intellect, and her wonderful smell. Now and then she turned to him and put a light hand on his arm to emphasize some point she was making, and her lightest touch made him want to drop the book bag, and grab and kiss her. He took in her incredible fragrance—a rich, mysterious potpourri that challenged his imagination. First there was the subtle, obviously expensive French perfume, then the earthy, animal aroma of a costly cashmere sweater, and finally her own porcelain skin, now infused with a faint flush on her high, wide cheekbones as she talked in animated tones about the auditions.

"Oh, it's going to be *wonderful*," she said with the first real excitement D. W. had ever heard in her normally low, well-modulated voice. "You and I are going to make this the best senior play this miserable little backwater town has ever seen!"

At that, D. W. felt the first tug of dissonance he had ever experienced in his feelings for her. He loved the fact that she was including him in her vision of making the play a huge success. However, his excitement over this awareness dimmed against another, more unsettling awareness that she considered herself superior to this place, the town that had spawned and nurtured him for the last eighteen years. Oh, he could name its faults a thousand times over, if anyone asked him to—in fact, he realized that he often had. But for her to do so in such a supercilious way, struck him as somehow churlish—not in keeping with the grace he attributed to her.

Whatever his misgivings, he had to file them away as they arrived at the school gymnasium, which doubled as an assembly hall. One end of the gym had a small stage that had been added well after the original school structure was built. D. W. had often thought it was the worst built stage he'd ever performed on. It creaked and groaned under anyone walking across it, forcing performers to raise their voices to be heard over the noise.

But entering the echoing gym with Breanna and eyeing the clumsy stage today, he suddenly found it the most picturesque and quaint structure he had ever spied. Even from the doorway, D. W. could sense the combined air of excitement, expectation, and anxiety that filled the air.

The entire senior class, all thirty-eight of them, milled about the room in various stages of unrest, preparing for their auditions in their own individual ways. Some were reading from their scripts or reciting lines to each other, and others were sitting quietly and breathing deeply. The smell of newly shellacked floors, an annual ritual observed by the school janitor preparing for spring commencement ceremonies, mingled with the pungent odors emanating from the boys' locker room nearby and the combined flop sweat of dozens of adolescents preparing to make good out on stage. D. W. found the aroma strangely intoxicating—something elemental, like the wind, and rain, and new-mown fields.

They really care about this thing, he mused. Something about that awareness touched him deeply in a way that he could never have articulated. Nonetheless, he felt a strange surge of goose

119

bumps wash over his neck and shoulders, seeing his classmates so worked up over tryouts for a school play.

Looking around, he saw students he had known since grade school practicing scenes with each other as if winning a role in their senior play was suddenly the most important goal of their lives. In the front of the big hall, D. W. watched perky Ginger Adams, captain of the cheerleader squad, emoting heavily as Emily in the graveyard, intoning dramatically with all the wrong inflections.

Listening to her treatment of the scene, he longed to go up and shake her. He had read, reread, and loved this play since he had stumbled across it one day in the Lanesville library when he was twelve years old. Palmer's Ridge still wasn't big enough have its own library. Ginger's recitation reduced its subtleties to maudlin mush, and made him furious.

"People! People, pull-eeze!" A shrill voice broke into the gathering. It was Mr. Phillips, clapping his small white hands and beckoning the crowd to the front of the gym. "We will never get out of here on time if we don't get started right now." Seeing the small crowd acquiesce and surge forward, he softened a bit. "That's it, that's it, chickens. Come on up here and let's get this thing sorted out."

In response to Mr. Phillips's shrill, effeminate voice, D. W. saw Breanna send him a piercing look beneath raised eyebrows. "Maybe I could land the stage manager's role after all," she whispered, and again, he burst out laughing. She subdued him with a disapproving look.

"All right now," Mr. Phillips said. "Looks like we're all here now and ready to get to work at last."

D. W. and Breanna sidled up behind the crowd and surveyed it from the back of the room. He risked a furtive glance at her, expecting her to make some further disparaging remarks about his hometown and classmates, but he was relieved to see her following Mr. Phillips's directions with close attention.

He looked at his lifelong peers, sitting on battered folding metal chairs in front of him here and thought to himself, "What must Breanna be seeing now?"

There in the front row sat Amos Dewberry, the rather dimwitted star quarterback of the football team, hunched over his frayed copy of the play, reciting lines under his breath. Ginger sat beside Amos, tossing her bleached blonde curls and pinching her pink cheeks to make them even pinker. She was clearly set on capturing the role of Emily and ending her high school days with the accomplishment of having starred in the senior play, the honor etched forever behind her name in the school's tiny yearbook. A dozen or more students had obvious designs on lesser roles. Curt Kissinger was mouthing the lines of Howie Newsome, Grover's Corner's sole policeman, and stodgy softball star Paul Gartner was clearly after the role of Constable Warren.

D. W. watched them all trying their best to pay attention to Mr. Phillips's directions while still looking at the lines they hoped to recite shortly. An unexpected feeling of tenderness came over him.

"Listen up," Mr. Phillips said, intruding into his reverie. "We always have lots of people vying for the same lead roles. This year, for once, can we please do a quick survey and see who wants what roles, and hopefully bypass some of the usual trials and tribulations?"

D. W. was relieved. He looked over at Breanna and saw from her affirming nod that she too appreciated what Mr. Phillips had done. They could have spent all night reading lines for every single part, but Mr. Phillips had cut through that painful process in an instant.

Naturally, every girl in class put up her hand to audition as Emily, and as they did, Mr. Phillips rolled his eyes and sighed.

"Well, it's obviously going to be a long afternoon," he said with a dour look. "How about the boys? Who wants what parts, starting with the lead, the stage manager?"

In contrast to the girls, not a single boy raised his hand. D. W. looked around the room and was surprised to see every other male staring straight at him.

"Who *me?*" he asked the assembled gathering. "Nah, not me. I'm reading for the part of George." He glanced over at Breanna and warmed to see her nod approval.

Mr. Phillips coughed into his hand. "We'll see about that," he said with a tone D. W. found ominous. "But let's go on and get started or we'll be here all night."

Mr. Phillips gestured the group closer to the little stage. Once they had rearranged the ancient folding in a semi-circle there, he squared his thin shoulders, and took out his legal pad and notes.

"All right, then, all you Emilys. We'll go in alphabetical order. First up, Ginger Adams."

D. W. cringed as he watched Ginger flounce onto the stage, holding her copy of the play tight against her buxom chest with one hand, and twirling her peroxide curls with the other. She turned and faced the audience, dropping her usual simpering smile and adopting an almost ludicrous mask of tragedy in its place.

"I want to read Emily's final scene in the graveyard," she said with a soulful look. D. W. grimaced at the thought of having to listen to her butchered delivery of those lines again.

"Of course you do," Mr. Phillips said wryly. "I'll read the other parts, then. Let's start with Mrs. Webb chiding Emily at breakfast."

The teacher pulled open his script and promptly fell into the role of Mrs. Webb. D. W. caught Breanna's eye again, and she gave him yet another knowing smile, causing him to stifle a laugh.

Ginger played the part of Emily with a valiant effort, reading the lines where Emily pleads with her mother to stop and look at her. As she wailed, the entire assembly fought to suppress giggles, but Ginger was blissfully unaware of the unintended impact she was having on the crowd. When she reached the last line, she put down her script and placed hands on either side of her face, making little spectacles around her eyes with her circled fingers. She had obviously thought this added gesture a brilliant piece of theatrical business, but Mr. Phillips gasped.

"What in the world are you doing?"

Ginger dropped the persona of Emily and turned to Mr. Phillips with a nervous giggle. "I was ad-libbing. You know, Emily wants them to really look at each other, so I was making eyeglasses with my fingers."

"Well, stop it right now," he replied. "I think that'll do for you, young lady. Who's up next?"

Alyson Anderson smiled sympathetically at Ginger as she passed her, lumbering up to the makeshift stage. D. W. watched the plywood flooring sag as the morbidly obese Alyson took center stage.

"I want to do the scene where Emily asks her mom if she's pretty," Alyson told Mr. Phillips.

"Perfect," the teacher replied, and D. W. thought he heard the beleaguered teacher trying hard to contain his characteristic sarcasm. Despite the old man's curmudgeonly ways, D. W. knew that Mr. Phillips had a tender heart, especially for his drama students.

"Start wherever you wish," the teacher said. "I'll pick up behind you."

Alyson began with the line where Emily asks Mrs. Webb if she thinks she's pretty. D. W. heard his male classmates shift in their seats and whisper snide comments, and a sudden rage took hold of his heart. There was nothing he hated more than people who teased others about things that they couldn't help, like their weight or facial features. He turned to his buddies and sent them a threatening glare. The hurtful comments stopped in an instant and several of the boys flushed with shame.

Listening to Alyson read, D. W. realized that she had the part down really well. She had just the right delivery, the right intonation on each word, and the right respect for each nuance of the scene. It was too bad, he thought, that she didn't look the part at all. He realized, too, with a little stab of anger that the world could be very cruel to people with weight problems.

He listened with true respect for Alyson as she finished the scene and applauded enthusiastically for her when she was done, despite knowing that she would never get the part. The thought occurred to him then for the first time in his life that this world that he loved, the world of the theater, had some definite drawbacks. It could be mercilessly superficial and focused on outward rather than inward beauty.

"Nice job," Mr. Phillips said as Alyson stepped cautiously down from the stage. Turning to the crowd, he spied Breanna.

"I believe you're next, Miss Banet." She nodded, flashed her signature Mona Lisa smile, and strode confidently to the rickety steps.

"You're forgetting your script," Mr. Phillips said.

She turned and gave him an almost pitying look. "Thank you, but I don't need it. I know the part by heart."

"Very well, then," Mr. Phillips said in a measured voice. "It seems we're in for a rare treat this afternoon. Proceed then, Miss Banet. What scene do you want to read?"

"Actually, I want to do a montage," she replied.

Mr. Phillips raised an eyebrow. "A montage?"

"Yes," Breanna said. "It's a collection of brief moments linked together to convey a larger or different message about the piece."

The teacher threw her a withering look. "I know what a montage is," he said with ice in his voice. "But I don't recall inviting any montages for these auditions."

"Is there a problem?" Breanna asked, narrowing her eyes in a way that D. W. found half-frightening, half-thrilling. "I don't recall reading anything prohibiting a montage either."

D. W. loved seeing Mr. Phillips meet his match, as both the teacher and the whole assembly realized that Breanna had him there. The other students watched their sparring with avid interest, eyes bouncing back and forth between the two antagonists. It was almost as if they were watching a table tennis tournament, waiting for someone to falter and forfeit the round.

D. W. observed Mr. Phillips's body language with a keen eye and thought that he saw the old man blink, as if he were thinking better than to square off with such a forceful young woman this early in the play production. He soon found that he was right, when the teacher threw up his hands, then placed them on his hips, and assumed an almost injured air. "Whatever you want, Miss Banet! Perhaps you'd like to direct the play as well?"

Breanna smiled sweetly at him. "Oh, that won't be necessary Mr. Phillips. I'm sure you know exactly what you're doing with this kind of thing."

D. W. watched as the message struck its target. Mr. Phillips stomped to a metal chair and threw himself into it. "Carry on, please."

"Oh, and one more thing," Breanna said. "I need D. W. up here with me."

"Anything!" Mr. Phillips shouted. "Only please get on with it."

D. W. felt his heart almost burst with pride at the honor of being summoned to assist Breanna in her reading. He leapt to the stage, and tried to suppress the overwhelming urge to wiggle like a puppy.

Breanna turned to him and whispered in sotto voice. "We're going to reveal the character of Emily in a different way, all right?"

D. W. nodded, dumbfounded. He was in love with her and completely in her power at that moment.

"What do you want me from me?" he whispered, hating the nervous squeak in his voice.

Breanna gave him a smile. "Just try to keep up with me."

D. W.'s heart fluttered, but it was too late to back down. He was up on stage with the most charismatic, gifted woman he had ever met, and they were about to go to work together on a shared interest . . . no, more than that, a shared passion. Whatever it took, he was going to keep up with her. He was going to rise to this and whatever other challenges she presented, and be all that she needed him to be.

D. W. watched her, trying to suppress the adoring look he knew he must be wearing, as Breanna turned upstage, her back to the audience for several moments. He watched as she lowered her head, closed her eyes, and took a deep breath. Then she turned and faced the audience, and when she did, D. W. almost lost his balance at the transformation he saw.

Breanna took several tentative steps toward the footlights. D. W. wasn't quite sure how she did it, but her posture exuded an innocent adolescent energy that was both excited and girlish. She held her hands down at her sides, balled into little fists one moment, then clasped them at her heart the next moment, somehow conveying in the juxtaposition of these actions all the wonderful, frightening contradictions of youth. D. W. was mesmerized, thoroughly enjoying the sight of her turning into Emily Webb right before his eyes. Then she turned to him and gave him his first challenge.

She simply said hello, looking down in a demure way. D. W. answered hello back, knowing that he was answering in the persona of George Gibbs, Emily's love interest, and eventual husband in the play.

Breanna raised her arms high above her head and turned in a circle on the stage. As she continued literally turning into Emily right before their eyes, she delivered the line where Emily says she can't focus on her homework at all because the moonlight is so terrible.

D. W. knew at once where she was in the script and picked up on his next lines. However, he found that he wanted nothing more in the world than to drop their stage roles and talk to her in earnest about how moonlight truly can be so terrible at times. It was something he had noticed often, staring out at it through the little window over his bed on the nights when he couldn't sleep. But now certainly wasn't the time to do any such thing. He had to help Breanna get through her reading.

They went on to run the lines where George asks Emily for help with his math homework, and she says that the problem he can't figure out is the easiest one of all. D. W. was warming to the scene and looked forward to running the next several lines with her. However, he soon realized that Breanna had a game plan all her own. She turned upstage again and closed her eyes for another moment. He stood by, trying to get ready for whatever she might throw at him. When she turned, she leveled a pouting look at him and tossed her hair. She delivered the line where Emily says she thinks all men should be perfect, since her father is and George's father seems to be as well.

Thankfully, D. W. knew the scene by heart, as he did most of the play. He rose to the challenge of meeting her every nuance and whim, whether in the character of Emily or that of her own true self. He loved this layered interaction he was having with her, all under the auspices of trying out for a play.

Suddenly a thought occurred to him. Perhaps she was doing more than enlisting his help auditioning. Maybe she was sending him a message about their real-life relationship. Was it possible she was inviting him to court her? Dare he hope for such a miracle?

He could see that she had shifted scenes and moods again. When she turned her back to the audience, she waved him away, signaling to him that she didn't need him for this next segment. He stepped back a few paces, respecting her wishes, but feeling a quick stab of rejection nonetheless. When she turned back to the audience for the final piece of her montage, he understood exactly why she had to jettison his support. She had an actor's task to accomplish and she had to do it alone.

D. W. had performed in school, and summer camp productions most of his life, so he knew more than a little about acting, but he also knew that all of his experience had been as an amateur. Breanna's performance today was something truly remarkable, far beyond the small time productions where he was top dog. For the first time, he was in the presence of true genius. He was under the spell of Breanna Banet, and felt sure he would be reading glowing theater reviews about her one day.

D. W. watched as Breanna turned to the little audience one last time and delivered the most powerful theatrical moment he had ever experienced, despite the fact that it was only an audition. He had watched her become Emily Webb in the last fifteen minutes. Now his skin crawled with goose flesh as he watched her say goodbye to Emily. She turned to the audience and looked every single one of them in the eye, a rare risk for an actor to take. But he understood why she chose to play the scene as a direct address, as she became Emily once again in the final moments of the play.

Breanna delivered the line where Emily says she can't go on, that life goes by so fast people never have time to look at one another. She did so softly, with a slight catch in her voice. D. W. knew that the script called for Emily to break down sobbing here, hiding her eyes in her hands. But he saw Breanna make another choice about how to play the scene, and he knew she had made the right decision, to do it more subtly. She bowed her head and bit her lip, letting her hands and arms go limp at her sides, while silent tears trickled down her cheeks.

She looked directly at the audience, and whispered the moving lines where Emily says goodbye to clocks ticking, Mama's sunflowers, and food, and coffee, and waking up, and sleeping. D. W. had been so engrossed in Breanna's performance that he never considered what the audience might be experiencing. As she looked out into the crowd, his eyes followed hers, and he was amazed.

Every person in the gym, even the school janitor who had been emptying wastebaskets at the back of the room, watched Breanna with total absorption. Their eyes were riveted on her beautiful face. Their heads were tilted slightly so that they could take in her every word, her every shading. Their mouths hung open in expectation or were covered with their hands as they suppressed soft sobs. Even Mr. Phillips seemed to be speechless for once. The man gazed at Breanna with a benevolent look, smiling the broadest, sweetest smile D. W. had ever seen on his normally cynical face.

Breanna's powerful performance drew his attention from the crowd as she delivered the next poignant lines, some of his favorite of all literature. It was the scene in which Emily wonders whether people ever fully appreciate life. He shivered, hearing her speak the moving words in the sweet, heartfelt voice of Emily, saying that earth was too wonderful for anybody to realize, wondering whether any human beings ever realize life while they live it.

D. W. knew that the next lines of the play called for a response from the Stage Manager, so he stepped forward to stand beside her.

Breanna took this intrusion from him in good spirits and went with it, reaching out a hand to him and smiling sadly. In her last words as Emily, she told him she was ready to go back to the cemetery. She extended her hand to him for several moments, as if waiting in the character of Emily for the Stage Manager to guide her back to the graveyard. Then she dropped her hands, turned her back to the audience again, and signaled to them with a ten-second freeze that she was done.

D. W. would never have expected what happened next in a million years. The audience jumped to their feet, clapping and whistling and shouting their approval. He looked out at them, a little startled by their reaction, but still savoring the accolades on Breanna's behalf.

Mr. Phillips strode to the front of the gathering, and addressed the crowd. "We can do auditions for the role of Emily all night long if that's the way you want it. Or we can end them right now and settle the matter. What's your decision?"

All of the students, even Ginger and Alyson, chimed in unison, "Breanna! Breanna!"

Mr. Phillips seemed vastly relieved. "All right," he said and D. W. felt his heart swell. He knew that Breanna had secured the lead, thanks mainly to her amazing talent, but also, at least partially, through his supporting role. He felt inordinately proud to have been a part of her audition.

"Thank you so much," Mr. Phillips continued. "You have saved us several hours of pure torture. Now, for another decision. I feel that D. W. is clearly the best choice for the role of Stage Manager. Can we agree on that too, or do we have to go through hours of auditioning to make that choice?"

D. W.'s heart sank. "But I want to play George," he protested.

"Not me, thanks," Amos called from his seat. "Too many lines to remember."

"Same here," Paul chimed in. "I vote for D. W. He's the man."

Voice after voice rose up, supporting their opinions, and as they did, Mr. Phillips turned to D. W. with a smile. "So, Mr. Singer, do you hear your fans calling you?"

D. W. looked over at Breanna. She looked back at him and smiled her encouragement. He knew in an instant what he was going to do, though it would mean he would have less interaction with her in rehearsals than he had hoped for.

"Okay, Mr. Phillips. I'll play the Stage Manager."

"Great! Now let's get on to the other roles." Mr. Phillips waved them away, and turned his attention to the rest of the class.

D. W. was disappointed he couldn't play George, but he was soon distracted by the sight of Breanna hurrying from the stage without him.

"Hey, Breanna, wait up," he called, but she proceeded on her way without turning to acknowledge him. Maybe she didn't need him anymore, now that she had finished her audition and gotten what she wanted from him. D. W. stuffed his worst fears into the back of his mind and went down the wobbly stage steps behind her as fast as he could.

D. W. heard the auditions resuming in the gym as he and Breanna made their way through the halls. She seemed lost in her own thoughts, walking briskly toward the nearest exit. He called her name and implored her to wait for him, but she ignored him. When he finally caught up with her on the front steps of the school, he was out of breath and puffing with a mixture of exhaustion, hurt feelings, and mounting indignation. He put a hand on her shoulder. "Breanna, please!"

She finally stopped and turned to him, but he paled to see the look on her face.

"*Excuse me?*" she said, glancing at his hand on her shoulder. He released it immediately, but still couldn't let her go on without some sort of explanation.

"I'm sorry, but I don't understand. I've been calling you and following you and trying to get your attention for the last five minutes."

She seemed genuinely surprised. "Were you? I was thinking about the audition, about how well it went and how strongly the audience responded."

D. W. softened. After all, she had a right to bask a bit in her own glory, didn't she?

"It was amazing," he agreed. "You were amazing."

She seemed to see and hear him at last.

"You're so kind, but it was just an audition. There's more to be done with this role than that little performance."

To his surprise, she took his arm in hers and started walking with him toward her car in the nearby parking lot, chatting about the role of Emily.

"What do you think about the wedding scene? Where Emily asks her father to take her away so she doesn't have to marry George after all? I've always thought it a bit implausible for a small town girl to balk at marrying her high school beau, and ask her sainted father to rescue her from him. It seems a bit too Freudian to me."

He was under her spell again, mesmerized by the combined forces of her intellect, her touch, and her apparent regard for his opinion, despite the fact that she seemed to be unaware he existed half the time. "Gosh, I never thought about that," he mumbled, hating the fact that he couldn't come up with a more substantive answer.

She flashed him a frustrated frown. "Well, you need to," she declared, tapping his arm with her fingertips in a peremptory way. "You're the real star of this play, after all, sir, so you need to understand every aspect of it." With that, she graced him with a beaming smile that stole his heart again, and finished off any hope he'd had of protecting it from being broken by her. He looked down at her with an adoring expression on his face and found himself thoroughly tongue-tied.

They reached her shiny silver Mercedes sport coupe, the only auto in the student parking lot that wasn't a beat-up jalopy or rusted out pickup truck. She opened the door and tossed her books into the backseat. D. W. let himself savor the rich, elegant smell of the leather upholstery. He knew his mother would never buy such a car for him, no matter how much money his father had left her. She even refused to let him drive their aging Cadillac, distrusting his driving skills and reminding him constantly that he needed to make more A's if he expected to get behind the wheel of that sacred inheritance. He knew better in his heart, though. She only wanted to make his life miserable in any way that she could.

Breanna got into the driver's seat with a ladylike tuck of her dress and toss of her flaxen hair. "Can I give you a ride? Your house is right on my way."

D. W. wanted nothing more in the world than to take her up on her offer, but surprised them both by declining. "Naw, thanks. Think I'll head back to the gym to watch the rest of the auditions."

"Are you sure?" she asked. "You could be hours back there. Long, *painful* hours," she laughed.

He felt himself pulling away from her again, wanting to distance himself from the superior tone of her voice and smug smile on her face. Even a goddess might have clay feet, he was beginning to suspect.

"I know, but like you said, I need to know everything about this play, so I better get back there and see what the rest of the cast is shaping up to be." He closed her car door. "Off with you then."

She looked up at him with a small puzzled frown. It seemed to him that maybe this afternoon hadn't gone exactly the way she had planned, but she recovered quickly.

"*Ciao*, then," she said with a nonchalant shrug. She pulled out of the school parking lot with an airy wave, leaving him behind with nothing but the acrid smell of exhaust fumes.

He watched her exit onto the county road in front of the high school and speed away in a cloud of dust. Struggling with his mixed feelings for her, he turned to go back into the school. He knew beyond a doubt that he had never met anyone quite like Breanna—anyone as beautiful, and talented, and totally charming. She was almost certainly one of a kind.

He had also begun to suspect, though, that nothing would ever come of his infatuation. Spoiled rich kid and child prodigy that he was in this "backwater town," as she had called it, he knew that she was way out of his league. She came from a world where money was taken for granted and only power, intelligence, and sophistication mattered. He also knew that he could dream about her and pine after her until he withered up and died, but that nothing would ever come of it. She was meant for another life, with another man, someone as rich and powerful and sophisticated as she was.

The insight caused him considerable pain. He wanted to drop to the ground, double up, and scream to the high heavens.

However, some core sense of self-respect and rationality came to his rescue.

He forced himself back up the front steps of the school and down its empty hallways, back to the gym. There he found a very frustrated Mr. Phillips and all of his classmates, still struggling to make their way through the remaining auditions.

"Hey, D. W., welcome back."

"You come to help us out?"

Mr. Phillips turned his way and gave him a sympathetic look. "We could certainly use some help. And it seems maybe you could use some, too, right about now."

D. W. looked him deep in the eyes. "Put me to work," he said, holding out his arms at his side. He watched as Phillips struggled to suppress a grin.

"Oh, *pull-eeze*," the older man trilled in response, turning to the class. "He should know better than to say that to me, of all people. Right, chickens?"

His classmates burst into good-natured laughter, and then went back to the business at hand. A couple of his peers came up to him and asked with shy smiles if he would read with them, ". . . like you did with Breanna."

He said yes to every request, glad to have the distraction for his aching heart. As he returned to the stage with his peers time and again that evening, he was surprised to look out from behind the footlights and find Mr. Phillips looking at him, almost fondly.

PART II

TO WAR...AT HOME
AND ABROAD

CHAPTER 8

BROKE, BUSTED, DISGUSTED

D. W. hated standing in lines, and the one today in the bursar's office at Indiana University seemed a mile long to him. He had just finished registering for the second semester of his sophomore year, and was excited that he was going to be able to take some real acting courses at last. He had only to pay his tuition and then he was free to do as he pleased for the rest of the day.

Scanning the women in the line next to him, he spotted a willowy blonde who reminded him a lot of Breanna. Though not quite as striking and arresting as Breanna, the girl was definitely pretty. He feigned a terrible coughing fit, and was pleased when she turned his way to see what the commotion was. She gave him a small, serene smile, also a lot like Breanna's. He smiled back, pointing to his throat with a shrug of his shoulders and an apologetic look.

He decided that waiting in line wasn't quite so irritating after all. The pretty girl kept glancing over at him, smiling, and he kept glancing over at her, smiling back.

However, matters took a turn for the worse when he finally got to the front of the line and handed the clerk his registration form and the check his mother had given him when he was home for Christmas break. The clerk took the check, looked at it closely, and compared it to a list in front of her.

"I'm sorry," she said loudly. "This check is no good. We'll have to have cash or a money order for you to complete your registration."

D. W. was still intent on his relentless flirting with the pretty girl now at the next window. "Uh . . . what was that?"

The clerk bristled. "I said, we've been getting checks returned on this account for months. You still owe the university tuition and board for last semester. There's a hold on your registration for this semester until the outstanding balance is settled."

D. W. tore his eyes off the girl beside him and grabbed the metal bars of the little screen separating himself from the clerk. "But that's impossible. My father's one of the richest men in Indiana!" Then he caught himself. "Or he was anyway. There's got to be some sort of mix-up. My mother just gave me this check."

The clerk softened a bit. "Is your mother named Alexandra?"

A cold chill went down D. W.'s spine. "Yes . . . yes, that's her," he whispered. He looked down at the list on the clerk's felt pad, saw the red circle around a name, and accepted at last that it was true. Somehow his mother had managed to sabotage him yet again.

In his last years of high school, his grades had improved, but were still far from stellar. On graduating, he had assumed he wouldn't be able to get into any decent college or university, much less one of the best state performing arts schools in the nation. But somehow the fates, and a number of "good fairies," including Miss Triplett and Mr. Phillips, had conspired to help him earn admission to IU.

He had completed more than a year, studying material that he really enjoyed. He was even doing quite well in his classes, despite cutting them every time he felt he could risk it to have coffee with winsome girl at one of the bohemian bookshops down on the town square. In spite of his good luck and hard work, though, his mother had reached out at him once more with her silver-plated hook to drag him down.

He stared at the hapless clerk and wondered if would ever be free of the web his mother had always spun. Would he ever be able to be truly happy and carefree without wondering every moment when and where she was going to strike next, and rob him of whatever small happiness he had managed to find?

The pretty girl in the next line put away her checkbook, gathered her purse to her chest, and hurried away, clearly uncomfortable with the scene that had played out beside her. He felt quite sure, thanks to his mother, that he would never have coffee with her.

The clerk coughed a little nervously. "I have a note in your file to send you in to see the bursar." She motioned him through the heavy Dutch-door beside her station. In a daze, he stepped through the swinging walnut portal and into a virtual hell of unpaid bills and unresolved family drama.

As he sat before the bursar for the next half hour, D. W. thought several times what a kind and diplomatic man he was. However, nothing the compassionate man did could distract him from the truth that his mother had bankrupted them. The bursar put one unpaid invoice after another before him, noting how often his mother had been billed for his expenses, and how often the bills had been either totally ignored or paid for by checks that bounced.

"By all rights," the man concluded, "we should have contacted you and suggested you end your studies last semester, but we try to work with families when we can. Did you not wonder why you didn't get your grades at the end of that semester?"

D. W. sighed. "No, not really," he admitted. Thinking of the pretty girl he had been ogling out in the line at registration, he added, "I've kind of had my mind on some other things lately."

He left the bursar with all the dignity he could muster, and a promise to begin making payments on his balance as soon as he could find a job. As he wandered back to his dorm room, countless questions and recriminations raced through his troubled mind. How could his mother have gone through so much money in such a short time? Why hadn't he stepped up to the plate and been more of a man, quizzing her about the status of the estate and offering his help? What in the world were they going to do now?

Somewhere along the way in the years since his father's funeral, D. W. had realized that his mother didn't love him—that she never had, and she never would. Some days the realization hurt; no, more than that, sometimes it truly wounded him. Other days it was merely a statement of fact, like the acknowledgement of any truth—the sky is blue, the grass is green, and Alexandra Singer is incapable of loving her son.

Ruminating, he went back to his dorm room and packed his scant belongings, then traipsed down to the Greyhound bus station, and booked a ride home. Four hours later, he lit into his mother the minute he walked through the front door of the house.

"What in the world?" he shouted at the top of his lungs from the front foyer into the upper recesses of the house. He didn't see her anywhere and rightly assumed she was hiding from him.

"I mean it, Mother," he ranted, bounding up the twisting staircase. "I need to know what in the world you did to squander hundreds of thousands of dollars in a few short years, so that I can't go to school anymore, you surely can't stay in this house anymore, and the both of us are probably going to spend the rest of our sad, sorry lives paying off debtors."

He reached the second floor and was able to see into all of its rooms from the center of the hall; he was puffing and sweating and fighting to get his pounding heart under control. His mother was still nowhere to be seen. He stepped slowly into her room, trying to avoid looking at the photos that filled the walls. There were pictures of his folks together in younger, happier days, hugging each other, and smiling and waving from canoes and steamships, and carriages in Central Park.

Like the bread crumbs and stones Hansel and Gretel left behind them, a sorry trail of wrinkled receipts and crumpled bank statements led D. W. to the hideout his mother had chosen in the linen closet beside the master bathroom. He tiptoed to the door, reached it, and threw it open. There on the floor of the closet, clasping her hands in prayer, was his mother. The sight repelled him.

"Sweet Jesus," she whispered in a hushed, frightened voice, her eyes clenched shut and her lips drawn taut with the drama of the scene. "Please save me from this angry, ungrateful boy. You know I've done everything in my power to give him a good upbringing and send him out into the world a good, wholesome, Christian young man. Now he's come home, upset with me over money, the 'root of all evil.'"

With a mighty effort, D. W. stifled his rage and even managed to reach out a shaking hand to her.

"Mother, please," he said, with his best effort at civility. "Let's not do this scene, okay?"

He watched as his words sunk into the tinted, permed head, and she seemed to regain her composure. She looked up at him and gave him a little smile.

"I'm so glad you're going to be reasonable, son."

"Why, thank you, Mother," he was able to say with some grace, still holding out a hand to her. He noticed with some satisfaction how she bit on this hook and took his extended hand, rising to her feet and looking him square in the eye as she did.

"I never meant any of this to hurt you, son," she said, with tears beginning to fall. "It has nothing to do with you, really. It was just that I never had any say over anything in my marriage. Your father always paid the bills and managed everything. When he was gone, suddenly I could do whatever I wanted to do with all that money, and it . . . well . . . it kind of went to my head."

D. W. continued biting his tongue as he escorted her into her bedroom and planted her on the blanket bench at the foot of the massive four-poster bed she had seldom shared with his father.

"What *did* you do with it, Mother?" he asked, trying to keep the venom out of his voice.

She let out a little sigh and then giggled like a schoolgirl. "Well, that's the thing. I can't say that I really know . . . exactly." She gestured at the chaos of receipts and invoices littering the room. "I've been trying to figure it out."

D. W. scanned all the paper around them that gave evidence to his mother's folly and felt a rising fury. Alexandra saw his glowering look and seemed to grow frightened of him again.

"Now son, don't take on that way. There was this and that . . . things we needed." She winced anew at the look on his face. "All right, things I *wanted*, but you wanted them too, remember? The slate roof, and the new kitchen, and the antiques in the parlor and dining room. You told me how much you liked them, remember? Remember?"

D. W. did remember and felt humbled at the recollection. He had been pursuing a fruitless courtship of Breanna at the time, and he had enjoyed being able to invite her to dinner at his newly refurbished home. He had wanted to show off the grandeur his mother had brought to the sorry household that had been so neglected and loveless for years. It had never crossed his mind to ask her whether they really had the money to spend on all the lavish renovations and purchases. His father's legacy had sounded so huge to him, once upon a time when he was younger, and money had seemed so plentiful. Now he realized what his pride and lack of awareness had cost him, and he wanted to cry at the thought.

He sucked in a deep breath, and trying to keep his composure, rallied every bit of acting skill in his repertoire. "So, how bad is it?" he asked, surprised at his almost chipper tone. He wasn't prepared for her response.

Alexandra laughed bitterly. "Oh, it's bad, all right," she cried. "We're penniless." Something about uttering the awful word seemed to bring her to her senses. "Penniless . . ." she repeated the word again, her face crumpling. "Penniless!" With that, she emitted a wail of grief, letting her tears stream, so that they made little rivulets in the thick makeup on her cheeks. Eventually, she sobbed so hard that she lost her breath and fell into a genuine faint. After making sure that she wasn't choking on her own tongue, D. W. let his mother's frame loll across the silk-covered blanket bench and stood up to survey the mess that was now his inheritance.

He ambled through the over-furnished, yet still somehow

empty rooms of the house that his father had inherited from his father, another successful businessman who had also seemed incapable of loving his wife and children. He stepped over the detritus his mother had left on the polished parquet floors. The sad trail of bills, evidence indicating that disaster was looming, had all been ignored by his mother until they had reached a critical mass. He found himself at last on the gabled third floor, on the top landing of the majestic stairway that wound down three stories into the marbled foyer below—the foyer that had been plain oak flooring until two years ago when his mother had decided she wanted to install marble tiles.

D. W. leaned over the banister and looked down at the shining stone floor. It would be so easy, he realized, to trip and fall over the banister and break his neck on that lovely marble flooring. He looked all around him at the grandeur of the house he had grown up in, the house where he couldn't recall a single moment of peace or comfort. Slowly he started to lift a leg over the banister to test his weight against its cool polished surface.

Soon he found that he was all the way over it, dangling from the graceful curved length of wood, standing on the thin edge of flooring below it, holding onto the railing behind him with sweaty fingers, looking down three stories into the foyer below and wondering, could he really do it?

A bronze statue of Venus rising from the sea rested on the newel post at the bottom of the staircase. D. W. figured that if he positioned his fall just right, he could impale his body neatly on her. He let himself hang further over the stair rail and imagine what it would feel like to end his life in this way. No one would really care after all. Not his self-absorbed mother, lying now in her room downstairs, grieving her own losses and worrying over her dismal future, totally unconcerned that her only child had no future. Oh sure, Miss Triplett would cry a little bit over him, but she'd taught thousands of students over the years. What would the death of only one of them matter?

D. W. leaned deeper into the chasm separating him from the third floor where he teetered now, and the first floor where the sculpture beckoned him to join her and spill his guts on her demure, bent head. He closed his eyes and let himself hang even more loosely from the stair railing, finding his fingers slipping ever so slightly from the burnished wood. As he did, his heart raced so hard that he felt it would burst, the blood coursed through his eardrums and beat so loudly he was sure it would waken his mother downstairs.

In the midst of his rising resolution to follow through, he remembered a scene from one of his favorite movies, *Rebecca*. In a low, seductive voice, Mrs. Danvers, the malevolent housekeeper, was hypnotizing the second Mrs. DeWinter to jump from a high window to her death. Just at the moment she was about to succeed, warning flares and horns from a nearby shipwreck interrupted Mrs. Danver's spell and the young Mrs. DeWinter escaped unharmed.

No flare or ship's horn went off for D. W., but something equally important and life-saving did. For, as he was dangling over the stair railing, seconds away from dropping and impaling himself on the sculpture three stories below, a vision came to him that stopped him. It was a pair of beautiful jade-green eyes.

D. W. couldn't make out a face around them, but he knew that they belonged to someone he had yet to meet. In them, he saw a depth of sadness, compassion, and concern for him that he had never encountered before—not from anyone in his life, not even Miss Triplett. He also knew that those eyes were sad and concerned because of what he was about to do. As long as those eyes were on him, following his actions, he couldn't possibly follow through with his suicide plan. To his surprise, the awareness made him furious.

"God damn it!" he shouted. "I can't even die to get away from her!" But the bathos in his own situation eventually won over his anger. "God damn it," he whispered with a self-conscious chuckle, throwing his right leg back over the railing and onto the floor of the upper hall. "So where does that leave me now?"

A loud snore punctuated the oppressive silence of the house and D. W. realized that his mother must have moved from her melodramatic faint into a deep sleep. "Good riddance," he murmured as he began roaming the third floor. He soon found himself in his old bedroom, the nursery, as his mother preferred to call it. He wandered about the room, marveling at how small his childhood bed seemed now. He came to the shelf that held his GI Joe collection. There he stopped, startled, as if he were seeing the dolls for the first time. A wisp of a thought emerged at the back of his mind, and soon took full hold.

The handsome, vacuous faces of the dolls stared back at him, sporting their familiar small, taut smiles. He scanned the variety of uniforms they wore, some in full parade attire, others in khaki green army fatigues, still others in paratrooper jumpsuits with parachute packs on their backs. It was as if they were sending him a message, one that was almost shouted out to him.

He had the answer to the question he had put out into the cosmos. He would go into the military. Somehow, somewhere, some branch or the other—whichever would have him first—he would sign up as soon as possible, maybe today.

That's exactly what he did, that very same afternoon. He left his mother still snoring on the foot of her bed, hurried down to the town square, and found the army recruiter's office by the Greyhound station. Once enlisted, he returned home only long enough to pack his bags and dig out the family attorney's phone number. He left it with his mother, giving her firm instructions to call the man first thing next morning to begin bankruptcy proceedings.

Then he gave her a true tongue-lashing, the first in his life, venting all the sadness, hurt, and rage he felt at her treatment of him over the years. He didn't let her open her mouth once to speak a word in her defense or utter any justifications. He let it all rip, figuring, "Why the hell not?"

When he finished, he gave her a curt goodbye, announced his enlistment as he was leaving, and slammed the massive paneled front door behind him, with all the drama she had taught him by her example.

CHAPTER 9

ON A WING AND A PRAYER

D. W. leaned back into the worn upholstery of the ancient DC-3 airplane taking him and twenty other nervous new recruits to basic training at Fort Polk in Louisiana. He tried for the tenth time since boarding the plane to focus on the *Newsweek* magazine he'd picked up in the airport gift shop before leaving Louisville earlier that day. It was no use; the words on the pages swam and blurred before his tired, aching eyes.

He hadn't slept a minute last night, remembering all he had said to his mother right before leaving home. His face still stung with shame at the memory of his own angry, hurtful words, no matter how much she deserved them. He would go to his grave, he felt sure, remembering the stricken look on her face as he told her how much he hated her. He struggled to put all thoughts of the awful confrontation behind him and dove once again into an article about the progress, or lack of it, in the mounting Vietnam conflict.

The article detailed how badly the fighting was going. Trying to imagine what it must be like for the men there, he found that he really couldn't fathom what it must be to experience such an ordeal. He was aware for the first time that the war movies and GI Joe games he had loved so much as a kid had nothing to do with the grim realities of combat. Now, in all likelihood, he was headed for combat himself.

His father had been a veteran of World War II, but had never spoken of his wartime experiences. D. W. wasn't sure whether that was because his father had such terrible memories, or because his father had never spoken to him about much of anything on any topic.

Thinking about his father as a veteran, D. W. found himself distracted again from his reading, reflecting on how the battered little DC-3 was something of a veteran itself. He knew about the craft from listening as a child to old men chatting at the corner cafe, some of whom had piloted them. From them, he'd learned that the well-built, all-purpose planes had been the workhorses of several branches of the military in World War II, and the Korean War.

Years later, Ozark Airlines, a small regional airline providing budget puddle-jumper services to mid-westerners, had bought a fleet of the plucky prop airships and reconfigured them into a passable passenger airline fleet. Ozark offered airfares that were little more than train or bus fares, so they were a popular choice for the military when they wanted to transport soldiers quickly and cheaply.

The planes' cabins weren't pressurized, so they had to fly at low altitudes. Because of the wind turbulence the little planes encountered on many flights, stewardesses spent much of their time aloft handing out paper airsick bags, and offering flyers paper cups of chicken soup to soothe their stomachs, or Juicy Fruit gum to clear their popping ears.

D. W. stifled a grin as the strap holding the soup cans in the plane's little galley gave way with a jolt when the craft hit a strong crosswind. Cans of Campbell's chicken broth went rolling down the center aisle, bouncing between the seat legs and sending a very harried stewardess scrambling behind them, trying to catch the cans before they all made their way to the back of the plane. D. W. reached down and caught one of the errant cans as it rolled by his seat, then offered it with a broad smile to the frustrated woman as she worked her way past him.

"Thanks, sir," she said with a wan smile, blowing a sweaty strand of hair out of her eyes, and shaking her head. "I am way overdue for my vacation."

D. W. tried to go back to his reading, but to no avail. He looked up from the dismal words that reported ever-mounting losses in a war in which he was destined to serve. He glanced about the cramped cabin and wondered if his fellow passengers were entertaining the same pessimistic expectations.

We're a sad bunch for sure, he thought with a grim face. They sprawled and lolled in various degrees of dishabille, making a tangled mess of the crowded cabin with their outstretched arms and legs. Their garish tie-dyed shirts and wide bell-bottom jeans suddenly looked ridiculous to D. W., even though he had worn them himself until recently.

A quick stab of grief, rage, and remorse took hold of him again as he thought about all that he had lost in the last few days. No matter how guilty he felt for attacking his mother the night before, he would never forgive her for what he had experienced at the bursar's office at school.

He found himself peering out the window of the aged Ozark airliner at the picturesque, rolling farmland below, lying in winter fallow now. The scratchy intercom came to life, waking the recruits. "This is your captain," a deep bass voice announced.

"We'll be approaching the Bowling Green airport in fifteen minutes for a short layover, so please fasten your seatbelts in preparation for landing."

D. W. heard groans from some of the young men around him, and immediately knew why. As a regional commuter service, Ozark's planes normally took off and landed numerous times during most flights. The frequent ups and downs made flyers who were already airsick feel even worse.

He glanced across the aisle at a lanky recruit sitting there, and saw that the guy was clearly fighting nausea.

"I don't know whether I'm on an airplane, or a rollercoaster," the fella moaned.

Just as the word's were out of his mouth, a collective gasp erupted from the port side of the cabin, followed by several cries of "Holy shit!" Startled, he looked in that direction and saw that the port engine was emitting thick black smoke and making heart-sinking coughing noises. Seconds later, in what seemed like an eternity to the frightened onlookers, it began shooting flames as the propeller struggled to keep turning. While the terrified men watched wide eyed, it died altogether, and the left side of the plane dipped with a stomach-wrenching lurch.

D. W. fought the overwhelming urge to vomit and void both his bladder and his bowels. The frantic stewardess raced down the aisle and into the cockpit. D. W. found this even more unsettling. Shouldn't she or the captain be addressing them all, uttering calming assurances, as it always played out in the movies when a plane encountered distress?

A smug older recruit turned and began berating the group. "What a bunch of pansies. You all need to learn something about aeronautics. Anyone who knows anything knows that these old warships can land fine on one engine. So quit your hysterics and buckle up, boys. We're gonna make it to basic training late, but no one here is gonna die." He chuckled to himself in derision.

Just then, the starboard engine began to sputter, emitting a greasy black cloud of smoke. As it did, the plane made an immediate, distinct dip in altitude, sending all of the men's stomachs rolling. All heads turned right and watched in agonized suspense as the last functioning engine fought to keep the plane aloft.

"Oh my God, we really are fucked!" the previously smug recruit screeched, his voice rising into a wail. D. W. took grim satisfaction in seeing the superior young man reduced so quickly to a mass of quivering nerves.

The captain's voice came to them again over the scratchy intercom. "This is your captain," he said, sounding none too confident to D. W. "We've encountered a little engine difficulty."

Oh, really, D. W. thought and almost laughed out loud at the captain's masterpiece of understatement. Still, he reminded himself, that guy up in the driver's seat was their only hope of getting down to terra firma in one piece. *So God help him*, he prayed in a silent prayer.

As he did, the irony of the situation wasn't lost on him. Only a few hours earlier, he had been dangling over the edge of the third-floor banister at his home, planning to jump. Now here he was, about to die in a tangled, flaming heap of metal and men and Campbell's soup cans. He liked his other plan better.

The captain continued. "Fortunately there are farms in the area with crop duster airstrips and Bowling Green's tower is directing us to one of those. Please buckle up and stay calm."

D. W. found some measure of comfort in the message. All he had to do was try to believe it.

He turned and looked at the fellow in the seat beside him. The guy looked to be all of fifteen years old, sweating profusely and clearly fighting back tears. Something in the boy's dark blue eyes and open face tore a huge hole in D. W.'s heart.

Well, there's at least one person here more scared than me, he thought. *I might as well try a little damage control.* Faking a nonchalant smile, he stretched and yawned.

"Third time this has happened to me this year," he lied. "It always ends up the same. They bring you to some Podunk airport and make you finish your trip on a bus. I don't know how the guys that run this operation sleep at night."

"Honest?" the kid asked. "So you've had this happen before and made it through okay?"

"Oh, please, this is nothing. Ask me some time about the snowstorm in Chicago two years ago. Now there was a predicament."

D. W. watched out of the corner of his eye as the younger man tried to relax and settled back into his seat. "That's good to know. Thanks for telling me, man."

Right then the plane lurched sharply, and the young man let out a small yelp, despite himself. "I'm sorry. I don't know what's come over me."

I do, D. W. thought. *You're dying, and you know it, and we all know it, and we're all trying to pretend that we don't know it, that this isn't really happening, and that we have a snowball's chance in hell to survive this situation. But that isn't going to happen. Not today anyway. We're going down, in a cornfield, or a hayfield, or a tobacco base somewhere, in a cheesy little plane on our way to training for Vietnam where we were probably going to die anyway.*

He caught himself and realized he was working himself into a panic that he might not be able to reverse. *No sense in that. If you gotta go down in a plane with a bunch of sweating, stinking strangers, you might as well try to hold onto a little dignity.*

He looked over at his companion and saw that the kid was so absorbed in his own terror that he hadn't even registered D. W.'s reaction.

"So, where're you from?" D. W. asked him. The kid seemed not to hear him at first, but soon shook himself back to the present.

"Uh . . . I grew up in Mountain Home," the kid answered, as if he'd had to think hard to remember. "Mountain Home, Arkansas. But I've been doing construction in Salem, Indiana, the last year or so."

"I know Mountain Home. Been there myself a time or two on the way to a summer camp I used to attend."

The kid seemed to remember his manners. "How about you?"

An old memory of another lost and frightened younger friend came to D. W. and he had to smile. "Nowheresville."

"Huh, never heard of it." The kid went back to watching the remaining working engine. D. W. leaned over and joined him in his vigil, their faces only inches apart as they peered through the tiny porthole.

"Come on! Come on, baby . . . *live,*" he whispered through clenched teeth.

The kid seemed to find this amusing. "You think that'll help?" he asked with a little grin.

"Hell if I know," D. W. grinned back. "All I know is it sure can't *hurt.*"

The kid sobered a bit and nodded. Then he turned to the window himself and began chanting through his own clenched teeth. "Come on, baby . . . live. Live. Live!"

Soon the sight of these two talking earnestly to a struggling engine caught the attention of the rest of the men in the cabin. Laughter rippled through the group for a moment and then died as suddenly as it had started, replaced by a whispered prayer, barely audible from somewhere deep in the rear of the cabin: "Come on baby . . . *live*."

D. W. looked over his shoulder to see who the new convert was, but he couldn't find him. That was okay. He didn't need to see a face. It was enough to know there were three of them now, praying to the fickle flight gods to resurrect their dying engine. Then it happened.

Something about the sheer desperation in their shared life-threatening situation cut through any last reserves of self-consciousness in the group. A veritable chorus of male voices rose around D. W. and his new friend, at first whispering, then demanding, at full volume: "Come on baby . . . live, live, *live*."

When the change finally happened, it seemed to D. W. that he must surely be imagining it. The engine was an inanimate, man-made metal contraption that had no spirit or life of its own. Yet somehow, the more the men talked to it, the more it appeared to actually respond to them.

As the voices continued to rise up all around him, D. W. realized that something remarkable was occurring. It would be years before he could fully understand or describe it, but the glimmer of an insight struck him at the time; maybe there really was such a thing as a collective consciousness, an idea he had encountered for the first time in a Psych 101 course back at IU. Maybe people really could tune in to each other and channel their energies together to make things different in the physical world. Maybe prayers could be answered. Maybe failing engines could be cajoled into functioning properly. Maybe even broken hearts could be repaired.

Under the prayer vigil, the sickly engine continued to chug along sufficiently to keep the plane aloft, though it flew at an alarming angle and rapidly descending altitude. D. W. looked out the cabin windows on the other side of the banking plane, and saw a cluster of white frame houses and large barns a couple of hundred feet below them. The scratchy intercom crackled to life again and confirmed his guess.

"We're approaching a runway which should accommodate our needs, so we'll be landing shortly. Please make sure your seat belts are buckled and follow the stewardess's instructions closely."

A happy roar went through the cabin as men shook hands and even hugged each other. Then the harried stewardess appeared in the front of the plane and put a damper on their celebration.

"Please put your heads between your knees and cross your arms tightly over them in case of a crash landing." The men looked at each other and lost their relieved smiles.

"But I thought we were home free," one man said.

"Yeah," another chimed in. "The captain said this airstrip could handle us fine."

She raised a hand like a school crossing guard. "No arguments, please," she said, and rushed to the back of the plane to take her own seat. The men threw nervous glances at each other as they assumed the crash landing position.

Crouching in his seat, D. W. heard a stifled sniffle and turned to see the kid in the next seat shaking with suppressed sobs. Uncrossing his arms, he put his right one over the kid's head and held it there. The kid turned his head sideways and gazed at him with grateful eyes. D. W. winked at him and put his head back between his knees, but left his arm over the kid's.

Mere seconds seemed like hours to the men as the plane continued its final descent. The flagging engine hummed along, and D. W. thought it had an almost valiant sound. Then he felt the nose of the plane rise at the same time the tail dropped, and he knew it was time for touchdown. The next second, they all felt the tires kiss the runway and heard the brakes squeal. The plane bounced twice, and then settled firmly at last, to taxi down the narrow corridor. The captain killed the engine as the plane rolled to a complete stop, and for a long moment, complete silence filled the cabin.

"God almighty," someone finally said, and laughter and happy chatter erupted everywhere. D. W. raised his head and looked all around him. Men unbuckled their belts, jumped out of their seats into the aisle, shook hands and clapped each other on their backs.

D. W. looked over at the kid again who was staring back at him with a beatific face. "We made it," the boy said.

"Told you this was nothing," D. W. lied again.

"You weren't scared at all, were you?"

"Honestly? I've never been more terrified in my life."

The kid frowned. "No kidding? You sure didn't show it."

"Acting," D. W. said. "I've had a lifetime of practice at it and it looks like it's going to be my life work, one way or another."

While he was kidding, D. W. soon realized he'd experienced another transcendent moment of some kind. The thought took hold and amplified in his mind, as he unbuckled his seat belt and shuffled out of the slanted fuselage with the others. Acting would be his life work after all.

He knew it just then, with a complete and comforting certainty. It didn't matter whether he attended a university or not. There were thousands of gifted actors performing all over the world who'd never had a moment of formal training. They did what they did through a sense of calling and natural instinct, so he would be one of those.

Oh sure, a theater or voice degree would have been a nice plus on his bio, but it wouldn't have ensured him anything. He would still have had to try out for every part and win it by being better than the others trying out for the same role. Mulling all of this over, he lost sight of what he had been doing, but came to himself at last on the runway outside the plane.

He looked all around him and thought he had never seen a more beautiful spot in the world. It was a warm mid-winter afternoon in the rich farmland of Western Kentucky, and a pale mist hung over the rolling fields. D. W. spotted several sleek horses grazing in those fields, taking leisurely steps as they nuzzled the grass. An unexpected urge came over him then to go grab some of that grass, feel it, smell it, and maybe even taste it himself.

He walked to the edge of the landing strip and leaned down to pluck a handful of the turf, still green in the mild winter weather. Raising it to his nose, he drew in its rich perfume and then lifted his hand high over his head, letting the blades sprinkle down over his upturned face and shoulders. He closed his eyes and let the sweet smell of the grass and the unforeseen serenity of this place and this moment wash over him. He knew that in a few moments he would have to re-enter the real world. Just as he had predicted to the kid earlier, they would have to find transportation of some kind to complete their trip, a bus or a train. For now, though, all he cared about was the feeling of peace and renewal he was experiencing, the first sense of hopefulness or well-being he'd had since leaving IU. A voice startled him out of his reverie.

"Acting again?" He turned to find the kid watching him with a quizzical look.

D. W. had to chuckle at himself. "Naw, not this time."

The kid walked up to him and stopped there, seeming to need something from him. Finally he coughed and made a self-conscious start.

"Back there, in the plane, when it looked so bad . . . do you think you could teach me to do what you did? You know, acting so calm when everyone else was falling to pieces? Because I think we're all going to need that in the place we're going after boot camp."

D. W. had a quick flashback to Toby Schumann, the boy who had almost drowned at camp. Remembering that experience and the other kids in his class who had needed his help getting through senior play, it occurred to D. W. that somehow, in spite of his checkered past as a problem child, he had always been a sucker for the underdog. No matter how messed up and confused his own life might be, people sought him out for mentoring. Miss Triplett had tried to talk to him about this phenomenon several times over the years, urging him to be more aware of his impact on others and his potential to be a positive influence. He had thought that she was just trying to get him to behave better, but subsequent events seemed to prove her point.

He came around and realized that the kid was blushing, obviously embarrassed about his question. "Sure," he said, with some bravado. "It's acting, not rocket science. They teach animals to do it in Hollywood."

The kid laughed and seemed to overcome his embarrassment. He stretched forth his right hand. "Jodie Lucas. I'm pleased to know you."

D. W. reciprocated and began leading them back to the airplane where it appeared a crowd was gathering to figure out next steps. "The first thing you need to know about acting is that people give you their permission to do it. They actually ask you to take them somewhere imaginary. So it's all about an interaction you have with your audience."

The kid listened intently but shook his head, signaling he didn't get it. *That's okay,* D. W. thought as he continued chatting with him. *We've got weeks of boot camp ahead. There'll be plenty of time.*

Somehow, merely through having someone else to look after again, he found a new purpose to help him forget how unhappy he had been.

CHAPTER 10

ONE DAY AT A TIME

Landing Zone Two Bits
Near Bong Son, South Vietnam

Jodie tiptoed through the hot, humid evening air toward the dugout bunker that he shared with seven other men. He stooped, picked up a couple of hefty stones, and inched to the doorway, where he scanned the dim interior, looking for the cat-sized rats that plagued their lives.

Sure enough, he spotted two of them scurrying about the footlockers, sniffing for food or anything else worth eating, which was almost everything the men owned. He lobbed his missiles at the rodents, killing one outright, and sending the other one scurrying for his hole in the shadows. As he did, he wondered for the hundredth time if he would ever conquer his dread of the revolting creatures. He often had nightmares about them nibbling on his toes, or worse yet, his face, while he slept.

He quickly surveyed the bunker, and reassured it was clear, strode to his bed. He glanced at the doorway to make sure none of his bunkmates were coming, and reached under the mattress for the diary he had kept since arriving there months earlier.

So far he had managed to keep his journaling a secret, and he hoped to continue that way. He knew that if it were detected, the razzing he would get from his buddies would be brutal. Then the question occurred to him, did they really not know about it, or was their lack of hazing another result of D. W. watching out for him? He often thought that he would never have managed to survive so far without the friendship of the older young man. His diary was full of entries about it.

The atmosphere in the bunker was musty and oppressive, plus the dead rat still lay on the floor. He decided to risk climbing onto the roof of the bunker to do his writing tonight. All of the other men were at a USO show presently—he could hear some Diana Ross wannabe singing a passable rendition of "You Can't Hurry Love"—so he felt reasonably sure he could get an entry completed before they returned.

He clambered up the sand bags and earthworks that surrounded the bunker, reached the roof, and looked out appreciatively over the unusually peaceful landscape. The surrounding hills were a lush dark green, and the Bong Son plain between them lay bathed in pale blue moonlight. Several farmers still tended their rice fields, taking advantage of the light, and the rare respite from gun and mortar fire.

Jodie wondered whether they were Viet Cong, and realized that they very well could be; one never knew with these people. The short-timers, so named because they were close to going home, said it best: "They might smile at you one minute, then throw a grenade at you the next, even the women and kids."

Nonetheless, he felt a twinge of sadness, knowing that the work the farmers were doing would probably be undone. Action in the area was escalating quickly, and villages and farms were being laid to waste.

Despite months of seeing the horrors these people inflicted on

US troops and each other, he couldn't get over the ambivalence he felt toward them. He had come to think of it as his Dr. Jekyll/ Mr. Hyde complex. One minute he wanted them all dead, the next he pitied them for their bad luck, being caught in this crazy war. After all, weren't they, like he and his comrades, merely trying to protect their homes and interests? Then another of their frequent ambushes or atrocities would occur, and he would pray for every Viet Cong to die a horrible death.

As always before writing, he leafed through the pages of the diary, looking at previous entries and reflecting on the changes he had experienced during his tour of duty. It often seemed to him that he had aged a lifetime in a few months. He smiled a little self-consciously as he reviewed the first entry. It had felt so momentous and dramatic to him then, yet sounded so juvenile now.

MARCH 2, 1967

The Beginning. I arrived in Vietnam today at 2:00 a.m. after a pretty good flight from California to Japan. It was 81 degrees in the middle of the night, and the air was so wet and heavy I had trouble breathing. Or maybe I was just scared? We're here in the Cam Ranh Bay and the mountains that surround us on all sides are beautiful and grand, nothing like what we call mountains back in Arkansas. This is my first entry in a diary I plan to keep while I'm here. Though I never wanted it, I plan to make the most of this experience. I want to come out of it a better person. I want to come out of it a true man. I want to come out of this knowing I can deal with whatever life throws my way. Most of all, I want to get out of here alive and in one piece.

He leafed through several more pages and stopped at a later entry. Once again, he had to smile at his youthful enthusiasm.

APRIL 1, 1967

April Fool's Day and how it fits. We're in An Khe now in the Central Highlands, being told we're moving south to Qui Nhon soon. Except for the rattle of gunfire in the hills, you would think you were in a tropical paradise. It's lush and green and hot. God, is it hot! I thought I knew hot growing up in Arkansas, but I never saw anything like this. It's not uncommon for it to be 110 degrees in the shade, and as they used to say back home, "It ain't the heat, it's the humidity." The slightest effort makes you sweat like a horse. And the work we're doing right now is awful, tearing down old barracks that stink and make you sick from the mold. But it's better than what they had us doing last week . . . latrine duty. Whoever thought up the idea of burning human waste had to be crazy. Of course, D. W. made a joke of it, saying, "The good thing about burning shit is it's a great motivator to find something better to do with your life." I don't know how he does it. I think maybe as long as he's around I can somehow manage to stay sane here . . . maybe, just maybe.

Skipping many pages ahead, he read the first passage that didn't bring a smile to his lips. In fact, it made him break out in goose bumps, remembering the events it described.

MAY 23, 1967

We're in LZ Two Bits now on the Bong Son Plain, and it's a true hellhole. Everywhere you look, you see nothing but tents, ramshackle buildings, and raw, red earth. The bunkers are dark and dirty and the choppers land and take off so close to them there's a constant cloud of dust in the air. But that's not the worst thing. "IT" finally happened . . . I killed a man, maybe lots of them, and all in just a few seconds, making the whole thing seem even more horrific. We were out on patrol in heavy brush and came under fire, but we struck back with so much more firepower nobody could have survived it. Then, after it was over, all you could hear was the hum of insects. D. W. and a couple of other guys went in to check the body count, but I hung back. I didn't want to know. It feels awful to have taken a human life, even if it is the enemy. I keep telling myself if we hadn't killed them, they would have killed us, but somehow that doesn't help. For once, even D. W. couldn't say anything to make me feel better. When I found him later, he was down on his hands and knees, retching into a ditch. I put my hand on his shoulder and he looked up at me. I don't think I've ever seen anyone look so sad, angry, and lost, all at the same time. He always tells me he's scared to death when I ask him how he acts so calm, and from now on I'll believe him. Strange thing is, I think I respect him even more after tonight. A man should puke his guts out after killing other men . . . and I wonder now why I didn't.

Jodie needed to clear his head, so he put down the diary, looked up again at the moon, and down again at the plain. The dizzying contrasts were surreal and crazy-making. In many ways, he found this alien land one of the most beautiful he'd ever seen, at least outside the base. In other ways, though, he found this country riddled with such abject poverty and mindless cruelty that it was totally repugnant to him. Those were the times he felt his tour of duty would never end.

Time to get writing, he told himself, *or the guys will catch me up here and give me hell.* However, for once, he found himself struggling with writer's block. Finally it occurred to him to merely comment on the moment, and from there he found himself waxing philosophical.

JUNE 15, 1967

I'm sitting on the roof of the bunker, because hot as it is up here, it's even hotter down there, watching the moon wash over the fields below, and some farmers try to make the most of the light. Normally the night belongs to "Charlie" (the VC), and they fill it with mortar and gunfire, till you think you'll go insane. But this one is calm for a change. There's some pretty good music coming from the USO show across the base, and, wouldn't you know it, the song that sticks in my head is the Supremes' "You Can't Hurry Love." What a joke on me. Sometimes I wonder if I'll ever find love. I've been homesick and heartsick a lot lately. I miss the folks terribly and hope they write me again soon. But there's no girlfriend for me to write to or get written to, and I feel the absence of that more and more over here. Other guys get letters sealed with lipstick kisses and dotted with hearts, but no girl has ever appealed to me much, or come after me either. Sometimes I doubt that they ever will. Funny thing is, there are prostitutes all over the place here, and they come on to us all the time.

He heard the finale of the show beginning, a rousing rendition of "God Bless America," and realized the guys would be back soon. He began scribbling more quickly to finish up his entry.

> D. W. and I went into the village the other day to drop off some laundry, and all the girls there in the laundry are prostitutes. One of them was all over D. W. and she asked him, "So, how much you love me, soldier boy?" He blushed and said, "Well, you're awful pretty darling,' but I'm sorry, I don't love you." She just shrugged and said, "No matter, you die soon." We both laughed our heads off at the time, but the more I think about it, the more it troubles me. I sure hope that girl isn't some kind of psychic, because if anything ever happens to D.W., I'm a goner.

A roar of applause and cheers rose up across the base signaling the show was over, and it was time for him to wrap up his writing. He closed the diary, stuffed it into the back of his pants and rose to exit the rooftop. Before he left, he took one last moment to savor the remarkable evening.

Looking out over the plain, he wondered, *why can't it always be like this? Why can't people just live and let live? And when will I ever get home . . . if I ever do get home?*

Then he heard the shuffle of many boots coming down the lane, and hurried back to the bunker to return his diary to its hiding place.

CHAPTER II

A DANGEROUS PLACE AND TIME TO BE ALIVE

Landing Zone English
Near Bong Son, South Vietnam

It was November 1967, and D. W. had been in Vietnam more than seven months. Since arriving in country, he had considered himself lucky to be alive. But he became increasingly restless and depressed during the months that back home would be autumn, his favorite time of year.

It didn't help that the area around LZ English was a hotbed of Viet Cong activity, and "Charlie" seemed to be hell-bent on killing and harassing the US troops in every way imaginable. They lobbed grenades or mortars and sent sniper fire into the base at all hours; few soldiers ever got a decent rest. They crept into the men's bunkers at night and slit their throats. They even released rabid dogs and cats that roamed the base and bit the soldiers, many of whom had to undergo painful shots.

To make matters worse, the topography of the region was difficult to defend. It was hilly, and crisscrossed with ravines and waterways. Numerous roads and bridges had been constructed to make navigation possible. The bridges especially were the targets of relentless encroachment by the enemy.

It was monsoon season and the constant rains gave the enemy a further advantage. Their strikes were more effective in weather where visibility was poor and roads were mired with mud. In addition, the frequent gray skies lowered the men's moods even further. The impact on morale was devastating. Men's nerves were frayed, their tempers were short, and their tongues grew sharp.

Like many apparently confident men who seemed equal to any adversity, D. W.'s acting abilities had a limit, and he was nearing it now. Always the consummate showman in the past, he developed a hand tremor and stammer that made him feel awkward and diffident, striking fear in his heart. His glib tongue and smooth ways had always been his strongest defenses, but these were crumbling.

He began imagining he was seeing things, and his nights on guard duty were torture, for he had trouble judging when he was hallucinating or seeing an actual VC. On the rare nights that he was able to fall asleep, he had terrifying nightmares about being wounded, losing limbs, or becoming horribly disfigured. He would wake up screaming, and run his hands over his face and body, amidst the groans and curses of his bunkmates.

Always one of the most well-liked soldiers on the base, he felt his popularity slipping. Americans weren't used to guerilla warfare, but they were learning in Vietnam that men had to be as sharp and trustworthy as possible in this type of warfare. There was no storming of beaches by thousands of men, with warships behind them pounding shells into the enemy lines. Here war was waged in close quarters among blinding elephant grass and towering bamboo cane. Soldiers had to keep their senses and stay closely in tune with each other. Any troop who wasn't totally on his game posed a risk not only to himself but to his fellow soldiers as well. Anyone who displayed signs of weakness often became the target of distrust and derision.

"What's up with you, Singer?" a disgruntled bunkmate asked after one of his particularly loud nightmares. "You better get your shit together or Charlie will have your hide."

D. W. wasn't sure which hurt worse, the contemptuous comment or the chorus of snickers that followed it. Only Jodie remained steadfast in his loyalty and support. Still, a subtle reversal was developing in their friendship.

Whereas D. W. had always watched out for and mentored Jodie, now Jodie sheltered and nurtured him, as best he could anyway in such an adrenalin-fueled climate. In an ironic twist, news crews from the states showed up soon after Thanksgiving to film the men's maneuvers on the big tanks called Dusters. Having heard of D. W.'s theater background, his commander sent the war correspondents to interview him.

However, with the cameras rolling and the microphone in his face, D. W. found himself speechless for once. Jodie stepped in and gave a masterful interview that made his family wild with pride when it aired in the states. Unfortunately, it only made D. W. feel worse.

Under the present troubled conditions, both within himself and on base, D. W. felt ill-prepared for the frequent patrols he and his unit were sent on to flush out the VC from the surrounding hills. The request he had made recently for R & R in Australia had fallen on deaf ears. There was too much action going on in the region, so he had no other choice but to try to pull his own weight.

Things started really heating up on December 7, and it struck the men as no coincidence that it was the anniversary of the Pearl

Harbor attack. Nearby LZ Tom was hit hard, and the enemy moved from there to the coast, only miles away, where they had fortifications and were dug in tight. The men mobilized all the manpower and firepower LZ English had to offer in a battle that lasted two days with numerous casualties.

D. W. and Jodie were among the infantry accompanied by one of the massive Dusters, but the big tank's lumbering weight and prodigious gun did little to reassure D. W. His nerves were so shot he had difficulty keeping his teeth from chattering. As usual, Jodie saw what was happening and tried to lend a hand.

"Come on, old man," he teased. "Think of this as an adventure—something to brag about to our grandkids when we're old and fat."

D. W. knew what he was doing and appreciated his intentions, but gave him a sour face and middle finger nonetheless. "That's if we make it through this farce and get the chance to have grandkids, which looks doubtful right now."

Jodie was determined to be optimistic. "What good does it do you to assume the worst? All that gets you is a shitty attitude, when you're already so scared you could shit. So then everywhere you look, all you got is a great big load of shit . . . shit, shit, and more shit!"

D. W. had to smile at that. "I gotta admit, kid. I taught you well. Remember all that stuff I told you about how to keep your cool and act the part until finally the act becomes the real thing? Only problem is, I was totally full of shit when I told you that."

Soon they had to cut the banter. They had been working their way across a coastal plain with good visibility, letting them draw a deep breath or two. Up ahead, though, was a bridge over a wide ravine, and they tensed and raised their M16s at the sight of it.

Just then, dozen or more VC sprang up over the ridge and launched a volley of grenades their way. Others kneeled and sprayed gun fire at them.

D. W. and the others threw themselves to the ground and positioned themselves near the Duster to counterattack. Aircraft came to their support, spraying the ravine with bullets, and the Duster's guns began blasting away. Within seconds, the US troops were engaged in a full-blown firefight, the first D. W. had experienced.

He was lying on the ground near the Duster, pumping rounds at the VC, when a grenade detonated close enough to raise a mound of earth that thrust him into the air and sent his weapon flying. He landed hard on his back, deafened by the blast, blinded by dirt, with the wind blown out of his lungs. In the next several seconds, more grenades detonated around him, so that all he could do for the time was clasp his arms over his head and pray. It seemed to him as if the whole world were exploding.

Eventually, despite the ringing in his ears, he heard someone screaming his name. It was Jodie, sounding very far away, though they had been only a few feet apart moments before. He propped himself up on his right elbow and wiped the dirt from his eyes with his left hand, blinking and searching for his friend. When he finally spied him, he wished he hadn't.

Jodie was down about twenty feet away from him. His pot helmet had been shredded by shrapnel and he had a gaping head wound that poured blood over his forehead and eyes. D. W. wasn't sure, but he thought that the boy didn't look all there. He couldn't see his right arm or his legs at all.

"I'm coming," he shouted and began crawling Jodie's way. Bullets continued pelting the ground around them, though the

Duster and air support were doing a noble job of giving the enemy hell. He reached Jodie's side after what seemed like an eternity, and stretched out a hand to let him know he was there, since the boy couldn't see through the blood in his eyes.

"I'm here. It's me, D. W."

Jodie tried to speak but had lapsed into such deep shock he was incapable of communicating. D. W. ran his hand over the boy's body as lightly as he could, trying to assess the extent of the damage. He was relieved to find there were no limbs missing after all; they were just covered with so much earth that it had appeared they were gone. The chief injury seemed to be his horrible head wound, and he shuddered to see a glimpse of gray brain matter amidst the blood under the shattered helmet.

As D. W. examined Jodie, he was oblivious to everything else. It was as if he had gone into suspended animation, and in that suspended state, he was suddenly strangely calm. The fears and self-doubt that had crippled him for months seemed far behind him. He felt as if he were both invisible and invincible.

Somewhere on the edge of his blurred awareness, he vaguely heard the continuing cacophony of the guns, and the muffled shouts of other men. Finally one of those other voices reached through his altered state and got his attention.

"Singer, is that you?"

D. W. turned in the direction of the voice and saw his lieutenant, Conner Olson, lying on his back against a berm. His left thigh was open to the bone.

"Yes, it's me," D. W. shouted. "I'm over here with Lucas. He's wounded real bad—out like a light."

"Then get the hell over here and give me a hand," Olson ordered. "I'm not out like a light and I hurt like hell!"

D. W. turned back to Jodie and saw that he was still breathing, fairly steadily, considering his condition. His field training had taught him in situations like this to tend first to the soldier who was able to communicate and possibly still fight. The best thing a soldier could do for a man who was totally down was get the medics to him as soon as possible. He patted Jodie on the shoulder.

"Hang in there," he whispered, fighting tears. "We'll get of here, one way or another. I promise you."

Turning he crawled like a crab toward Olson and reached him right as another grenade landed nearby, sending another load of dirt over them. When the dust cleared, they blinked and surveyed the latest damage. A number of men lay still all around them.

Olson pointed toward the bridge and D. W. turned to see what was happening there. "Looks like we're turning things around," the officer grunted.

Sure enough, the enemy seemed to be taking some hard knocks. There were still quite a few of them, doing their best to inflict all the damage they could, but the Duster was doing its duty and gaining the better of them.

D. W. turned back to Olson. "Thank God. If we hunker down tight here, we should get relief soon."

Olson grabbed his chin and gave it a hard squeeze. "Like hell," he spat. "We're getting the advantage over those fuckers. Get up and go after them, Singer!"

D. W. felt his newfound sense of calm slipping away. "But . . . but, I've lost my rifle."

Olson reached beside him and tossed his own lightweight M16 to D. W. "Well then, here, by all means, please feel free to take mine."

D. W. caught the weapon, but still looked uncertain. Olson

shook his head and smiled with disdain. "What is it, Singer? Still running from those nightmares?"

The remark struck D. W. with the force of a stomach punch. In an instant, he went from uncertain to determined to angry to enraged. The strange calm he had felt moments ago was replaced by a killing fury. At first it was directed at Olson for insulting him so deeply, but soon it refocused on the men who had done this to all of them, the men back there at the bridge.

The metamorphosis must have been evident in his eyes, for Olson's sneer softened into an approving smile. "Now then . . . that feels better, doesn't it?"

D. W. nodded, shouldered his weapon, and stood to face the enemy. He felt the explosive white rage mounting in his chest, and found himself embracing it and harnessing it. Adrenalin coursed through his body and made him feel superhuman. He heard a blood-curdling banshee cry coming from somewhere, and then realized it was coming from his own throat.

He felt himself barreling forward toward the bridge, howling like some feral animal. All the while, he felt the trusted weapon in his arms, spraying the startled VC and cutting them down, almost as if the gun was acting of its own volition. In the midst of this bloodlust, he was surprised to find that it could feel very, very good to kill someone. The sick remorse that had crippled after the first time he did it was completely gone.

As he continued charging forward, he saw that most of the enemy were down, but he kept coming at them, shooting the whole way. He had almost reached a point where he thought he could stop when a whistling sound came his way, and he knew what it meant. Then, as if in slow motion, everything went very white and still.

CHAPTER 12

FACING FACTS

Nineteen-year-old Corrine Kelly hated her night-shift job as a nurses' aide on the convalescent ward at the military hospital at Camp Zama in Sagamihara, Japan. She hated it almost as much as she hated her physician father for insisting she take a position there, saying it would toughen her up.

At four foot eleven, and barely ninety pounds, "Cory," as she was known to family and friends, had never had any desire whatsoever to be tough. The youngest of four siblings in an Irish Catholic family, she had no greater ambition in life than to have fun, make plenty of friends, and spend as much time as possible keeping everyone she knew happy, by doing whatever they pleased.

Cory's martinet father was the chief surgeon and the most prominent physician ever assigned to the military hospital at Camp Zama, near Tokyo. He had done his time in the medical trenches back home—conducting research, publishing papers, and speaking at national conferences—and Michael Kelly knew his reputation and worth to the struggling, undermanned army of the day. He manipulated that to his advantage with shameless zeal.

Dr. Kelly's life would have never turned out as well as it had if not for the perfect combination of cockiness, charisma, and back-to-back wars. He was a short, muscular, bullet of a man who prided himself far more than he deserved to on his energy and fitness. Despite his best efforts to ruin his health in every imaginable way—drinking and womanizing at every opportunity—he was brilliant in his field, and seemed, in fact, unable to make a misstep. No matter where he worked, or what challenges he faced, he always succeeded, and made a name for himself as a brilliant military physician. The impact on his already bloated ego was incalculable.

The other thing Dr. Kelly had to his advantage was his incredible gift for making quick, powerful connections with his patients and peers, all of whom thought he was the second coming of Christ. Only his family knew the real man.

Like many families with an abusive parent, the Kellys had learned how to manage a difficult home life. Cory's mother had been her father's chief nurse during World War II, so she knew how to manage his moods and anticipate his needs to prevent unpleasantness . . . at least most of the time. Cory's older siblings all had lots of hobbies and activities outside the home, and had learned to avoid trouble by being scarce.

Only Cory seemed unable to develop strategies for dealing with her father. In fact, she seemed to be constantly in his way, and thus became the target of his ire.

"Cory! Why don't you go somewhere and make yourself useful?" he would bark at her when she was little. When she was older it became, "Surely you don't plan to wear *that* dress outside of this house, do you? You look like a tramp."

She became a shy, self-doubting young woman, but she also learned how to anticipate others' whims and to placate them, exactly as her mother had done. She became popular at school, despite her shyness, because she was always trying to make other people feel good.

Because of her father, Cory also came to loathe bullying of any kind, and developed a raging lioness inside to fight it wherever she encountered it. She normally showed this side of herself outside the Kelly home, at school or socializing with friends. However, when she was sixteen, the time came that it erupted in a direct confrontation with her father, and their relationship would never be the same.

Her father had berated her mother all day for one imagined fault or another; the laundry wasn't folded right, the kitchen floor wasn't shiny enough; the gravy in the pot roast was too thin. He delivered this last complaint at the dinner table with the bellow of a mad bull. Cory's siblings sat with their eyes downcast, silently poking at their food with their forks. Her mother sat frozen, looking down at her hands in her lap. Cory felt paralyzed until she saw a tear fall from her mother's eye onto her folded knuckles, and a blinding rage took hold of her.

Before she knew it, she jumped up, threw back her chair, and grabbed the carving knife from the pot roast plate. Stabbing the blade into the table, she leveled a steely gaze at her father, and bellowed back at him, "Then why don't you get out to the kitchen and fix something yourself!"

She would never forget (and always cherished) the look on his face. Clearly shaken, he was speechless for once in his life. More than that, she saw something else in his eyes, something between fear and respect. Having expected him to beat the living daylights out of her, she was surprised by what actually happened next.

He blinked several times, cleared his throat, and reached for his water glass with a shaking hand. He managed to squeak, "Well . . . I think . . . I think . . . we've had quite enough of that kind of talk for one night, young lady."

She almost laughed at the ineffectual response, so totally unlike his usual harsh words. They finished the meal in silence, but when it was over, her father helped her mother clear the dishes. Cory had learned one of the most valuable lessons of her life. Sometimes people have to fight, no matter how scared they are, and no matter how uneven the odds—because often an aggressor is only another bully and bullies are always cowards at heart. It was a lesson she never forgot, and one that would come to her aid many times in the years ahead.

Her father never berated her mother again, at least not in her presence. And he also treated Cory differently . . . not pleasantly or respectfully, but warily, as if he didn't know quite what to expect from her, and was afraid to find out.

Leafing through a *Seventeen* magazine during her mid-shift break, Cory had none of these matters on her mind. She was thinking only about how wonderful it must be to be a writer and interview rock stars for magazines. *Someday, dear God*, she prayed, *let me get out of this miserable family with its military housing and commissary shopping and see the real world before I'm too old to enjoy it.*

The double doors at the end of the hall swung open with a loud bang and startled her out of her daydreams. Vince, an orderly she had come to loathe for his incessant unwelcome flirtation, was negotiating a gurney through the doorway. At the nurses' station, he stopped it abruptly enough to elicit a groan from its occupant.

"Another new arrival from the sunny land of South Vietnam," he said with a grin, popping his gum, and winking at Cory. "Just out of surgery, needing tender loving care." He looked deep into her jade-green eyes and smiled a leering smile. "I hear young Corinne Kelly has lots of TLC to give . . . is that true, babe?"

"Sure, *babe*," Cory purred, giving him a coquettish wink in return, and coming around the counter of the nurses' station. "How's *this* for TLC?" she asked with a demure smile, then kicked him in his ample rear.

"Aw, shit!" he yelped, running for the door. "I've been attacked by a leprechaun! Lemme outta here! Where's the charge nurse? Where do I file an assault report?"

Cory listened to Vince continue his theatrics through the halls of the hospital, furious that he was waking patients who needed their sleep. She cursed him under her breath and hoped the young man occupying the gurney was still too fuzzy from whatever anesthetic he had received in surgery to hear the commotion. She came around to the side of the gurney and looked into the young man's bandaged face. Gazing into his tawny eyes, she saw in an instant that he was awake, in excruciating pain and terrified. She had seen that almost crazed look in the eyes of incoming patients before.

Eyeing the big frame on the gurney, she took in the sorry landscape of his body. He seemed to have bandages almost everywhere, especially around his face, where the only visible features were the soft brown eyes—eyes that she had to admit to herself, were very, very attractive indeed; eyes that looked deep and with anguish into her own. He tried to speak through the packing in his mouth and managed to produce little more than a garbled grunt.

Cory's heart went out to him. "It's okay. We'll get you settled in a room shortly. Try to relax. You're safe now."

Looking down into the beautiful eyes, she wasn't prepared for what she saw. Large teardrops formed in their corners and flowed into the bloody bandages around his mangled face. She put an arm over the pillow behind his head.

"Honest," she said. "You're going to be okay."

To her surprise, these reassurances only seemed to make him more agitated. He shook his head slightly and struggled to speak through jaws that had been wired shut. Finally he managed to form some barely intelligible words through the bandages and wires.

"Is it really you?" he croaked, and stared at Cory with a beseeching look.

The question made no sense to her, but that wasn't new. Combat survivors who had just come out of surgery were always asking her all kinds of crazy things. Was she an angel? Was she their mother? Could she make them a cheeseburger? She decided he must still be under the influence of the anesthetic and needed to be humored.

"Yes, it's me. Cory."

He struggled to speak again and obviously found it maddening that he couldn't. He kept trying to form words, was unable to do so, and tossed his head in frustration.

"Thanks . . . for . . . stopping me . . . from jumping," he eventually managed to get out in short, gasping breaths. He seemed to decide it was better not to talk anymore and closed his eyes.

Cory glanced up at the morphine drip hanging from the pole by his gurney and plunked the plastic tubing several times with her index finger to make sure a steady flow continued. She knew he was going to need every single drop of the painkiller to get through the night. She also knew it might very well be hours before they had a bed open for him. She had paperwork to complete, so she wheeled his gurney beside her chair and returned to her notes, looking up frequently to see how he was faring.

During the next several hours, she was relieved to see him fall into a fitful, drug-induced sleep, but as the morning drew nearer, he became more restive, tossing and turning, and muttering various names she could only assume were his family, friends, or combat buddies. Breanna, Jodie, and Miss Triplett figured most prominently in his rantings. He also kept up a lively dialogue with "Ma," and though it was hard to tell exactly what he was saying, he became particularly agitated when he mentioned her name.

After working her way down to the last of her paperwork, Cory looked up at the clock and saw that her shift was almost over. Physicians and the morning crew of nurses and aides began straggling in. As they did, they all passed by the young man's gurney, gave him the once-over, and looked grim as they checked his chart.

Suddenly a voice barked from the end of the hall, startling everyone. "What's this man doing in the middle of the corridor? Get him out of here at once!"

Cory didn't have to turn to see who it was. Dr. Michael Kelly was here to start his rounds and she knew that, as usual, he was sure to find something amiss on the ward. Thank goodness she was due to go home soon.

Dr. Kelly strutted up to the new patient and grabbed his chart; he gave it a quick perusal and began to shout orders. "Room 103 has three men ready for discharge. Get them out of here now, and put this man in one of those beds, stat!"

As always, when observing her father in action professionally, Cory watched with a mixture of anger and awe at the way people jumped at his every command. They seemed genuinely scared of him, but also wished to please him and earn what scant praise he tended to give. Then in the next instant, he would take the hand of a patient and talk in reassuring tones, clearly making the patient feel better solely his gentle touch. Cory watched him doing exactly that with the young man she'd been tending.

"Looks like you're pretty banged up, fella," he said, putting a hand on the young man's shoulder. "But you're in the right hands now. We're going to pull you through this thing. Don't you worry about that." Then he was off down the hall to attend to other patients.

Cory watched as the young man's troubled brow relaxed at her father's calming influence, and found her eyes welling up. *Why can't he be that way with his own family?*

Several aides scurried about the ward, following her father's orders to clear a bed for the new arrival. Within minutes, one of them was wheeling the young man's gurney away from the nurses' station, and into a nearby room. As the new patient passed, Cory tried to catch his eye to give him an encouraging smile, but he seemed to be sound asleep. Grudgingly, she had to hand it to her father; he may be an absolute tyrant at home, but at least he knew his business. She glanced up at the clock, saw that it was time for her to clock out, and hurried to make her escape before her father returned.

*　*　*

As the aide wheeled him away from the pretty young nurses' aide, D. W. wasn't sleeping at all. In fact, he was wondering whether he would ever be able to sleep again. Though there were confusing blank spots in his memory about what had happened to him over the last several days—blank spots that would mercifully remain with him for a long time to come—his mind was nonetheless filled with all kinds of horrible sounds and images.

He knew that he had survived a terrible firefight, a firefight that most of his platoon had not survived. He had seen too many of them fall around him before he took the shell that finally brought him down as well. After that hit, everything was a blur—everything except the excruciating pain he felt from the shrapnel that had pelleted his body pretty much everywhere, but especially in his chest, neck . . . and face.

His face . . . D. W. had never admitted it to a soul, but he'd always known he was a handsome young man, maybe even extremely handsome. It didn't take much insight on his part; all he had to do was take note of the admiring glances of almost every woman he'd ever passed on any street. But he'd also always felt it a matter of personal integrity to downplay his good looks, to not let his ego get away from him, or become stuck up. Nonetheless, there had certainly been plenty of times, especially in his college days, when he'd used his looks to his advantage, flirting with girls every chance he got, and they had generally given him plenty of chances.

Now though, his face had been savaged. He didn't know the full extent of the damage, but he knew it was serious. The extensive bandaging around his cheeks and jawline, and his wired-together jaws told him so; that and the involuntary reactions of the medics who had treated him at the field hospital when they first surveyed his injuries. He knew that when a seasoned medical professional winced looking at a patient's face, his injuries must be pretty bad.

So he had forced himself to close his eyes to shut out the sweet, sympathetic smiles the little nurses' aide had been giving him ever since he'd arrived. After years of knowing that women found him attractive, he couldn't bear the thought of a new and frightening future—a future where women pitied him because of his looks, if they could stand to look at him at all.

Settled in his room, he was glad for one thing—the morphine drip. Under its benevolent spell, he felt, if not complete escape from pain, at least a merciful dulling of it. Drifting in and out of sensibility, he found himself having fantastical dreams, even visions.

He was a counselor at a summer camp somewhere—he couldn't recall exactly where right now—and there was this kid there, Toby something. He'd known at the time that the kid had a huge crush on him, but he'd felt such immense empathy for the little guy, so alone and unlike his peers; it was a feeling he had wrestled with himself most of his life. Now the kid was in his room, at his bedside, talking to him, saying, "It's all right, D. W. My father is rich. He'll buy you a new face."

At that, he startled and woke briefly, then floated off again. Images of other people he had known through the years, and of himself at different ages and stages of growth, blew through his mind like a somnolent wind. Now he was a senior in high school, playing the Stage Manager in *Our Town* and reciting the final lines of the play.

He had never known exactly why this sweet, nostalgic play had always held such a strong hold on his heart, but now, in spite of his drug-induced haze, he understood completely. It captured so powerfully the idealized world of close family and friends, living simply, with the kind of love for one another for which he yearned. Would he ever find that world, he wondered, growing maudlin under his medication. Did such a world even exist, or was it just another impossible dream?

Thinking of family brought his mother to mind. He thought of her, listening with tears streaming down her face, as he had told her how much he hated her the last time he saw her; of her keening at his father's funeral and clinging to him with a vise-like grip; of her standing in his nursery doorway, silhouetted against the hall lights, fussing at him for not going to sleep, shouting, "D. W. Singer, you'll be the death of me. Now drink your toddy and go to sleep!"

He came to as someone entered the room to check his signs, and wondered if his mother knew yet that he'd been wounded. He also wondered, if she had been informed, did she even care? He wondered, too, if his broken face would give her yet another reason to reject him. And with that, he fell into a deep and dreamless sleep.

CHAPTER 13

TWO SIDES TO EVERY STORY

Betty Triplett put down the newspaper she had read for the tenth time that morning, but its front-page headline still reached out and grabbed her attention, pulling her eyes back to the newsprint time and again: "Hometown Hero Wounded in Vietcong Ambush."

Betty thought that she had experienced plenty of heartache over the years, as the oldest child of an impoverished, motherless family, and later as a career schoolteacher in a hard-scrabble rural community. She had seen family members die too young of malnourishment and diseases that could have been cured if they had only had access to adequate medical care. She had seen students come to school hungry and unwashed, or worse yet, battered and bruised, with no social services to help. She had seen her first one-room schoolhouse destroyed by a tornado, and had taught her students in a tent for several months, until the parents of her pupils had finished spring planting and could come rebuild the structure.

Yet these heartaches were nothing compared to the present one. The thought of D. W. Singer, the beautiful, gifted boy she had loved and nurtured like her own child, alone and injured on the other side of the world, broke her heart. And the article

193

described grave injuries, "especially to his face, neck and chest, along with a broken hip, broken legs, and several fractured ribs." It not only broke her heart, but angered her, as well.

Betty liked to think of herself as a doer. When hardships presented themselves in her world, she went to work solving them, and she usually succeeded, but there was nothing to be done about this one. She found it took great effort to keep from grabbing the hand-painted English teapot on her breakfast table and smashing it against the wall.

Her eyes wandered back to the newspaper again, and she read several more lines which made her even angrier: "Interviewed at her retirement home yesterday, D. W.'s mother, Alexandra Singer, expressed pride in him. 'He was always such a brave boy, it doesn't surprise me he saved the lives of his fellow soldiers. I always taught him to put others before self.' Though she is trying to contact him, Mrs. Singer reports she hasn't been able to speak with her son yet."

Betty sniffed. "I bet you 'taught him to put others before self,' you old witch," she said aloud. Suddenly an idea came to her, a way that she could actually do something significant to help D. W. rather than merely stewing in her own helplessness. She would contact everyone who knew him—that would be the whole town, even county—and collect their comforting messages to him, then put them all into a care package. She'd include some home-baked cookies and other treats, and mail them all off to him to cheer him up.

"Starting with *dear old Ma*," she said and chuckled with spite. She grabbed her purse and car keys, and headed out the door. She would never have believed at that moment the way the project would end.

* * *

Pulling into the parking lot of Whispering Pines, the retirement home where Alexandra Singer lived, Betty couldn't help but indulge in some satisfaction to find it such a shabby little place, a far cry from the biggest house in the region that D. W.'s family had owned for generations. She had never forgiven Alexandra for making D. W.'s life so miserable, and couldn't resist the temptation to gloat a bit over his mother's present misfortune. She felt sure, however, that no matter how reduced her circumstances might be, Alexandra would still be lording it over the other residents and playing the grand dame to the hilt.

After inquiring at the front desk, she found Alexandra's room and rapped firmly on the door. "I'm coming," the familiar voice called in response, and shortly Alexandra appeared. However, Betty wasn't prepared for the startling difference in the woman.

The once portly matriarch with the battleship-prow bosom was now a mere specter of her former self. She had lost fifty to sixty pounds, and the thick hair she had always kept dyed and stylishly coiffed was pure white and pulled back in a bun. The lost weight made the flesh of her face hang loose and jowly, and deep wrinkles creased her mouth and eyes.

Her eyes are haunted, Betty thought to herself.

It was clear to Betty that Alexandra had been crying heavily, not only recently, but likely for several days. "I'm so sorry," she stammered. "I've obviously caught you at a bad time. I'll come back later."

She was surprised at Alexandra's welcome. "Oh, no, please, do come in and have a seat."

Betty stepped into the tiny room and saw immediately how

reduced Alexandra's circumstances were. A single bed with a faded chenille spread, a large chest of drawers, a small writing stand with a battered office chair, and a white wicker rocker were the only furnishings. Limp lace curtains and cracked, fly-specked roller shades covered the sole window. The overall effect struck Betty as thoroughly dismal until Alexandra switched on a table lamp.

There on the walls, filling every available space, were hundreds of photos of D. W., almost like a museum exhibit, chronicling every moment of his life, from birth to young adulthood. There were professional studio portraits of him at yearly intervals from birth to graduation, probably annual Christmas or Easter photos taken to be sent to relatives. More to Betty's taste, there were countless snapshots of him as well, taken at home, at play, in the yard, on the stage at school, and on trips to various popular destinations—Niagara Falls, the Grand Canyon, and the Saint Louis Arch. They revealed D. W.'s impish charm growing gradually into his movie-star good looks of more recent years. Betty was taken aback at the sheer multitude of the photos, and a small, startled cry escaped her lips, "Oh, my goodness!"

Alexandra followed Betty's eyes and a nostalgic gleam came into her own eyes. "Nice, aren't they?"

"Most certainly," Betty agreed. "Who took all of these?"

Alexandra seemed surprised at the question. "Why, me of course. Except for the studio ones, that is. He *is* a good-lookin' young man, isn't he?" Then her face fell and her eyes welled up. "Or . . . *was*, I should say." She put a handkerchief to her swollen eyes and dropped into the straight-backed office chair at her desk.

Betty was surprised to find herself suddenly feeling true compassion for this woman who had always seemed so heartless.

She took a seat in the wicker rocker and reached out to put a hand on Alexandra's knee. "Now, we don't really know that . . . yet. These things often seem worse at first report than they turn out to be later."

Alexandra struggled to contain her tears and looked up at Betty with gratitude in her puffy eyes. "Oh, do you really think so? I'd give anything for that." Then she seemed to reconsider. "Not that looks are everything. I mean, after all, look at me." She let out a hearty laugh. "Who'd have ever thought Alexandra Singer could live one week without going to the beauty parlor? But I haven't been to one now in months."

Betty found herself laughing, too. In spite of herself, she was feeling another surge of empathy for Alexandra, and maybe a touch of something else . . . admiration. She would never have thought that this self-absorbed woman, who had seemed to hold her very special child in such little regard, would have steadfastly been saving photos of him throughout his life. Nor would she have thought that Alexandra would display them in her little room with such pride, as the only small glimmer of joy in the otherwise empty landscape that was now her home.

"Well, there's no sense in assuming the worst," Betty said. "What we need now is a good plan."

Alexandra seemed interested, but confused. "Like what? What kind of plan are you talking about?"

Though it pained her to admit it, Betty had to confess her own uncertainty. "Well, I'm still working on it. The newspaper said you've been trying to get information about D. W.'s condition, to contact him even, but that you hadn't had any success."

"Yes, I've been calling that army recruiter down on the square for days now and he never returns my calls."

Well, that explains that, Betty thought. "I think maybe we need to go over the local recruiter's head. I have some former students in high places in the military. Let me see what they can do for us."

"Good gracious," Alexandra burst into fresh tears. "Thank you so much. Would you really do that for me?"

Her gratitude made Betty squirm, remembering how poorly she had thought of this woman up until only a few moments ago. "Don't thank me yet. I don't know what I'm going to be able to do, really, and I don't want to disappoint you."

Alexandra was full of surprises this afternoon. "Just the fact that you'd try is all that matters to me. Especially knowing how hard you've felt toward me over the years. It means so much to me to know you're willing to get beyond all that."

Betty felt her treasured mastery of every situation slipping away from her. So many things were happening in this interaction that she hadn't seen coming, and she struggled to regain her equilibrium.

"I'm sure I don't know what you're talking about," she said, trying to sound as calm and matter-of-fact as possible.

Alexandra kept surprising her with unexpected grace.

"Aw, come on now, Miss Betty. I think we both know the real truth about these matters. This whole town thinks I'm the worst mother ever. I see it in their eyes and I hear it when they think I'm not listening. And truth be told, sometimes I think they're right. I wasn't a good mother to D. W. He was always so smart, I thought if I could hold him back a bit, maybe I could catch up with him one day, and then we could both get along really good. But he was too much for me, like his dad. And so there I was, this old frump, sitting at home alone, watching soap operas and quiz shows, and hating the whole world, while my husband bedded every young gal he could get his hands on, and my son just kept soaring higher and higher. I can't tell you how many times over the years somebody stopped me in the streets to tell me what a wonderful young man he was. Then I'd see that look . . . you know, that puzzled look, like they were wondering how he got to be such a fine young man, with me as his momma, and his philandering dad to boot. I can't deny it . . . it hurt me, it hurt me a lot. But I did the wrong thing with that hurt. I took it out on D. W. and I tried to get him to make things right. But he couldn't do that. He was only a kid, after all. How he could fix things that were wrong in his momma and daddy's lives when we couldn't even fix them ourselves?"

Betty was so riveted by this unexpected soliloquy that she was startled when something dropped onto her hand and broke her concentration. She looked down, saw that it was one of her own tears, and abruptly decided she had to do something.

"Alexandra, I came here to propose an idea to you, a plan that I think could buoy D. W.'s spirits at a time when he desperately needs support. I want to canvass the whole town . . . heck, the whole county, and state if I can reach them, and ask them to send messages of encouragement to him. Is that something you'd be willing to help me with?"

Alexandra squared her chin and straightened in her chair. "Well, of course I would. What kind of mother could turn down an offer like that?" Then her brow furrowed. "Only thing is, he can't know I'm involved. If he did, he'd only throw the whole lot away without reading a thing."

Remembering the sensitive little boy who had obviously yearned so deeply for his mother's love, Betty couldn't imagine what Alexandra was talking about. "I'm sure you're mistaken," she said.

"Well, like I just said, I know I'm not smart, but I do know what I'm talking about this time," Her eyes filled again. "He hates me now. He told me so the last time we were together, the night he enlisted and left town."

Betty still couldn't believe it. "Surely he was merely upset at the time. D. W. has a huge, loving heart. He couldn't possibly really hate you."

Alexandra was adamant. "If you'd seen the look in his eyes, you'd know, Miss Betty."

Betty conceded. "All right, but let's take one thing at a time. We don't even have a package to send yet, so let's get to work and cross these other bridges when we come to them."

Alexandra just nodded in response, but in her eyes and tentative smile, Betty thought she saw a ray of hope.

*   *   *

So began one of the strangest yet most rewarding experiences of Betty Triplett's long and storied career. She generated a call list with Alexandra, and each of them took half of the names to telephone. Betty left Whispering Pines with a plan to reconnect with her new confederate in twenty-four hours to review their progress.

The next day when she called Alexandra as planned, the woman had not only contacted everybody on her call list, but dozens of additional people as well that neither of them had thought of originally. It seemed to Betty that Alexandra had finally found a way to express her maternal instincts in a fashion that worked for her. She had never felt comfortable sitting on flimsy folding chairs at PTA meetings or bleachers at ball games, but this task she could do . . . calling people on the phone and asking them to write a supportive message to her wounded Vietnam vet son, recuperating in a convalescent center in Japan.

The response they got was nothing short of staggering, far greater than anything either one of them had anticipated, even in their wildest imaginings. The sheer volume of letters—not to mention homemade candies, cakes, and cookies, as well as collections of toiletries, popular magazines, and smiling snapshots of the senders—was far more than the package they had originally envisioned. It was going to take a huge crate to contain it all.

The day arrived when it was time to send it off, and Betty invited Alexandra to lunch. Her garage had served as the collection point for all of the letters and donations. A large wooden container stood in the doorway, waiting to be picked up by a delivery service. After they ate, Betty pulled out two labels and wrote on one of them the address she had gotten for the hospital where D. W. was convalescing. When she was finished with it, she handed the other one to Alexandra.

"We need a return address label," she said. "You decide what to write on it. You already know what I think it should be."

Alexandra took the label and pen in hand, and frowned. Then a resolute look came to her face and she began writing. When she handed the label back to Betty, she smiled. "You're an awfully hard one to say 'no' to, Miss Betty."

Betty looked down, saw that the label did indeed include both of their names, and laughed. "I know I am. How else could I have managed D. W. in class all those years?"

The doorbell rang and the two went out to greet the delivery man. When the crate had been loaded, and the truck was driving away, Betty saw that Alexandra's resolve seemed to be slipping. She reached out and put an arm around her shoulder.

"Do you think he'll really accept it?" Alexandra asked in a small voice. "Seeing it came from me, as well as you?"

"I'm sure of it," Betty said. "That boy is far too curious and nosy to turn down a package from home, especially one the size of a tank!"

They would find out later that she had once again been right.

CHAPTER 14

LOOKS AREN'T EVERYTHING

D. W. sat in the speckled shade under the boughs of a flowering cherry tree, reading the script for Arthur Miller's *The Crucible*. The USO had asked him to direct the play for his fellow patients' entertainment. Flicking fallen cherry blossoms from the pages of the manuscript, he let out a long yawn now and then.

Funny, he thought, *who would have ever dreamed it could feel so good to be able to yawn again?* Dr. Kelly had removed the wires from his jaws a few days before, and he couldn't believe the difference this single change made in his mood and outlook. It was probably the best he had felt since leaving IU more than two years ago. On second thought, he realized that wasn't quite right; there had been several other developments in his world recently that had also left him feeling pretty damn good.

He reached into the little satchel attached to the side of his wheelchair and fingered the letters inside it, enjoying the feel and the rustling sound of the paper. Remembering the day they'd arrived, in a packing crate big enough for a baby elephant, he broke into a big grin.

Have to admit, never expected that one. Maybe Ma's not quite as big a bitch as I thought.

Then he recalled that Miss Triplett had been involved too,

203

so he assumed she must have been the driving force behind the whole effort. Nevertheless, that had been a major turning point in his recovery. Hospital staff had commented on it in his progress notes: "Patient's major depression seems to be lifting a bit more each day as he continues to read through the numerous cards and letters he recently received from home."

One of the most surprising findings inside the care package was a letter from someone he never expected to cross paths with again, Toby Schumann. Apparently the boy had read an article in *The New York Times* about the battle at LZ English, which mentioned a soldier who had fought especially valiantly there, D. W. Singer of Palmer's Ridge, Indiana. Toby had contacted Alexandra and airmailed a letter to her to include in the package. As he reread it time and again, D. W. still couldn't believe the eloquence of the boy, not that he was really a boy any longer. He appeared to be growing into a very courageous young man.

Dear D. W.

I imagine you've forgotten me by now, but I'll never forget you. Believe it or not, a day never goes by that I don't think of you. How could it, when I still wear the tiger-eye amulet you gave me? In fact, it's become a talisman for me. Whenever I feel anxious or uncertain, I hold the stone in my hand and ask myself, "What would D. W. do?" And I always feel better.

I'm still living here in New York, in my sophomore year at Columbia. I'm planning to major in journalism, though the folks of course want it to be business, so that I can take over running their stores someday. I hate to disappoint them, but that's not going to happen.

It's got to be journalism because there are so many things going on that I want to tell the world about—stories of corruption, greed, abuse, and prejudice.

One that's foremost on my mind right now happened a while back at a little hole-in-the-wall bar here called the Stonewall. It's a gay bar, where police have been harassing patrons for years, conducting raids, arresting people, exposing them, or extorting bribes. Well, not long ago, we fought back . . . and I write the word "we" here with some trepidation, because I'm not sure you know that I'm gay myself. I tried so hard to hide it back at camp and everywhere else through the years, but I can't do that anymore. It's dishonest and shameful, and that's not the way I want to live my life. It's "not what D. W. would do" I tell myself when I hold the amulet.

Funny thing is the people at the bar who fought back first were the drag queens. Can you picture that? A bunch of hardened New York cops backed down by a mob of gay men dressed as women. It was too much! Rallied by the drag queens, together we all backed them down. And it became the start of a whole new way of life for us, a huge movement we're calling Gay Pride.

I'm chair of the chapter here at school and making quite a name for myself (and a pest as well) with school officials. But there's nothing new there, right? I've always fought bigots. Remember my cabin-mates at camp? Sometimes I ask myself, how did I ever survive that? Then I remember, I survived because of you. You literally saved my life, and I'll never be able to thank you enough for that.

So I'm hoping to pursue a career telling stories about people and events like the riot at Stonewall. Who knows, I may even have a book about them rattling about somewhere inside me.

Anyway, I'm writing here to tell you how much meeting you

all that time ago has meant to me through the years, how helpful it was to me to encounter another "problem child" who'd turned his life around, like you did. Following your example, I'm trying to do the same thing.

I hear that your injuries were "grave" but that you're recovering well now. Please know that you're in my thoughts and prayers, and will be forever.

If you're ever in New York and want to have a drink with an old friend, I know this groovy little place called the Stonewall . . .

Warmest regards,

Toby Schumann

D. W. finished rereading the letter, and then tucked it away. *Amazing, truly amazing*, he mused with a grin. He thought about all the nice guys he had known through the years, and wondered why he hadn't had more close male friendships, except for Jodie, who was recovering now in the states, and often wrote. But Toby had forged his way into his heart too, and he made himself a promise to write him back soon.

His thoughts turned to what was probably the best new development in his life lately . . . a four-foot-eleven package of energy and optimism named Cory. The nurses' aide who had sat beside him the night of his arrival at the rehab center and had somehow managed to get her assignment changed every time he was moved to a new ward. When she had turned up again and again, each time he was moved, he hadn't been able to resist teasing her a bit.

"I know I'm devilishly handsome and the scars just make me all that much more unusual and intriguing, but really, Miss Kelly, will you please quit throwing yourself at me?"

She had been standing at his bedside at the time, pouring him a glass of water, and had managed to spill most of it on him when he made the comment.

"Don't let your big head run away with you," she said as she dried him off. "I'm what they call a 'floater' in this hospital and that means they move me wherever I'm needed, shift to shift. It has nothing to do with you, believe me." And she had flounced out of the room.

However, he had checked with the charge nurse later that day and learned that Cory was fibbing. She had asked to be reassigned every time he was moved, and her father's influence at the hospital had helped her get her way.

But why, he'd wondered, looking at his mangled face in a tiny hand mirror—the only mirror they had allowed him to have since the bandages came off a week ago. Oh sure, it was true, exactly as they had told him it would be, that the redness and swelling went down a bit more each day. As that happened, the disfiguring did seem a little less daunting to him; plus, he knew, there was always the option of plastic surgery. He felt fortunate that his lips and nose and cheeks were essentially unaffected. The chief damage was to the flesh along his lower cheeks and jawline, where a patchwork of angry keloids crisscrossed his skin. It was the result of being cobbled back together in a MASH unit, by medics who were more concerned with saving his life than with saving his looks. In hindsight, he was grateful for that, but it had taken him awhile to get there.

For the first few days after the bandages came off, they had kept him on sedatives and prevented him from seeing himself. He had managed to sneak a look at his reflection in a darkened window by his bed one night and his howl of shock and despair woke the whole ward. Staff had put him on increased medication and a suicide watch for several days. It was only after a confrontation with Cory that things had taken a turn for the better.

He had isolated himself in his bed for days, refusing to eat or to get up for his physical therapy. Cory came to his room with a tray and set it down before him.

"I told you I'm not eating!" he shouted at her.

"Oh, don't worry, it's not food to eat," she replied in a measured voice. "It's food for thought. Maybe you need to know how some of the guys in the next ward are doing." She left the room without a backward glance.

Lifting the metal plate cover on the tray before him, D. W. found a stack of photos of horrifically wounded men . . . men missing eyes, noses, ears, segments of their skulls, the entire lower half of their face. He reached for an emesis pan and vomited into it repeatedly.

He coughed to get the nasty, bilious taste out of his mouth, and was surprised to find himself chuckling. *Well, thank you so much, nurses' aide Cory Kelly. That was a very productive therapy session. What's next in your photo album for me? Lepers, perhaps?*

He never refused meals again, and hospital staff commented again in his progress notes on the marked improvement in his mental status. He smiled, remembering the next time he'd seen Cory.

"Message received, loud and clear," he told her, and she gave him a dazzling smile.

"Just remember, looks aren't everything," she said. "Besides, you men are lucky. You can grow beards to cover up your flaws." She cocked her head, and gave him a speculative look. "Yes, a beard's definitely the answer. You'd look quite distinguished with one, I think."

He put a hand to his face and ran it over the scars there. "This is going to take one hell of a big beard." When he saw her frown again, he added quickly, "But I'm not complaining. God, I'll never complain to you again about anything. I'm too scared of the pictures you'd show me."

They had been fast friends ever since, and in the last few days, D. W. realized, they seemed to be moving somewhere beyond that, although he wasn't exactly sure where. He did know that he found himself looking forward to seeing her every day. No, it was much more than that, he had to admit; he waited for the first sight of her each day like a dog waiting for its master to come home. When she did appear, he couldn't help but break into a big, silly grin. Then he would find himself trying to come up with something witty to say to her, some comment about what she was wearing or the way she had styled her hair that morning. More often than not, his best efforts were more corny than witty, but she always favored him with a laugh anyway.

He thought that maybe he'd seen a fond, expectant look on her face, as well, now and then, when she first came onto the ward and scanned the halls to see who was present each day. Once, he hid behind a newspaper for a long time to trick her into thinking he was gone. When he put aside the paper at last and saw the sadness in her eyes, he felt guilty for his trick.

Remembering other girls he had fallen for over the years, he wondered what it was about Cory that he found so attractive. She certainly wasn't the stellar beauty Breanna had been, but recalling how cold and unfeeling he had eventually found Breanna to be, he decided that was probably a good thing. No, Cory was no Breanna, to be sure—but he decided he liked her looks better.

She was tiny, "no bigger than a minute," as they used to say back home in Indiana. Her pink-cheeked gamin face was dusted with pale freckles, and the short bobbed hair that framed it was a rich auburn red. He thought her jade-green eyes were definitely her best feature, and he would never forget where he first saw them—not here at the hospital, but in a vision that came to him as he dangled over the banister at his home in Palmer's Ridge, trying to rally the courage to jump to his death. He would never understand what had happened that night, although he knew it was a truly mystical experience of the type that changes peoples' destinies forever.

Looking up from his script, he saw those eyes again, only in the flesh, not in a vision. She almost ran to his side, it seemed, and held out a plastic cup of water, and a paper pill holder.

"Your three o'clock dose. Open the hatch."

He dutifully swallowed the pills and water, and surprised himself with his next blurted-out comment. "So what do I get for all this good behavior?"

As soon as the words were out of his mouth, he realized that they may have been wildly inappropriate. Cory did indeed seem taken aback by them for a moment, but her innate good humor took over and she played along.

"Why nothing, of course," she said with a arch smile. "After all, virtue is its own reward."

D. W. groaned and covered his face with his hands. "Oh, dear God. How very *Catholic* of you!"

She giggled, put a finger to her chin, and dropped a quick curtsy. "Best little girl in a blue-plaid jumper you ever saw." Then she glanced over her shoulder at the windows of the hospital behind them to see if anyone was watching. Once reassured they were out of sight of prying eyes, she leaned down over his wheelchair. Hovering there for a moment, mere inches from his face, she gazed deep into his eyes, her smile gone; and then she kissed him, on the lips—lightly, briefly, but more sweetly than he had ever been kissed before.

He leaned forward in his chair, hungry lips reaching for more, but she laughed and put her fingers over his mouth. "That's quite enough for today, Casanova. Remember, you're an invalid." With that, she ran back to the hospital, but just as she reached it, turned and gave him another one of her radiant smiles. In that instant, he became hers forever.

CHAPTER 15

I JUST CAN'T DO IT

D. W. had to admit to himself that he had been in love many times before, and that each time, it had felt like the first and only time he was experiencing true love. With each new romance, he measured all his previous loves against the intensity of the current one, and found them all sadly lacking. Somehow, though, that wasn't happening with Cory.

In fact, he couldn't even say yet whether he really loved her at all. He only knew that he felt more comfortable with her than with any other girl he had ever met. Plus, he had none of the angst and tension he'd felt with Breanna, who had always seemed to find something amiss in him.

Cory had seen him at his worst, right from the beginning. She had put up with his pain-fueled temper tantrums, emptied his bedpans, changed his dirty bandages, and helped him with sponge baths. Even now, he was no catch, still healing from his facial wounds; beginning his first awkward efforts to master crutches; and pursuing a punishing physical therapy regimen that left him exhausted, sore, and irritable many days.

No matter how difficult a patient he might be, though, she always greeted him with the same brilliant smile, the same unflappable equanimity. He didn't know it at the time, but she

213

had been raised to get along with one of the most difficult men on the planet, so he posed no challenge to her at all.

Then there was her laugh, a cascading peal of bell-like notes, tripping from her tongue, winding down to a throaty chuckle, and finishing at last with a contented little sigh. He had never heard anything quite so captivating before, and had become totally hooked on it, almost from the first moment. He found himself trying to think of ways to get her to laugh, just so that he could hear it another time. He had become quite the clown with her.

Although D. W. wasn't sure whether he was in love with Cory, everyone else on his ward knew that he was.

"Man, you've got it bad," his roommate Gary teased him one night after Cory had given them their evening medications and gone off to do her notes.

D. W. pried his eyes off the sight of Cory's retreating figure and turned to his buddy. "Huh? What are you talking about?"

"Oh, nothing," Gary replied. "Only that you pretty much sit up and bark every time that little girl comes into your sight. That's all, nothing really important." He turned and plumped his pillow and went off to sleep.

His comments got D. W. thinking. Was this indeed love? Was she the one he'd been searching for, yearning for, all these years? If she was, why didn't he feel more infatuated, even obsessed with her? In many ways, she was becoming his best friend, and though he certainly found her attractive, he couldn't say that he found her irresistible or unforgettable. Shouldn't those feelings be there if he was truly in love?

Sometimes he had to give up on all of this questioning, wondering, and yes, dreaming about Cory, and throw himself into the moment with her. And that was a very easy thing to do, because she had all of the unbridled curiosity and playfulness of a kitten. After observing these traits in her over several weeks, D. W. got an idea. She would be perfect for the part of Abigail, the young vixen who seduces John Proctor in *The Crucible*. He was surprised at her reaction when he posed it to her.

He pitched it to her as they sat at a picnic table on the hospital grounds one morning. "Hey, girl," he'd said, reaching his hand across the table to her. "You know that I'm directing the USO play coming up next month, right?"

She pulled her eyes from the sight of a large South Vietnamese family visiting their wounded patriarch nearby, and turned her attention back to him with a distracted air.

"Hmmm, what was that?"

"I said I'm directing the USO's production of *The Crucible* next month."

"Oh, that. Yes, I remember now. How are rehearsals going?"

"Well, not so hot. We still haven't finished casting all the parts, so we can't go too far with rehearsals until that job is done. And we're due to open in less than three weeks."

"Hmmm," she said, smiling absently. Her attention drifted back to the Vietnamese family who were clearly enjoying each other's company tremendously.

"Cory!" he said, raising his voice a bit. He grabbed her hand and forced her to make eye contact with him. "I don't think you're hearing me. I'm really in a tight spot. I need to cast someone soon for the role of Abigail, the young seductress who has an affair with John Proctor."

Present at last, Cory smiled and nodded. "And, so?" she asked, a puzzled look on her face.

"Well, you're perfect for the part! It's a natural for you. There aren't that many lines and they aren't too demanding. It's far more about Abigail's energy and vitality, which is exactly the kind of energy and vitality you have."

Awareness dawned in Cory's eyes, and she pulled back her hand with a look of true terror on her face. "No way!" she cried, putting a fist to her mouth. "I'll never go on a stage and strut and prance in front of a bunch of strangers, just for their entertainment. It's out of the question!"

D. W. wasn't prepared for this reaction. She was such a spontaneous person; he had figured she would also be a natural for the stage. He even imagined that she might be flattered and excited by the idea. Coming from the background he did, where winning the applause of an appreciative audience was the sweetest achievement in the world, he almost couldn't conceive of the idea that others wouldn't want the same thing.

"I'm so sorry. I had no idea you had such strong feelings. I thought you might see it as a lark, maybe even a chance to get to know each other a bit better. I'm playing John Proctor myself, you see." He decided to play the guilt card to see what might happen. "I thought maybe something was going on here between us—you know, something, well, a little, uh, romantic." He looked up at her and flashed his most charming grin. Seeing the growing consternation in her eyes, he drifted off into silence.

She drew a deep breath, and looked as though she were weighing whether to flee. Finally, she squared her shoulders and looked him in the eyes.

"I've been acting all of my life, and it hasn't been a good thing for me. Acting like I'm happy when I'm not; acting like I don't see the horrible, hurtful things that happen between people, especially family members; acting like the world is a safe and lovely place when I know it's not."

D. W. tried to reach across the table again for her hand, but she was having none of that. She kept her hands folded tightly against her heart, as if she needed their protection there.

"So, can I act? Yeah, sure, give me my lines, Mr. Director Man." She gave him a little salute that made them both smile in spite of themselves. "But do I want to keep acting?" Her resolve crumbled suddenly, and she put her face into her hands. "God, no!" she wailed. "Why can't I just be *me*? Why can't I just be *myself*? What's so wrong with the person I am that I have to always be *acting*, pretending I'm someone else—someone happier and more successful and accomplished than I am?" She put her tear-stained face into her folded arms on the picnic table. "Why is it that 'me' is never enough?"

D. W.'s heart went out to her and he tried to comfort her, but she leapt up from the table and started walking briskly back toward the hospital. Grabbing his crutches, he began limping after her, calling her name, trying to get her to stop.

"Cory, wait! It's no matter. I don't give a shit about the damned play."

At that, she broke into a run and was soon out of sight. He stopped hobbling after her, and shook his head in disbelief. "What the *hell*?" he said with a sigh. Then he realized that the little Vietnamese clan, as well as every other person on the surrounding grounds was watching him intently, obviously curious about what had gone down between them. Forcing a wry smile he didn't feel in his heart, he shrugged.

"Women! Can't live with 'em, can't live without 'em!" Rather than the appreciative laughter he expected, he was met with a resounding silence.

*   *   *

For the first time in his stay at the convalescent center, he didn't see Cory for several days. Initially he thought that maybe she wasn't scheduled to work, or perhaps she had gone on vacation with her family. When he heard the charge nurse talking to her on the phone one day, he knew she was still at the hospital, but working on other wards. Any questions he might have had about whether he was truly in love with her were immediately resolved; for the thought of her being so nearby, but not with him, broke his heart.

He spent the next few days trying to come to terms with the possibility of losing her, so early in their budding relationship, and thinking of ways to recapture her goodwill. He tried to lose himself in the work of producing and directing the play, but for once, the theater didn't feed his soul as before. Every time they came to a scene involving Abigail, the only part that still hadn't been cast, he remembered again that Cory was gone. There were times when he had to summon all the acting skills in his repertoire to keep from bawling openly in front of his players at the thought that she might be gone for good.

Days turned into weeks without Cory appearing on his ward, and as the opening night for the play approached, D. W. had to face the facts—she was out of his life forever, as quickly and quixotically as she had first appeared. It seemed impossible to him that the hole she had left in his heart could ever heal. He decided that once this accursed play was out of the way, he would indulge in a complete and utter breakdown, and ask to be transferred to the psych ward. The truth was, he honestly didn't think he could go on living without her.

Opening night came, and D. W. found himself pacing backstage, practicing his opening comments to the audience about some necessary accommodations that had been made to the production.

"My roommate, Ensign Gary Swindler, will be reading lines for the role of Abigail, though he has refused to put on a dress or kiss me in my role as John Proctor . . . that chicken!" Yes, that just might do it, he decided; it was silly enough to get a laugh, but also to elicit the audience's sympathy and support.

An usher came up and whispered to him that the auditorium was full. He looked to his little amateur cast gathered backstage who seemed to draw courage and strength from huddling together. He saw the looks of combined excitement, anticipation, and fear on their faces. He looked overhead and out into the wings, and saw that all the props and ropes were in place, exactly as they were supposed to be. Parting the curtains slightly, he looked out into the crowded hall, and saw that the footlights were on, and the spotlight was trained on center stage, where he would soon be making his remarks. The crowd was beginning to get restless. This was a convalescent hospital, after all; did they have to wait for everything, even their entertainment?

D. W. went to his cast and gave them each a big hug. "You're going to be great. Just go with the flow on this thing. It's an incredible play with an incredible message. You pretty much can't mess this one up, even if you try." With that, he threw back the curtains and went to front center stage. He had graduated from his crutches to a cane, yet the trip from backstage seemed incredibly laborious and slow. Still, something surprising happened along the way.

At first, he was perplexed by the vigorous applause that greeted him, before he had even done anything to earn it. Then it occurred to him; maybe all of those hours crooning love ballads with his little band in the canteen hadn't been such a waste of time after all. Most of the campus already knew him and appreciated his work as a singer and bandleader, so tonight was only going to be one more venue with a bunch of old friends.

"Thank you. Thank you so much," he called out to the crowd. "We are so glad to have you here tonight for a truly wonderful play, Arthur Miller's *The Crucible*. It has drama, it has sex, it has betrayal . . . hmmm, kinda sounds like things back home in Washington, where they can't decide what the hell to do with all of us guys over here." The whole auditorium erupted into wild laughter and applause, and D. W. knew that he had them in the palm of his hand.

"This being the last outpost of the civilized world and all, we've had to make a few adjustments in order to get this production together. You'll note as the play progresses that we've had to make some changes in the staging and script. We've obviously had to use minimal props and sets. In addition, certain roles couldn't be cast at all. For instance, lacking an interested applicant, the role of Abigail will be filled tonight by my roommate—"

"Corrine Kelly!" a sweet familiar voice rang out from backstage.

D. W. thought for a moment that he had imagined it, but when a great wave of laughter broke forth from the assembled crowd, he realized that they had heard it, too. Catcalls and whistles rose from the rowdy assembly.

"Damn, Singer!" someone exclaimed. "How'd you manage to land a female roommate?"

"Yeah, man, what's your secret? It's obviously not your looks!" someone else shouted.

Trying to keep his stage presence, yet figure out what was happening, D. W. laughed along with the crowd, but glanced over his shoulder into the wings. There he saw her, standing with his cast, looking terrified, to be sure, but also incredibly beautiful as well.

"Yes," he said, turning back to the audience. "The part of Abigail will be played by Miss Cory Kelly, daughter of our esteemed physician, Dr. Michael Kelly. By the way, she is not my roommate . . . yet . . . I'm still working on that one." He ducked back behind the curtains amidst a roar of laughter.

He went right to her and wrapped her in his arms. "What are you doing here?"

"Don't ask me to explain, I don't understand it myself. I just had to be here."

"But are you sure about this? I mean, are you really ready?"

"As ready as I'll ever be. I've been up all night for weeks now memorizing my lines. I'm still petrified, of course, but nothing new there. I'll survive one way or another. Can't say that I ever heard of anyone dying from embarrassment after making a fool of themselves on stage."

Her courage and humor in the midst of doing something so unpleasant for her touched him beyond words. He took her face in his hands and looked deep into her eyes until she seemed to grow uncomfortable under the intensity of his gaze. "Please, *please*," he murmured. "Don't ever leave me again."

She met his gaze with equal measure and nodded. "I won't.

Though I promise you, one day, you might wish that I would."

They continued holding each other tightly for a moment, but soon had to part. As Abigail, Cory had the first lines in the play and made her entrance immediately after the curtains opened. They let go of each other reluctantly, with a silent promise in their eyes to reconnect after the show. From his place in the wings, D. W. motioned for the stage manager to start. The entire cast and crew heard the curtains swish, saw the standing-room-only house, and felt the heat of the footlights.

He watched with pride as Cory walked onstage and delivered her lines like a seasoned pro. *No doubt about it now, she's the one all right.*

The stage manager came to his side and nudged his elbow. "She's really good," he whispered.

"Damn right, she's good," D. W. whispered back. "I'll tell you something else . . . I'm going to marry that girl someday."

CHAPTER 16

ANOTHER BRIDE, ANOTHER GROOM... AND MAKIN' WHOOPEE

They sat, as they usually did, on the park bench in the hospital courtyard that they had come to think of as their place, looking to casual passersby as they always did, a handsome young couple, hopelessly in love, and without a care in the world. And so it had been for them many times in the months before, but not this particular afternoon.

"It's for sure now," she said in a hushed voice, looking down at her lap. "I'm almost three weeks late, and I've never been more than a week late before."

She waited for his response, expecting some words of encouragement or support. When she heard nothing, she ventured a glance at him. She was troubled to see him looking off into the distance, stroking his new-grown beard, as if he hadn't heard the momentous news she had shared with him.

"D. W., did you hear me?"

He turned and gave her a big smile. "Of course I did, sweetheart. I was thinking."

"About what?"

"About what our baby's going to look like, of course."

She felt a flood of relief and leapt into his arms. "Oh, you big gorilla. I could kill you!"

He wrapped her tightly in his arms and nuzzled her hair with his lips. "Well, that wouldn't be very good, would it? Because there you'd be with a baby gorilla to feed, and no Papa Ape to bring you both bananas."

As always, he was glad to hear that unique bell-like laugh of hers, but especially now, as he realized that his shirt was becoming wet with her tears. He had been so happy to think of a baby on its way that it never occurred to him how frightening the idea might be for her.

Struggling to suppress her sniffles, she wiped her nose and sighed. "I wasn't sure whether you'd want it. I was afraid you might want me to get rid of it, or maybe even leave me. I know I could never have done the first thing, and I'm pretty sure I'd die if I had to face the second thing."

He turned her chin up to face him. "Then you still don't really know me, do you?" he asked, kissing her softly before she could answer.

They settled into their bench and snuggled for a while. Then he felt a little shiver go through her.

"Daddy is going to kill me . . . and maybe you, too."

D. W. had to admit that he hadn't yet thought about facing the formidable Dr. Kelly with this news, but now that he did, the idea was daunting. "Well, what's he got to say about it?" he asked with a confidence he didn't feel. "We're both of age, and we'll be married before he knows we're expecting. So what's the big deal?"

Cory looked up at him with excited eyes. "Oh, *really*? That's the first time you've mentioned marriage. Being the big bohemian that you are, I thought sure you were going to ask me to live as your common-law wife on a commune somewhere."

He stroked his chin for a moment and pretended to give the idea serious thought. "To tell the truth, I never considered that option. Now that you mention it, I agree it's a much better plan. Yes, indeed, I think we'll go with that idea, after all."

She punched him in his sternum, then settled her head into the place where she'd hit him. "Oh, dear," she murmured into his chest. "I do hate indulging in clichés, but I honestly think you've made me the happiest girl in the world today."

He raised her chin to face him again, and was pleased to see that the tears in her eyes were happy ones. "Oh, that," he said, "you ain't seen nothin' yet. I'm just getting started, little girl."

Disengaging from her, he rose from the seat, and then struggled a bit to drop to one knee. The multiple fractures in his hips and legs were all fully knit by now, but he still had tremendous soreness and stiffness. Once on his knee, he took her hands in his and looked into her eyes.

"Miss Corrine Kelly, will you do me the honor of giving me your hand in marriage?"

She burst into fresh tears, but also hearty laughter. "Yes, yes, of course I will! Only do get up, please, before you break your leg again, and I have to go back to emptying your bedpans."

PART III

BACK HOME AGAIN, IN INDIANA

Palmer's Ridge
Population 8,382
1970

CHAPTER 17

OUR LOVE IS HERE TO STAY

Cory hung up the phone after talking to her mother-in-law for the fifth time that day, and looked at the kitchen clock; it was only half past noon. Her heart ached at the news she had just received from Alexandra, and she wondered how in the world she would break it to D. W.

Right then, she heard the aging washing machine on the back porch start to cough and gurgle again, which it always did when it was about to break down. She rushed to it as fast as her pregnant body would allow. As she did, she knew she'd be lucky to get another month out of the decrepit old machine.

Arriving at the ailing patient's side, she opened the lid and readjusted the load of clothes so that they were more evenly distributed, then slammed the lid shut and gave the machine a good hard kick. Thank God, it fell into a steady hum as it went back into the spin cycle, and Cory indulged in the small hope that the satanic appliance might give her at least a few more weeks of service.

She scooped toddler Amy up from the floor and hurried into the kitchen to begin making D. W.'s lunch. The local radio station where he worked as a deejay gave him only a half hour break, so she always tried to have things ready for him as soon as he came in the door. Her only question was what to make for him. She nosed around inside the refrigerator, scanned the spare pantry shelves, and suddenly felt like Old Mother Hubbard.

How could two, young, fit people work so hard and have so little to show for it, she wondered sadly. She finally seized on a can of tuna, and that, along with some mayonnaise and diced pickles, eventually morphed into a fairly presentable serving of tuna salad, which she put out on a plate with some saltines and a glass of milk. Just about the time she got it on the table, D. W. waltzed through the back door, took Amy from her arms, and gave them both a swift peck on the cheek. Then he sat down at the kitchen table, situated the baby on one knee, and removed the napkin covering his plate.

"Gosh, how did you know, babe? Tuna salad was exactly what I was hoping for." He picked up several crackers and dove into the dish with relish.

Sometimes she marveled at the way that merely a glance or a smile or a frown from him could turn her inside out. Or the way that sweet, musky smell that came from his unwashed skin made her want to follow him anywhere, even at those times when she was angry at him. She had to admit, those times were multiplying.

After the whirlwind courtship and elopement that had enraged her father and titillated the whole army community, D. W. had earned a medical discharge. He was eager to return home to his roots in Southern Indiana. Despite the way he often described Palmer's Ridge as Nowheresville, Cory knew it had a hold on his heart, as he talked frequently and fondly of the people there.

But where was home for Cory? She had been such a vagabond, following her father all her life, that she had no place to call her own. She had accepted D. W.'s home as her own by default, but had come to regret the decision almost immediately after meeting his mother.

She didn't know their complete history, as neither of them liked to talk about it, now that they had forged a tentative truce. However, she did know that they had always struggled with a turbulent love-hate relationship. She found it perplexing, for when she watched them together, it was clear during the rare times they let down their guard that they adored each other. She saw the same vulnerable look in their eyes when they watched one another undetected, a look that seemed to yearn for closeness, but also feared rejection. The latter response still happened all too often, because one of them always said something to irritate the other.

No matter how well they seemed to be getting along at any given moment, hot words would eventually erupt and one of them, usually D. W., would storm out of the room with a volley of hurtful comments. On the other hand, they would always make up the next time they spoke, neither of them ever saying "I'm sorry" or addressing the latest conflict in any way. They would just pick up and act as if nothing had ever happened. The cycle replayed itself, time and again.

Observing all of this once they had moved back to the states, Cory got the first unsettling inklings that perhaps her prince had a few cracks in his crown. In Japan, she had seldom heard him utter a cross word to anyone. In fact, he was so steadfastly good-humored that he had been a favorite of everyone on base, even her irascible father, at least until the elopement. Now that they were back on his home turf, though, she shuddered at times to see how dark he could be, especially any time he had to deal with his mother, and that, unfortunately, was pretty much every day.

Cory tried her best to run interference between them and buffer the frequent tensions that surfaced. The effort often tied her stomach in knots. To her surprise, she had found that Alexandra wanted to be friends, right from the beginning. She soon came to understand why, when she realized that the woman was the town pariah, without a friend in the world, except perhaps for the forbearing Betty Triplett. D. W. had informed her that Miss Triplett was famous for accepting all challenging people, himself included, because it had been her life's work.

Cory had let Alexandra glom onto her, hoping it would make for a more peaceful family life for all of them, and she had been right, for the most part. Especially after baby Amy arrived, they had formed a new, unspoken bond, as two women, now two mothers, who both loved D. W., yet struggled with how to live with him. He was such a challenge, so vibrant and unpredictable, that he sometimes made Cory's head spin, helping her to feel some empathy for her mother-in-law.

Then, too, there was the way Alexandra related to the baby. Based on D. W.'s miserable accounting of her parenting, Cory never expected his mother to be such a doting grandparent. Sometimes when Cory's patience was exhausted with talking to Alexandra on the phone, she would ask her if she wanted to say hello to the baby, and her mother-in-law always replied, "Oh yes, please, do put her on the phone!" Cory would watch in amazement as little Amy's face lit up to hear her "Me-Maw," and the baby would babble back into the phone for the longest time, as if the two were having a perfectly intelligible conversation. She would hear Alexandra's coos and praise in response and was always touched.

On these occasions, Cory marveled that the woman who

had been so impatient with her son could so different with his child. She guessed maybe it was because Alexandra had worked through some of her inner demons with D. W.—or maybe it was that Alexandra was becoming more childlike herself as she got older.

Cory's father had disinherited her and forbidden any contact with her own family, so she felt it important for her children to have at least one grandparent in their lives. She was genuinely grateful to Alexandra for loving and cherishing the baby so much. Perhaps, she wondered at times, D. W. didn't really know his mother as well as he thought. Perhaps they ought to all give Alexandra a little more credit for being a real human being than they did.

Today, though, she was furious with her mother-in-law. She struggled with how to present D. W. with the news she knew was going to upset him. Sitting down across the table from him, she decided it was best to spill it all out.

"Your Ma called today," she began, and saw the little crease that always formed on his brow when her name was mentioned.

"Only once?" he asked with a smirk.

"Well, no, actually, now that you ask. It was more like five or six times."

"Lots of news today, huh? Let me guess . . . she won big at bingo last night, or no, better yet, she had a really good poop this morning?"

"Don't be crass. No, this is something serious, D. W." Cory's heart fluttered as he paused between mouthfuls and gave her a questioning look.

She plunged on. "She's received a letter from some state government office that deals with unclaimed estates. Seems your dad had some assets he'd hidden away, that didn't get attached when your mom filed her bankruptcy. She's talked to an attorney and he says they can be claimed, free and clear."

"But that's wonderful. Now maybe we can get a leg up in life."

"Not so fast. Seems there was a little house, a little place near Corydon . . . where your dad kept a mistress."

Her stomach lurched as she saw his eyes darken and the rising anger and confusion in his face, but she forged on. "There was also a little nest egg . . . a Swiss bank account, not much apparently, but enough to live on for a while."

He still seemed perplexed. "Enough for *her* to live on," Cory explained. "She's keeping it all for herself, leaving the retirement home and moving into the house as soon as she gets the money in hand."

Having expected an explosion, she was surprised at his response. The furrow between his eyebrows deepened, and his face went white. He handed her the baby, got up from the table, and went to look out the back door for a long moment. Then he turned to her and said in a forced breezy tone, "Well, good for her. It's her money, after all. She earned it putting up with my dad all those years. It's just my bad luck that I had to go to Vietnam, get shot up, almost lose my legs, and definitely lose my looks. So once again, she wins, I lose. Nothing new there, right?"

Cory was aghast. "I can't believe how calmly you're taking this," she exclaimed, breaking into tears. She began to pace the room, as the baby in her arms began to fret, too. "Here we are scraping by with hardly a dime to our name, and now she gets some money, but doesn't offer us a cent to help us out, like any truly loving mother would do. You're her only child. Amy is her first grandchild. But all she can think of is her own comfort!"

That brought a chuckle from him. "Welcome to the club," he said, taking her and the baby in his arms. He broke into the officious, radio announcer's voice he used when he was on the air. "Breaking news, it's official now . . . *everyone* hates Alexandra Singer. Young Corrine Kelly Singer was the last holdout, and she gave it a long, brave try, but she, too, has finally seen the light."

At that, she had to giggle in spite of herself. She burrowed her tear-stained cheek into his chest, and then she had a troubling thought.

"D. W., do you really think going into the army was such a terrible thing for you?"

As usual, he saw right away where she was going in her head. Raising her chin in his hand, he looked solemnly into her eyes. "Of course not, otherwise, how would I have met you?"

She smiled and burrowed even deeper into his big body.

"Forgiven?" he asked softly, kissing the top of her head, and when she looked up, he was pleased to see the old adoring look in her eyes.

"Damn you, D. W. Singer," she whispered, hoping the baby wasn't going to pick up on all of her cursing that day. "To save my life, I can't stay mad at you for more than two seconds."

Still looking into her eyes, he disengaged from their hug and held his hands out to her, inviting her to dance. She met his gaze, still holding the now peaceful baby on her hip. He put his arms around both of them, put his bearded cheek to her head and began to croon the old Gershwin tune, "Our Love is Here to Stay," as he led them all in a slow dance.

She leaned into him, giving herself up to him at that moment, but still pondering where things stood for them. They were young, hopelessly in love, and hopelessly broke. She had one of his babies on her hip (thankfully beginning to fall asleep), and another one in her womb (thankfully about ready to make its debut). His mother, the one person in the world who could have offered them financial help wasn't going to, and she had thoroughly burned her bridges with her father.

She thought about the stack of unpaid bills on her bedside table and their dwindling groceries, with a week still to go until payday. But, as always, she ended by thinking mainly about him . . . how big his heart was, how hard he worked, how brave and cheerful he tried to be, even though she knew he was tired and scared himself . . . and finally, how good he smelled. So, though she didn't know how they would manage, she figured she, too, was "here to stay."

Putting her finger to his lips, she changed the dance, and it was she who was leading him. Holding the now sleeping Amy in one arm, she guided him with the other as they tiptoed into the adjoining bedroom, where she laid the baby in her crib. Then she turned to him and with a playful shove, pushed him backwards onto their double bed. He seemed thoroughly pleased to be so dominated; she saw the evidence in the rising lump in the crotch of his pants. Walking slowly to the bedside she whispered seductively, "I may be eight months pregnant, big as a house, and broke to boot, Mr. Singer. But I am just the woman to make all your dreams come true . . . starting now." She slipped onto the bed beside him, and began covering his face, his neck, and every inch of him that she could access with feverish kisses.

He gladly reciprocated, but in between nibbling her lips and letting her nibble his, he remembered something. "I'm going to be late getting back to the station."

She took his face in her hands and gave him a somber look.

"Oh, yes, you are definitely going to be late. Very, very, late." With that she began tearing off his clothes.

Indeed, he was late . . . very, very, late, but it turned out to be the best thing that had ever happened to them. For in their hushed, passionate coupling, they somehow cemented their destiny. They may be going to hell and back, but at least they would be going together.

CHAPTER 18

SLOWING THINGS DOWN

Betty Triplett carefully parked her ancient Plymouth roadster in a handicapped space near the doors of the Palmer's Ridge IGA. She clipped the laminated handicapped sticker to her rearview mirror with a sigh. Despite having recently ignored her eighty-sixth birthday, she still found that she had to do everything a lot more slowly and cautiously than she once did.

Until recently, she hadn't minded growing older at all. In fact, she had actually enjoyed growing into the gracious "old girl" who had taught almost everyone in the county for six decades, and who was still greeted fondly by them wherever she went. However, this "slowing down thing," as she referred to it, really bothered her a lot—that and the constant pain of the arthritis that riddled her entire body, making even simple tasks pure torture at times.

Struggling to get out of the car, she heard a familiar, welcome voice call her name. "Let me get that for you, Miss Triplett."

She looked up to see D. W. Singer running to her side, trying as always to hide the slight limp he had brought home from Vietnam.

My goodness, she thought, *he gets better looking by the day. How smart of him to grow a beard to hide the scars.*

"D. W. Singer, what a sight for sore eyes." She laughed inwardly at the puppy-dog wriggle he did with his big shoulders at her affirming words. It was exactly as he had always done in her classroom. Toddling behind him were three pre-school aged children, each of whose christening she had attended in the last five years.

The eldest, five-year-old Amelia, or "Amy," was holding the hands of her younger brother, Buddy, and little sister, Colleen, leading them dutifully through the hazards of the store parking lot. This, despite Amy's own slight limp from the mild cerebral palsy that she had been diagnosed with when she was slow to walk.

Betty had been with D. W. shortly after they received the sad news and she had been surprised by the intensity of his grief. He had held her and cried into her shoulder like a little boy. Maybe he still was a boy in many ways, she'd thought at the time, robbed of a normal childhood by an absent father and unloving mother. Today, though, he looked handsome and healthy and on top of the world, with his little brood following behind him, appearing for all the world like a gaggle of goslings, trotting along after a gander in a barnyard.

D. W. took her arm and guided her toward the store with his usual courtly manner. "How have you been, Miss Triplett?" he asked, refusing to address her as "Betty," although she had invited him to do so countless times over the years. He looked over his shoulder at the kids and warned, "Watch this high curb here, Amy, honey. It's kinda steep; be careful you don't stumble."

Touched by his vigilance for his kids, Betty decided he didn't need any further worries about her failing health. "I've been fine, thank you," she lied. "And where's your lovely bride this afternoon?"

"She's studying. She's got a big exam coming up and is worried sick over it. Don't know why, though. She always aces them and has a 4.0 average."

"Good for her." Betty smiled. It was she who had encouraged Cory to go back to school after she observed how all of her children knew their numbers and the alphabet by the age of two. "That girl has a natural gift for teaching," she had told D. W. "We need to help her pursue a career in education."

She was touched by his enthusiasm and commitment to the idea. He immediately went out and got a second job, as a campaign manager for a local politician, so that Cory could afford tuition at the nearby community college.

"What about your own degree?" she asked him at the time. "What are you going to do about that?"

"Aw, Miss Triplett. You of all people ought to know, I've got this love/hate thing about education. Sitting at a desk, in a classroom, listening to some pompous so-and-so pontificate about thus-and-so just isn't my thing. If I could only find a school that'd give me credit for my life experiences, I'd probably have two, maybe even three degrees by now."

She had to concede the point, as she of all people certainly understood his learning difficulties. Yet she couldn't quite give up the fight.

"You'd have so many more career options with a degree," she said, and regretted the comment immediately. She saw his face darken and remembered how sensitive he was about his struggles to provide for his family. Still, he didn't seem to take offense.

"Oh, we're not too bad off as it is. They've made me station manager at the radio, and Councilman Pearce is paying me well to run his election campaign. Plus, I'm starting a little acting troupe over in Corydon at the Hayswood Theater."

She had read something about that in the local paper. As he guided her and his children into the grocery store, she asked, "How is the theater group doing? Are you finding talented players?"

"Uh, not so much, but I am finding a lot of excited people, all volunteers, who really want to be on stage, and dream about making it in the big time. So we're having a lot of fun together."

Betty was struck with the realization that D. W. was actually talking about himself, whether he knew it or not. He had been such a promising talent, with a rare gift for acting, a beautiful singing voice, and movie-star good looks. Starting a career with a degree from IU's respected theater program, he could have been on the fast track to his own success in "the big time." Fate, in the form of Alexandra Singer and the Vietnam War, had intervened and sent him on another journey. That journey had called on him to grow a beard to hide his facial scars, walk with a limp, work several jobs to support his family, and find consolation for his thwarted dreams by coaching a bunch of local amateurs in a small-town repertory company.

It broke Betty's heart to think what might have been for him. She knew that it galled not only her but the entire community, to see his mother now living in comfort, without giving him a hand. She had thought Alexandra was growing in grace when she was a pauper, but now that the woman had some money again, she seemed to have reverted to the same selfish character she had always been. Thinking of her now, Betty felt obligated to ask after her health.

"And your mother, is she well?"

D. W. smiled. "Of course not, but no one enjoys poor health better than Ma. She calls Cory six times a day to complain about some ailment or other. Cory's actually gotten quite good at making all the right sympathetic responses on auto-pilot. I swear that girl's a better actor than I am."

They both laughed, and then Betty had a more serious thought. "Well, what about that? I seem to recall hearing you once did *The Crucible* together, and it's quite a challenging piece. What about getting Cory involved in your theater group? After her studies are through, of course."

D. W. nodded. "Wouldn't that be something? How I'd like to have my own version of the Von Trapp Family Singers. We'd grow our own talent. But Cory has terrible stage fright. I think she'd gladly follow me over a cliff before she'd go behind the footlights again."

Betty poked a gloved finger at his chest. "Well, there's no sense pestering her to do something she finds so uncomfortable. However, I also seem to recall that you can be awfully persuasive at times. Who knows what the future might bring? You might have your little family theater troupe one of these days after all."

D. W. smiled again. "You've always had my number, Miss Triplett, that's for sure."

"And I've always been right, haven't I?" She indulged in a small, smug smile. She had been teasing him, expecting him to laugh, but she was surprised to see his face cloud.

"God, I hope so," he whispered, tears forming in his eyes. "Because you've always been the only person in the world who thought I'd amount to something someday—until Cory, that is. And sometimes I think all my grand ideas scare her a little bit."

He seemed to remember where he was and laughed at himself. "Well, look at me now, getting all maudlin, right here in the doorway of the IGA." Noticing the kids getting into the racks of candy near the checkout line, he called out to them. "All right, you little munchkins, let's get those groceries Mom wanted."

Betty put a light hand on his shoulder to delay him a moment. "You aren't *going* to amount to something someday. You already *are* something, and I'm so very proud of the man you've become."

He beamed the winning smile she'd loved since he was a little boy. "Thanks, Miss Triplett. I couldn't have done it without you."

They stood hugging for several moments, in an open display of affection that was highly uncharacteristic for them, but she didn't care what onlookers might think. She thought about all the children she had taught over the years, all the success stories and the failures. She didn't know why, but somehow this one young soul had grabbed her heart and held it like nobody else could, right from the moment she first laid eyes on him. Looking back over their years together, she realized that maybe he was the child she'd never had, and she began to feel a little maudlin herself. That was all it took for her to come to herself, and end their embrace.

"Now, off with you," she said briskly. "I've kept you long enough."

D. W. herded the kids to his side. "Okay, troops, say 'good day' to Miss Triplett." They each obliged in varying degrees of baby talk, waving little hands and giggling self-consciously.

Betty smiled down at them and waved back. "What lovely manners you have," she said, and watched them smile back at her over their shoulders as they toddled off beside their dad.

She sighed with a contented little smile. "Now, wasn't that nice?"

As she turned to get a grocery cart, she realized that she hadn't felt any arthritis pain the whole time she had been visiting with D. W.

CHAPTER 19

MILESTONES AND MILLSTONES

The Corydon Clarion, June 5, 1980

Local Family Has a Banner Year

By Sally Bromley

T he Singer family of Palmer's Ridge says 1980 has been a banner year for them so far. Residents of the region will recognize the family name from the work of household head, D. W. Singer, whose musical comedy productions have entertained countless playgoers at Corydon's Hayswood Theater for years.

However D. W. is only one of many accomplished family members. His wife and mother of their three children, Corrine Singer, recently graduated magna cum laude from Kentuckiana Teachers' College in Clarksville. Starting this fall, she plans to teach first grade at Saint Mary's Catholic Academy in New Albany, and is very excited at the prospect.

"It's always been my dream to help young people learn more about the world," she says. "I've always done it with my own kids, but now I can reach out and touch even more young minds.

Indeed she has helped her own children learn, for all three are star students, or so say their teachers at Palmer's Ridge Elementary. Ten-year-old Amelia recently won the regional spelling bee for the third year in a row, correctly spelling the word "perspicacious."

Not to be outshone by his older sister, eight-year-old Albert, or "Buddy," recently earned first prize at the Southern Indiana Science Fair for his realistic recreation of an active volcano, complete with flowing red lava.

Finally, youngest daughter, Colleen, just completed first grade, winning both a perfect attendance medal, and a special certificate for outstanding conduct.

"She's just getting started," supportive dad D. W. shared with a wink. "But we're already as proud of her as we are of the others."

Perhaps the Singer family's biggest event this year is yet to happen. The couple recently announced plans to renew their marriage vows at Corydon's Mother of Good Counsel Catholic Church later this summer. In preparation, D. W. is now taking instruction to join the Catholic faith, and will be baptized and confirmed by the time the wedding occurs.

"It's important that families worship together," he says. "Cory's faith is very special to her, and if it's good enough for her, it's good enough for me."

When reached for comment on this story, retired teacher, Betty Triplett, whom Singer calls his mentor, had this to say. "I'm so proud to have been a part of this talented young man's life, and consider our whole community lucky to have him as a cultural leader here."

*   *   *

Alexandra finished reading the article, tore the paper into shreds, and threw the wadded pieces across the room with a howl.

"What can that crazy boy be thinking now? There's *never* been a Catholic in the family, on either side, and I'll be damned if I'm going to let there be one now."

Going to her new Trimline phone hanging on the kitchen wall, she angrily dialed their number and waited for someone to pick up on the other end.

"What the—" she blurted, when a recorded voice answered: "You've reached the Singer family, but we can't come to the phone now. Please leave us a message and we'll return your call as soon as possible."

"What's the world coming to?" she muttered as she slammed the receiver back into its cradle. Obviously, this was a matter that was going to require more direct intervention. She went back to her La-Z-Boy recliner, plopped into it with a pout, put her chin in her hands, and began considering next steps.

I know, she finally decided with a smile. *I'll go to their little ceremony, throw myself on him, and beg him before God and the whole congregation not to shame his ancestors by becoming a papist. That ought to do the trick!*

She relaxed into her recliner, glad to have matters settled.

*   *   *

Across town, Betty Triplett put down the same article and smiled serenely. "How lovely," she murmured, reaching out to finger the leaves of one of the numerous African violets on the windowsill nearby.

The morning sun was beginning to fill the little Florida room where she sat having her coffee. She watched as its golden beams lit the cheerful muslin curtains and floral chintz slipcovers on the wicker chairs. This had always been her favorite place in the world—after the classroom, anyway. Looking about it now, listening to the calming, classical music on radio station WUOL from nearby Louisville, she watched with an almost childlike fascination as the sun turned everything a beautiful, burnished bronze.

All of a sudden, she had the strange thought. *I could die right this moment, and never regret a single thing. I've been a lucky lady and led a very happy life.*

She settled more deeply into the cushion of her chair, and smiled as her cat, Cheerios, jumped onto her lap. He began purring and kneading his claws into her terry cloth robe. Stroking his head and closing her eyes, she decided now would be a very good time to take a nice little nap.

* * *

That was exactly the way D. W. found her the next morning, after worried neighbors called him, concerned because they hadn't seen her out in her garden as usual the day before.

He was surprised when he walked in on her lifeless body to find that he was not more grieved. He had always thought that he would be beside himself when she finally left him; she had been such an important, even essential, part of his life. She was, after all, the only person in his youth who had shown him uncon-ditional love and support, though she had made her agendas for him clear from the start—to measure up to his potential and make good on the gifts God had granted him.

However, seeing her sitting there, looking almost regal, to grieve and keen over her seemed somehow wrong. If nothing else, Betty Triplett had been a great lifelong learner. She had known, he imagined, that her time had come, and was probably eager to see what she could learn from dying, the final adventure.

No, he decided, there was no need for grieving. She had lived one of the richest lives of anyone he'd ever known, and had touched countless other lives, enriching each and every one of them.

There was still one more thing that he needed to do, though, something that he had always wanted to do from the first time he saw her, in her Spartan classroom, all those years ago. Going about the prim little sunroom and drawing all the crisp cotton curtains closed, he came back to her chair and looked down on her with love. Then he kneeled on the floor beside her, and put his head in her lap.

CHAPTER 20

TROUBLE IN PARADISE

Cory dialed D. W.'s beeper number for the sixth time that night, and for the sixth time, got no response.

"Where could he be?" she wondered aloud angrily. Then she glanced anxiously at the sick children in the bed hoping she hadn't awakened any of them with her outburst.

Sure enough, they all seemed to be sleeping soundly, despite the fact that they were still raging with fever and soaking the bedclothes with sweat. She felt each of their foreheads, put cool damp washcloths over them, and tucked the covers around them more snugly.

Please let the fever break tonight, she prayed. Otherwise, she knew, she would have to get them to the hospital first thing in the morning, and they simply couldn't afford a big medical bill right now. *Hell*, she thought ruefully, *we can't afford even a small bill right now.*

Influenza had been especially bad this year, and she felt sure that's what the kids had now. She had seen her classroom decimated by it over the last few weeks, and had even lost a student to it the day before. She had come home that afternoon to find all three of them overcome with nausea and diarrhea. They were lying on the floor in front of the television where D. W. had left them when he went to work at his second job, shortly before her arrival home. They were so weak that she had to lift them each up to get them to the bathroom.

As soon as she got them settled and the worst of the mess cleaned up, she called him at work, furious. "What do you mean, going off and leaving our children so sick on the living room floor? One of them could have died there!"

"I swear to God, babe, they were all fine when I left."

Remembering that flu could come on like this in an instant, she gave him some grace. "Well, all right then," she grumbled. "Only *please*, get home as soon as you can tonight."

"But I can't, babe, remember? I've got that meeting with Tammy Cantrell. She's in French Lick playing the casino lounge and word is she's looking for a local manager to get her more gigs in the Midwest. Her big-time career's on the skids, and she's hungry for work. This could really be the chance we've been waiting for. If I can get in good with her, we might finally begin to make some real money for a change."

Cory strove with all her might to keep from lashing out and saying all the hurtful things she'd been longing to say for some time. There was always a Tammy Cantrell, some "next big thing," some pie-in-the-sky-dream he was working on. It was always "just right around the corner," that dream just about to come true, but not quite here yet.

The only problem was that his plans always involved him being somewhere other than home. Cory tried to count on her hands the times he had been there for dinner with her and the kids over the last several months, and realized that she couldn't fill even one hand.

She knew part of it had to do with him losing Miss Triplett. He had seemed so philosophical and accepting of her death at the time. He even gave the eulogy, and sang the "Our Father" *a capella* at her funeral, leaving the entire assembly in tears. But the changes in his behavior—the staying out late and talking about grandiose plans and schemes—began shortly after her death.

She found him sitting alone in the dark one night, nursing a bourbon and water, and tried to talk with him.

"What is it, hon?" she asked, curling up at his feet, and taking his hand.

"I gotta make something more of myself," he replied in a sad, deflated voice.

"But you're doing so well. We're still not rich by any means, but the money's coming in, the bills are all paid . . . or mostly anyway. We're so much better off than so many other people we know."

"Huh! That's not saying much in this little dump where half the town's on food stamps."

She left him alone that night to sort things out on his own and went to bed. When she awoke in the morning, he'd already left for the radio station. Looking at the empty bourbon bottle on the sink, she wondered how he could possibly do his early morning broadcast as usual without slurring, and turned on the station to see how he sounded.

Somehow, he managed to seem his usual, upbeat public self. It felt to her that the rest of the world got to see a lot more of that persona lately than she and the kids did. Remembering that anxious night, Cory wondered what kind of shape he would be in when he finally arrived home this evening. Would he have stopped for a couple of drinks at the little pub by the radio station, as he often did? Would he come home, already a little buzzed and irritable, as he also often did? Or would he burst in the door, singing loudly and bringing her a bundle of flowers he'd stolen from some neighbor's yard, as he sometimes did? She never knew what to expect from him, and there was nothing she could do. She would have to wait and see.

Then she felt a sudden flash of anger; there was that word again—*wait*. It seemed like the one thing she was always doing when it came to her and D. W.—waiting. But that, she knew after all, was the card she'd drawn when she agreed to commit her life to this complex man—a man she had met when he was as broken as any human being can be.

She had seen him claw his way back to normalcy after horrific wounds, both physical and mental. She'd even seen him become far more than normal, even exceptional. She remembered how brilliantly he'd directed and performed in *The Crucible* on the military base in Japan. He had made them a home, worked several jobs for years to make ends meet, and suffered the neglect of his mother, largely without grumbling. He had even endured his mother causing a scene at their Catholic renewal vows, throwing herself at him as he walked down the aisle, begging him not to become a "papist." Cory realized, remembering all of their history, rather than the last troubling chapter or two, that maybe he hadn't been such a worry after all.

She returned to the bedroom to check the kids' foreheads, and was relieved to find that they seemed a little less hot. After tucking them in again, she went to the tiny kitchen and put on a kettle to make a cup of tea. The pot was coming to a boil when she heard a key in the kitchen door and turned to see him standing in the doorway—no flowers or loud singing, but no smell of alcohol on him either. He eyed her with a guarded look.

"Is it safe to come in?" he quipped.

A half hour ago, she could have killed him for joking at a time like this, but the little epiphany she had just experienced as she reflected on all the ups and downs they had been through together softened her heart. She found herself rushing into his arms instead.

"Oh, D.W.," she sobbed. "I've been so scared. Jimmy Weller in my class died of this thing on Tuesday. And they were so very, very sick when I got home."

"And now?" he asked, his lips caressing the top of her head.

"A . . . a little better, I think. You come see what you think."

Wiping her eyes, she led him by the hand to the master bedroom where the kids lay sleeping. A nightlight illuminated the room with a rosy glow, and together they looked on the three angelic faces. He leaned down and touched each of their foreheads with a kiss, then looked up at her with a big smile.

"A little warm still, but almost normal, if you ask me. I don't think it's flu after all. Maybe some kind of twenty four hour stomach bug instead?"

She began to cry again, but this time with relief. "Oh, thank God," she murmured.

He came to her and put his arms around her once more. "I'm sorry I wasn't here when you needed me, and I know it's happened way too much lately. I'll be better about that, I promise. Just wait, you'll see."

The word "wait" hit her like a slap in the face, and she struggled to repress the urge to snap at him.

"If it's any help, Tammy Cantrell's just signed me to stage all of her shows here at the casino this spring. That'll really help with expenses."

Abandoning her pique, Cory said with joy, "Oh, my God, D. W., that's wonderful!"

They both turned as the kids began to rustle in the bed.

"Daddy, is that you?" Amy asked. D. W. was at her side in an instant, tucking the sheets under her chin.

"Yes, it is sweetie, but you need to lie real still now, okay? You've been real sick."

The girl nodded drowsily and snuggled herself back to sleep. Cory gestured to him to follow her out of the room, and closed the door behind them as they left.

Back in the kitchen, they fell into each other's arms, kissing feverishly. Something about the terrible fear she had felt earlier and the tremendous relief she felt now morphed into an intense erotic attraction for him. He was so big and strong, towering above her as he always did. No matter how frustrated she might be with him at times, she always felt, surely, no *real* harm could ever happen to her, or to any of them, as long as he was there.

She let her trembling hands wander his bearded face and thick body, pressing the hot flesh, smiling a little to herself at the realization that there was a good deal more of it than there had been a few years ago. Finally her roving hands locked around his jutting manhood, now straining the pleats in his pants, and she felt that she had to have him in her, all the way to the hilt, right here, right now.

He sensed her urgency and responded in kind with his own frenzy. Tearing off their clothes between kisses, somehow without breaking their embrace, they wrestled together onto the vinyl-topped table in the center of the little kitchen. She let out a little gasp as the cold plastic met the bare skin of her back, but the heat of his body as he entered her soon warmed her and overcame that small moment of discomfort. Now completely naked, stripped of all their clothes, as well as all pretenses and defenses, they fell into the ages-old rhythm of two people in love, two people needing to join their bodies and souls together, needing comfort, needing safety, needing each other to secure all of these things. When they climaxed, at the same time, as usually happened for them, they had to bite their tongues to stifle their cries of pleasure, for fear of waking the sleeping invalids in the next room. But they couldn't suppress the giggles that ensued afterward, as they realized the ridiculousness of their contortions on the rickety table.

D. W. chuckled into Cory's ear. "With the belly I'm growing, we're lucky I didn't bring the whole house crashing down on us with that pounding."

"Hmmm," she purred back into his ear. "Just more of you to love." She wrapped her arms and legs all the tighter around his body.

He pulled back a bit and looked into her eyes. "Honest?" he asked, and she was troubled by the concern in his face. He was still inside of her, the two of them marinating in each other's body fluids and fragrances, but she understood right away, that he had doubts about her attraction to him.

Taking his face in her hands, she looked back into his worried eyes. "Honest. There's no one for me in the whole wide world but you. And no one like you in the world for me. You're . . . you're one of a kind"

He seemed mollified, but still uncertain, as he nestled deeper into her encircling arms. "It's just that I feel like a stranger in

257

my own body sometimes. First there was losing my looks in Vietnam. Now I feel like I'm losing my body. I can't stand the sight of myself in the mirror most days."

She realized suddenly, perhaps for the first time, that this man whom she loved, who had fathered her three children, who had made her crazy with joy and frustration, was more tender and vulnerable than she had ever perceived him to be. The insight struck her with mixed emotions. Part of her wanted him to be the strong one. She didn't want to have to manage and shelter and protect his sensitivities; she wanted him to do all of that for her. But her stronger nurturing and loving side rushed to his defense, wanting to shield him from any hurt that she could, and restore him to the confident, even cocky self that he usually projected.

Disengaging from him gently, she kissed him long and hard, then led him from the kitchen into the adjoining living room. There she pushed him firmly onto the sagging sofa and knelt between his knees.

Taking his rough hands in hers, she looked into his eyes again. "Now listen, to me, D. W. Singer. You are my husband, my lover, the father of my children, and most of all, my best friend, and no one gets to put down my friends, including you. I love you. I love everything about you. Oh, yeah, sure, no one can make me crazier than you, and oh, my yes, how you can do that better than anyone I ever knew, even Daddy, and that's saying a lot."

She paused as she saw his eyes welling up, and wondered if maybe she'd gone too far, but she decided to press on.

"It would all be so much easier if you weren't so damned intuitive, because, yes, it's true, I haven't been happy with you lately. I've been dissatisfied and discontented, feeling like you're never home anymore and, worse yet, like you're never really here even when you're here. It seems like we're always waiting and hoping, for that next big deal. Meanwhile, bills need to be paid, and lunches need to be made, and laundry needs to be done. Way too many of those times, I look around for you and you're nowhere to be found."

He put a finger to her lips to shush her. "I know, babe, I know, but this deal with Cantrell is going to change all of that. It's a really big contract and it's just in the next county. I can manage all of her appearances, hold her hand through her concerts, and still be home with you and the kids for dinner every night." At her skeptical look, he added, "Well, by bedtime anyway."

For some reason, at that moment, all the heat of her indignation went out of her like a popped balloon. All she wanted in the world was to fall into his arms and spend the night, as well as the rest of her life in their grasp. So that's what she did—fell into his arms and never uttered another word.

How can this be? she wondered, as she nodded off to sleep. *A few hours ago, I hated him. And now I'm totally in love with him again. I must be schizophrenic.*

Six hours later, they both woke to the patter of little feet in the kitchen. "Mama, Daddy," little voices called out. "We're hungry."

D. W. excitedly grabbed Cory's face in his hands. "They're going to be okay." Seeing her quiet, knowing smile in response, he decided she was the most beautiful woman in the world. Together, they got up and made pancakes for the kids.

CHAPTER 21

THE AWFUL TRUTH

January 12, 1990

Jodie Lucas, M. D.
Lucas, Miller & Sims, Neurology Associates
Riverside Medical Towers
1400 Wisteria Way. Suite 314
Arlington, Virginia

Mrs. D. W. Singer
210 Upland Road
Palmer's Ridge, Indiana

Dear Cory:

This is to thank you for your hospitality when I visited there last week. It was a rare treat to be in a strange town for a conference, and still have a delicious home cooked meal. I had wanted to take you and "the old man" out to some elegant restaurant in Louisville, but I'm glad you insisted we eat at your place instead, as we all had a far better meal there than we would have at any restaurant. D. W. has often said that you're a wonderful cook and hostess, and he sure had that right! If it's not top secret, my wife, Jenny, would love to have your recipe for Beef Bourguignonne. It was the best I've ever tasted, and I've been raving to her about it ever since I got home.

Forgive me if I'm being presumptuous here, but I feel like I

*know you well, even though we only met recently, because D. W.
has written me so much about you over the years. So, at the
risk of giving offense, I'm going to take a leap of faith here, and
express some concerns that arose for me during my visit. I'd also
like to ask that you keep this letter to yourself, as I don't want
D. W. to feel like I'm going behind his back. I thought about
saying this directly to him by phone or letter, but felt that you
would have more influence over him. From the worried look
in your eyes several times that evening, as D. W. kept pouring
himself drinks, my guess is you may harbor similar concerns to
the ones I want to express here.*

*Cutting to the chase, I'm troubled by D. W.'s health, both
physical and mental. Even before my visit, I was wondering
if he was okay, because the frequency and the tone of his letters
has changed. He doesn't write as often, and when he does, it's all
very superficial—as if he's hiding something from me.*

*Then, seeing him for the first time in years, my worst fears
were confirmed. He doesn't look well, and the old light in his
eyes is gone. He still jokes as much as ever, but the jokes are
different now. They all have a cynical edge . . . gallows humor,
so to speak. When I was leaving, and he lost his balance and fell
off the porch, you looked terrified. I'm relieved he didn't break
anything, as that was quite a bad fall.*

*I won't presume to know what life is really like for you there
these days. My assumption, though, is that if what I saw in a
single evening was bad, worse things could be happening. I'm no
psychiatrist, but I do know when a person appears to be unwell
and unstable, and that's how D. W. looked to me last week.*

*I'd like to venture a suggestion, and a hope that you'll seriously
consider it. The University of Louisville has an excellent medical*

school that has produced numerous outstanding psychiatrists who practice in the region. I heard several of them speak at the conference I just attended. I wish you'd encourage D. W. to see one of them soon, as well as his primary care physician for a thorough physical. I'm truly worried about him, as I'm sure you are, too—even more so than me. If I can be of any help in this—getting names and numbers and such—please let me know.

I'll close this by repeating my sincere thanks to you for a lovely evening, and expressing my hope that I've not given offense by being so frank. I only go there out of my deep love and respect for your husband, who literally saved my life, in so many different ways. It was D. W. who kept me sane in Vietnam, who backed down the Viet Cong, so that I could be airlifted to medical help, and who later encouraged me to study medicine and specialize in Neurology, after my brain injury in the war. I owe him a debt I can never repay, but I'd like to try to do something in return for him.

Please keep me posted, and, again, don't hesitate to ask if there is anything I can do to help. You will all be in my thoughts and prayers in the time ahead.

With warmest regards,
Jodie

* * *

D. W. stood in front of the imposing Greek Revival façade of the Actors Theater of Louisville. Built during the city's boom in the nineteenth century, the structure had originally been a bank. Now it housed one of the most respected regional theater troupes in the country. Plays that debuted at Actors had won numerous prestigious awards, including Pulitzers and OBIEs. Many had gone on to run on Broadway and been made into movies, television films and radio productions.

As a youth, he had dreamed of a career in "the big time." Once it had seemed that he might even have a chance at it. Then, right or wrong, he had felt he had no other choice but to go into the army, and that had led him down another path. Looking back, he wondered sometimes why he hadn't simply gone out and gotten a job when his mother bankrupted them, but then he remembered he hadn't been thinking very clearly at the time. He had narrowly averted committing suicide, after all, and the dauntless GI Joe dolls on his bedroom shelf had seemed to beckon him to join them in a life of adventure.

Well, some adventure it's been all right, he mused wryly, staring up at the high Ionic columns of the theater. He found them both imposing and intimidating. Anxiously he wondered, *Can I really go through with this thing . . . after all this time?*

Actors was conducting general auditions presently, looking for character players for a variety of productions coming up in the season ahead. The theater was known for encouraging new talent and had a broad outreach that welcomed performers, experienced or not, to try out. Numerous big stars had gotten their start at Actors, and all of them spoke fondly of their time there, citing the valuable training and experience it gave them.

Lately D. W. often felt that his life had ground to a total standstill. He loved Cory and the kids more than life itself, and he had worked like a yeoman to provide for them through the years. However, for some time he had been fighting an old demon, one that he was able normally to hide through his acting skills—depression.

He had lapsed into it in Vietnam right before he'd been wounded, so deeply that he'd felt on the verge of a major breakdown at the time. He still shuddered to remember how awful it felt to imagine seeing things and not be able to speak without stuttering—worse yet, to have others notice these frailties and judge them as weakness. It might be the twentieth century, but most people still didn't have much understanding of mental illness.

Mental illness—the very words made him squirm, particularly when, as time went by, he felt that he may truly have a problem. Recently he had begun hearing things again, and the return of the troubling wartime symptom frightened him. He would be out in the yard, mowing the grass, and hear someone call his name. The voice was familiar, but he couldn't quite place who it was. He would go to the kitchen door and ask Cory if she'd called him. She'd say no and look worried.

"Are you sure you're all right, hon? Maybe you should go get your hearing checked."

He sniffed off the suggestion and reasoned everyone thought they were hearing things now and then—only he didn't believe his own rationalization. He knew something was going on in his head, something wrong, maybe terribly wrong.

He couldn't control his own turbulent thoughts and feelings. Sometimes he felt as though he were going completely insane. He would find himself engaged in deep internal dialogues with old friends, some long dead and gone. He would find himself ruminating on a past insult or slight by someone who didn't even matter to him. He would wake up in the night terrified and shaking, without remembering a specific nightmare that would have induced such a reaction. Worst of all, he felt a constant sense of impending doom, and was endlessly scanning his environment for imminent threats.

All in all, he was miserable, but still couldn't rally the courage to talk to anyone about it, even Cory . . . or perhaps especially Cory, because she of all people would be the most deeply unsettled by his condition. He merely kept trying to hide his symptoms, stuffing the feelings further into the back of his mind; and the more he did, the worse things got.

He found that sometimes the only solace was in drinking, and even that didn't really solve anything; it just eased the pain long enough for him to fall asleep. Sometimes it felt not so much that he was putting himself to sleep by drinking, but knocking himself out with it. The toll on his physical and mental health was mounting.

Like his father, his hair had turned white prematurely, making him look older than he was. He had put on a lot of weight and developed high blood pressure. Now his cheeks became bloated and his eyes red and puffy. He could hardly stand his own face in the mirror, which only exacerbated his depression and sense of living a wasted life.

He may have thought he was successfully hiding things from Cory but he was wrong. One night she cornered him when she found him finishing off a fifth of bourbon in the night.

"D. W. you have got to go see the doctor. You're obviously not well, and you're only making it worse trying to drink it away."

"Okay, okay, babe, I'll call him tomorrow," he slurred, but it was only to placate her. He never made an appointment and he lied when she asked about the doctor's advice. "He says I'm fine. I just need to lose some weight."

He could see the doubt in her eyes, but she let him off the hook nonetheless.

Then an unexpected ray of hope came his way. He stumbled onto a notice in the paper about tryouts at Actors, and a bit of the old audacity he once felt came alive again.

I may be putting on the pounds, but I can still play character parts. I'm a natural for Cat on a Hot Tin Roof *or* The Man Who Came to Dinner.

Soon he found himself standing in front of the theater, trying to rally the nerve to enter it. He wished he hadn't felt the need to resort to taking some false courage by having a nip or two of bourbon on the way there, but he still felt clear headed and was sure that he hadn't drunk enough to affect his audition. Taking a deep breath, he pulled open the massive door of the theater and entered the cavernous lobby.

Once inside, he surveyed the polished marble floors and vaulted ceiling. He felt like Dorothy approaching the Wizard's throne room . . . or more aptly, the Cowardly Lion whose knees buckled on the way there. Still, he was determined to take a shot at this opportunity, and had just enough of his youthful idealism left to make him believe that he might make a go of it. He squared his shoulders and put on a confident face, as he strode to the main auditorium where the auditions were being held.

On arriving there, he began to have second thoughts. The room was filled with people, mainly young, good-looking ones. There were a few older folks, but they were certainly a minority. He suddenly felt very foolish and irrelevant.

He found some comfort in seeing that the director conducting the tryouts was someone he knew. He had once interviewed Tom King on his radio show, and had found King to be a genuinely kind and likable guy.

At least Tom won't laugh in my face if I fall flat, he reflected.

King called the auditions to order, and he and several assistants began polling the group to see what parts they wanted to read, and whether they had their own materials, or were open to improvising. D. W. had brought the script for *A Christmas Carol*, although he knew that he hardly looked the part of the scrawny Scrooge. However, the piece had a poignant resonance for him. Like Scrooge, he was struggling with an unfulfilled life, and found himself compensating, not with money, as Scrooge had, but with overwork and alcohol. Plus, he knew the lines by heart and was certain he couldn't stumble over any of them.

As the auditions began, he watched with envy at the range and depth of the talent present. These were no rank amateurs hoping for a little time in the limelight. No, these were skilled performers, most of them probably alumni of one of the many strong theater schools in the region.

They're good, they're damned good, he thought, as one after the other did stellar readings. The rest of the gathering seemed to think so too, judging from the enthusiastic applause after each of the performers finished.

By the time his turn came, he was a bundle of nerves. Nonetheless, he forced himself to stand tall, thrust out his chin, and strode purposefully to the stage. Remembering another audition from his past, he'd decided to do a montage, reading brief parts from several scenes in the play.

He began with the scene where Scrooge delivers his sour appraisal of Christmas to the two gentlemen who visit him to solicit a donation. King and another assistant read the other parts, and he thought when he looked up that he saw a certain appraising look in the director's eyes. Dare he hope that it was approval?

He went on to the scene where Scrooge is left at boarding school for Christmas until his little sister comes to rescue him. The crowd chuckled a bit as King read the part of the sister, and again D. W. thought that maybe things were going pretty well after all. The whole experience was actually beginning to be fun.

He closed with the only possible choice, the scene where Scrooge vows to change his life. No matter how many times he saw the scene, it never failed to move him to tears. That happened again with today's audition, and he felt that his shedding actual tears during his performance gave it an extra punch.

When he was done, he was pleased to hear what he considered to be a polite round of applause—maybe not as loud or long as some of the other performers had received, but it seemed pretty good to him. He returned to his seat with a mixture of relief and hope, and sat through the remaining auditions, able to enjoy them now that his trial was over.

King closed the auditions by telling the group that his staff would be in touch with them, and thanked everyone for coming. D. W. tried to approach him to thank him in return, and see if he remembered him from their previous meeting, but the man was swarmed by other performers all doing the same thing. Finally he gave up and left the auditorium.

On his way out, he decided to stop in the restroom and take a little celebratory swig from the flask tucked in his coat pocket. He went into a stall, sat down on the commode, and pulled out the flask. Before he could take a sip, he heard the door open and the sounds of two other fellows stepping up to the urinals.

"I think things went pretty well, don't you?" one asked the other.

"Yeah, me too. You did great with that reading from *Rent*. I think you've got a really good chance landing something juicy."

"I don't know. The competition was pretty stiff. I don't think I've ever seen such a strong group of tryouts."

"I agree . . . well, except for that old fart. What the hell was he thinking?"

"I know! At first I thought he was up there as some kind of joke or something, but then he got so worked up, it was obvious he was serious."

"Exactly. What an ego, too. Imagine, getting the chance to audition at Actors and having the gall to do three readings instead of only one. Who does he think he is?"

"And those readings! Have you ever seen such blatant overacting? Can he really imagine he's got talent? Somebody needs to tell him to stay home next time."

The two snickered and went on to other topics. Meanwhile, D. W. crouched in hiding, his body shaking uncontrollably, his face burning with shame, as his whole world collapsed around him.

The men chatted on for a bit as they finished up their business. Then D. W. heard them exit, and he finally let himself go. As the racking sobs took over, he tried to recall if he had ever felt more devastated or cried so hard. This was pure hell, and he saw no way out of it.

Here was the awful truth, delivered like a knife in the heart by the careless words of strangers. If it were a family member or friend, he might be able to talk with them, change their minds, do another audition, and do it better this time.

As it was, he'd been damned in the court of public opinion. There was no negotiating a different outcome. He had to live with the verdict . . . only how? Having devoted his life to performing, one way or another, the prospect of leaving that behind was incomprehensible.

He had to suppress his sobs when the whoosh of the door signaled another man had entered. Thankfully this one was alone, so he wouldn't be opining at the urinal about how bad D. W.'s performance was. He guessed that whoever the guy was, though, he probably thought the same thing.

I bet the whole damn bunch thought the 'old fart' was a joke.

Finally alone again, he found that the effort to stifle his sobs had actually taken the wind out of them a bit, and he was able to take a deep breath at last. He wiped his nose on his sleeve, looked down at the flask in his hand, and considered what to do with it.

Was this the culprit that had sabotaged his audition? Had he been more under the influence than he realized? Was Cory right—that he was developing a serious drinking problem?

He knew that the only honest answer to all of these questions was yes, but everything in him shouted no. This bottle was the only friend he had right now, or at least the only one that could offer him any comfort. Defiantly, he pulled off the cap and emptied the flask in three long gulps. Then he sat, waiting for the merciful haze to take hold.

* * *

It was dark by the time he left the theater. To his further shame, he had actually gotten locked in and had to find a security guard to let him out. At least the world-weary guard took no issue with his explanation about falling asleep in the men's room.

"Believe me, bub, I've seen stranger things in this job."

Back in front of the theater, he realized he was still too buzzed to get behind the wheel of his car. No sense adding to his woes with a driving-while-intoxicated offense. He decided to clear his head by taking a stroll of the newly revitalized area around the theater.

It was late April, and the city was in the midst of its biggest annual event, the Derby Festival, culminating in the running of the Kentucky Derby. As often happened in the region, spring weather could be capricious, and a cold damp breeze filled the air and stung his face. He was glad of it though; the better to sober him up.

He roamed awhile on the Belvedere, a terraced open-air concourse between the 1960s' kitsch towers of the Galt House Hotel and the sweeping, sensuous lines of the Kentucky Center for Performing Arts. At its northernmost edge, the terrace looked out over the expressway and Ohio River, a good hundred feet below. There he paused to look at the view, standing by the statue of General George Rogers Clark, Louisville's founder and co-leader of the Lewis and Clark Expedition.

He turned and looked up at the compelling statue, showing Clark dressed in frontiersman garb and striding boldly forth where no white man had ever gone before. *Now there was a life well-lived*, he mused. The thought only worsened his gloom. "Unlike my own," he said out loud.

He turned back to the river and watched the cold, gray current wash swiftly by, carrying flotsam in its foaming waves. He glanced to the east and saw the Second Street Bridge lit up in preparation for the Derby. Only the weekend before, it had been the site of Thunder Over Louisville, a fireworks display the city boasted was the largest in the nation. He knew the bridge was also a favorite jumping off point for suicidal people.

At that thought, the irony of what he was experiencing suddenly struck him. He looked down at the expressway traffic speeding by below, and out at the dark river currents rushing past.

I'm George Bailey from "It's a Wonderful Life," he realized with a start. *I could just wait for a great big eighteen-wheeler to come along, lift my leg over this ledge here, and drop down right in front of it. And that'd be the end of it.*

Once planted, the idea mushroomed in his mind. He had a little life insurance policy that would take care of Cory and the kids. There would be his veteran's death benefits, including free tuition for the kids to any state university. They also had a mortgage insurance policy that would pay off the house, and the family would be able to live there rent free. He was worth more to them dead than he was alive. Yes . . . the more he thought about, the more sense the idea made to him.

If he did jump, he knew there would be no Clarence the angel to salvage the situation. He also knew there would be no jade-green eyes to implore him to stop this time. Cory seemed literally and figuratively miles away from him these days. He knew the distance was his doing, not hers, but that didn't make any difference. The end result was still the same . . . even she couldn't help him.

He turned and looked all about the Belvedere. There were a number of other people there, some couples walking hand in hand, others kissing on one of the many concrete benches. There was a wino weaving in circles, singing "Happy Birthday to me," at the top of his lungs. There was even a wedding party having their pictures taken by a photographer who kept coaxing, "A little more to the left there, sweetie, and flash us that dazzling smile!"

Everyone seems to be having a grand old life except me right now, he thought, lapsing into abject self-pity. *Hell, why not feel sorry for myself? Nobody else does.*

He looked down again at the expressway, and then turned once more to the crowd behind him. Finally he let out a sigh.

Unless I want to ruin someone's wedding memories for the rest of their lives, I'm not going to be able to do it.

The puzzling question occurred to him, why would that thought stop him, when thinking about Cory and the kids didn't? Then, just by asking himself the question, he realized the truth; he really was mentally ill. Much of his thinking made no sense at all these days. The scornful fellows in the restroom had him pegged. It had been incredibly presumptuous of him to do three readings instead of one today, and he was crazy to have drunk alcohol before such an important audition.

He didn't know what to call his particular brand of mental illness, but a psychotherapist would have said that he had post-traumatic stress disorder. Countless Vietnam vets suffered from it, and most, like him, didn't understand why decades' old traumas could still be affecting their lives so painfully.

All he knew was that he was more miserable and hopeless than he had ever been. Yet he was also so tired and depleted that he didn't have the energy to do anything about it, even killing himself.

He took a deep breath, removed the empty flask from his breast pocket, and gave it another long look. He could go replace it at one of the many liquor stores all over downtown Louisville. Yes, that might be the ticket . . . tie on a really good one and sleep it off in the back seat of his parked car.

Then he remembered the audition earlier that day. Hadn't this "old friend" already caused him enough trouble, not only today, but in his life overall? Like it or not, he knew what he had to do.

"So long, partner," he said, and threw the flask with all of his strength into the river. He saw it hit the water with a splash, and turned to leave.

He didn't feel any better for this one act of good judgment today. In fact, he felt even more depressed, considering the grim possibility of having to face his meaningless life without alcohol, or worse yet, having to seek psychiatric treatment. He found some comfort, though, in making a pact with himself to never subject himself to such humiliation again.

On an impulse, he raised his fist to the sky and bellowed, "As God is my witness, I'll never audition again!"

All activity froze on the Belvedere, followed by an astonished silence, as every pair of eyes there stared at him in shock. He hurried to the exit stairs as fast as he could, before someone really did think him insane and call the police. He may have just had to face the frightening reality that he was crazy, but he still wasn't ready for anyone else to know.

CHAPTER 22

CLIMB EV'RY MOUNTAIN

Nine-year-old Emily Hutchinson stood in front of the Hayswood Theater in Corydon, Indiana, reading and re-reading the call for players to audition for Singer Productions' upcoming performance of *The Sound of Music*. She had seen the movie a hundred times, like every other little girl in her class, and they had even acted out their favorite scenes in their own little backyard productions. But the thought that she might actually earn the chance to perform in a real theater production of it had never crossed her mind. It was too grand a fantasy to ever come true.

Yet here was the notice, posted beneath the glass frames on either side of the ticket booth, calling for young players to audition that evening for the parts of the Von Trapp children; all of the other parts were cast. From her constant viewing of the 1960s' film on her family's worn VCR, she knew by heart every line that every one of the Von Trapp children ever spoke. There was only one problem; Emily had a terrible stutter.

Like many stutterers, hers manifested most when she was nervous, and there was nothing that made her more nervous than the idea of auditioning in front of a crowd of strangers. However, today something deep within her, something she didn't quite understand, drove her to walk to the theater and stand before it, reading all the posters and *dream* . . . dream of being a great actress, or at least, of getting up on stage and playing a part successfully. God knew she hadn't had much success of any other sort, in her short life.

Born the youngest child, and worse yet, a female, in a male-dominated family, she had been indoctrinated from her earliest years in the belief that women couldn't do much of anything important . . . not hunt, or fish, or farm. They were best relegated to the household, the domain where they could do what little good they were capable of—cooking, cleaning, and washing laundry for their men.

She could look at her middle-aged mother and see the toll this life had taken on her. The woman was old before her time and clearly beaten down to submission by her chauvinistic husband and sons. She wore a faded old housecoat, tied up her graying hair in an unflattering ponytail, and shuffled about their unpainted clapboard farmhouse in a worn flannel housecoat, from dawn to dusk, seldom venturing from her little world, which grew smaller every day.

Every now and then, though, Emily would catch her mother looking at a sunrise, or sunset or a brilliant flower growing somewhere in the tangled yard about their dilapidated house. At these times, a look of such rapt appreciation, even awe, filled her mother's face, that Emily knew the beaten-down woman was in the midst of a powerful spiritual experience, and she would look at her with a special tenderness.

I'll never let them do that to me, she swore to herself. *They may have gotten to her, but they won't do that to me.*

In that spirit of resistance, she was standing in front of the theater, reading all of the posters and considering going into the lobby to sign up for auditions. However, the longer she thought about it, the more she trembled at the prospect of following through on the idea.

She had about decided it was time to admit defeat and turned to go home, when a bearded, burly, white-haired man came out of the theater and began scanning the sidewalk. A small, pretty woman hurried to keep up with him.

"I can't believe it," he began to bluster. "Where is everybody? I thought sure we'd have dozens of kids lining up by now."

"Come on, D. W.," the woman said in a soothing voice. "It's early still. They're probably all at home having supper. I told you that six thirty wasn't a very good time to get kids out of the house on a weeknight."

"It's the only time I had," he said, his voice rising even louder and his face beginning to turn red.

"Hon, please," she said, putting a hand on his arm. "Remember your blood pressure. It's not good for you to get so worked up."

Emily decided maybe she'd better make herself scarce, and began to inch backward toward the nearby alleyway. As she did, her movement attracted the man's attention, and he turned to her.

"Well, at least there's one here, anyway. What's your name, young lady?"

Despite her heart thumping in her chest, she was able to squeak without stuttering, "Emily, sir." Most words starting with vowel sounds weren't too hard for her, but she dreaded his predictable next question.

"Your last name, please?"

Beginning to blush, she struggled to get out the hated H sound. "It's uh . . . it's uh . . . Hu . . . Hut . . . Hutchinson, sir."

The man looked at his wife and muttered under his breath. "Oh, please, God, no. Not this. Help me out here, Cory."

The little woman looked angrily at him, but turned and smiled sweetly at Emily. "Are you Sarah Hutchinson's daughter? And Darryl, Seth, and Tom's little sister?" Emily nodded shyly, and the woman walked up to her and took her hand.

"I'm so glad to know you," she said warmly. "I'm Cory Singer, and I taught all of your big brothers. My, what a handful they were. Your mother was such a big help, though, always volunteering to be there for field trips and parties and such. I haven't seen her since Tom graduated. How is she doing?"

"She . . . she . . . she's fine," Emily replied, knowing she was lying, but also knowing this was not the time or place to do anything else.

"I'm so glad," Cory said. She seemed to feel her husband's impatience mounting at these pleasantries, and turned to him with a wry smile. "So, D. W., what parts do you think Emily should audition for tonight?"

Emily watched the subtle, but nonetheless obvious communication between them. She was used to it. She had watched people struggle with how to respond to her speech impediment for years, and had grown adept at reading covert messages in people's eyes and body language. She knew the man was trying to figure out how to tell her there was no way he was going to let her audition for his play; also, that the woman wasn't going to let him get away with handling this situation in such a dishonorable manner.

To her surprise, the man suddenly turned to her and gave her a long, hard stare, looking as if he had just remembered something important. He came to her, and knelt down on one knee, groaning softly as he did.

"Emily, have you ever heard of a country music singer named Mel Tillis?"

"No, no sir, I ha . . . ha . . . haven't," she confessed.

"Well, no matter," he said, waving his hand. "It's only that, well, you and he have a lot in common. Tell me, do you sing?"

She nodded eagerly, smiling.

"Then give me a few bars of your favorite song from the play we're doing."

She saw the kind glimmer in his eyes, and without hesitation, launched into the opening bars of "Climb Ev'ry Mountain," singing every note to perfection and never stammering once. The clear, sweet voice rang out across the square and several passersby stopped to listen appreciatively.

As he listened, the man smiled up at his wife and she gave him a big smile in return. When she was through, Emily was relieved that he put a hand on her shoulder, and gave her an approving nod.

"That was beautiful, absolutely beautiful. Now, can you try something else for me, please? I want you to tell me your name again, your whole name, but this time, pretend you're singing while you say it."

Baffled, but still wanting to do whatever she could to please this strange man, she complied, imagining she was singing her name. "Emily Hutchinson," she said, and it came out flawlessly. As she realized what had just happened, she laughed out loud. "It's Emily Hutchinson! Emily Hutchinson!" She shouted it, over and over again, until people turned to look.

The man rose stiffly and turned to his wife. "Cory, I think we've cast the first of the Von Trapp children, and auditions haven't even started yet. I think Emily would make a wonderful Brigitta, don't you?"

The little woman just nodded and beamed up at him. Then, as

if on cue, other children began appearing, jostling and giggling and poking one another. The woman cocked her head at her husband and raised an eyebrow. "I think you've finally gotten your wish . . . lots and lots of children, all wanting to 'act out' for you. Oh, and by the way, did I mention that I need to be getting home to make dinner for our own children? You have fun here tonight."

As she started down the sidewalk, he came running behind her like a puppy.

"Aw, come on now, babe, you're not really going to leave me alone with this crowd, are you? They'll eat me alive! Come on. Stay till we get rolling, maybe fifteen minutes, half an hour?"

Emily watched them as they worked their way down the street. The woman was shrugging her shoulders and insisting she was going home; he was bargaining and pleading. Though she had only now met them, she had the feeling that they engaged in this banter all the time.

The growing crowd of rowdy children did indeed seem to Emily to call for some adult handling. She was glad to see the woman throw up her hands, laugh a captivating bell-like laugh, and agree to come back to help with the night's proceedings. For some reason, Emily felt the need to crow, and made an announcement to the crowd, employing her new strategy of pretending to sing as she spoke.

"For your information, the role of Brigitta has already been cast." It came out in a faultless, flowing voice.

The man and woman were back in the midst of the children. With just a few soft, authoritative words, the woman had the group in a line and heading into the theater. As Emily followed the last of them through the door, she saw the woman look at her husband and heard her say, "You owe me big time for this, D. W. Singer."

Emily tagged along behind them, curious to know more about this unusual couple, one where both the woman and the man seemed to share equal, though different powers. She had never seen anything like it before. Little could she know then that her time with them in the weeks to come would begin a whole new chapter in her life.

CHAPTER 23

MURPHY'S LAW

D. W. sat at his usual director's station in the last row of the theater, watching his cast plod through their dress rehearsal. The show was due to open this weekend, and the house was already sold out for the first night, but D. W. wasn't excited about that.

As expected, since everything that could go wrong had gone wrong with this production, his players were doing a perfectly miserable job tonight. Because it was a dress rehearsal, he was duty bound not to say a word or intervene in any way. He had to sit through the whole performance, listening to every miscue and off-key note in silence.

The effort was taking a considerable toll on him. His stomach burned, despite the two and a half rolls of Tums he had chewed since the rehearsal started. He also knew, from the way his face tingled, that his blood pressure must be going through the roof. Then, too, there was that newest and most perplexing of symptoms, one that had appeared only recently . . . a sharp pain shooting down the inside of his left arm from the shoulder to the wrist. It had come on him a couple of times recently, and then mercifully passed after a few minutes. He didn't know what it meant, but it scared him more than he liked to admit. He had no intention of sharing that information with anyone, not even Cory.

Almost as if his thinking about Cory magically produced her, she slipped into the next seat and reached out to squeeze his right hand.

"Isn't there some old saying about how bad dress rehearsals mean great opening nights?" she whispered, trying to sound bright and cheerful. It was hard for her, because she, too, could see that the performance onstage was clearly sub-par.

"Yes, there is," he whispered back in a dejected voice. "But I don't think that's going to save us. This is absolutely the worst thing I've ever produced. I'm thinking about pulling the plug on the whole production."

Cory looked at him, saw that he was serious, and felt a prickle of alarm. He had never talked about scuttling a performance before. In fact, "the show must go on," had always been his mantra. Somehow they always did, and somehow they always succeeded. He had gotten countless rave reviews in the local newspapers, and occasionally, even some honorable mentions in Louisville's award-winning paper, *The Courier-Journal*. He must be having very grave doubts indeed about this production to consider cancelling it. Determined to pull him out of his funk, she squeezed his hand again.

"Oh, it can't be all that bad," she said in sotto voice, but just then, she heard the girl playing the oldest Von Trapp child, Liesl, butcher a lyric and sing totally off-key. *Oh my God*, she thought, *it really is all that bad.*

She glanced again at D. W. and watched him wince at this latest misstep. "How can we go on tomorrow night with this kind of performance?" he muttered into the hand covering his face. "I'll be the laughingstock of the whole region. No one will ever come to see anything else I produce."

Cory struggled with how to respond. She knew very well, having spent more than twenty years with this man that sometimes she needed to let him have his say, no matter how melodramatic he might sound. Usually, if not always, once he had vented his spleen, he came back to the problem at hand, ready to tackle it again. Generally, he was able to solve it in the end.

However, as she continued to hear the dropped lines and sour notes issuing forth from the stage, even she began to despair. Then a thought came to her, as she remembered the task that had brought her here in the first place. Pulling out the contents of the brown paper bag she had brought with her, she waved them at him.

"What's that?" he asked in a disinterested monotone.

"The programs I put together for you," she said, managing to sound excited. "I just picked them up at the printers, and they're wonderful, D. W., truly wonderful. Look."

She handed him one, and when he stared at it without opening it, she took it back from him and began reading to him. "The role of Gretl is played by six-year-old Nancy Smart, a first-grade student at Salem Elementary School. Nancy's mother tells us that *The Sound of Music* is her favorite movie and she is so excited to be performing in the play. While this is her first experience on stage, Nancy says she hopes it won't be her last. "I want to become a great actress when I grow up.""

D. W. grunted and continued sighing into his hand. Undeterred, Cory read on: "The role of Max Detweiler is played by sixty-two-year-old Wilbur Strong, owner of Corydon's only hardware store. 'I haven't been on a stage since my senior year high school play,' Wilbur says. 'But this has been the most fun I've had in years. I can't wait to hear what Singer Productions will be doing next. I plan to try out for anything and everything an old man like me can play.'"

"Oh, that'll be great," D. W. groaned. "He was the last cast member to learn his lines and he's still flubbing them."

Cory pretended not to hear him, and went on reading the players' bios to him. One after another described how proud and excited they were to be performing in the production, and most gave D. W. accolades for his direction.

"Corydon High senior, Gilbert Strong, (yes, Wilbur's grandson) plays Rolfe in the production, and he says the experience has really changed him for the good. 'I never liked history so I didn't know much about the Nazis until I got this part. Playing Rolfe has helped me understand how even good young people can be swayed by bad influences. I thank Mr. Singer for pointing out stuff like that to us while we were learning our roles."

Cory was pleased to see D. W. seemed to soften a bit hearing that one. "He confided to me he's been experimenting with drugs lately. So maybe some good might come out of this debacle after all." He chuckled grimly, dashing her hope that she was getting through to him. "Now I'm a social worker. Good thing, too. I'm going to need a new job because I'm a flop at this one."

The final rendition of "Climb Ev'ry Mountain" was beginning, signaling the end of the rehearsal, and Cory had to admit that she was relieved. Another minute of this torture and she was afraid D. W. might run out of the theater screaming. The little stage was too small for elaborate sets like a mountainside for the Von Trapp family to climb their way out of Austria, so the actors climbed up the aisles of the theater instead. As they reached the last row and passed them, Cory was touched to see their happy faces. They may have butchered one of her favorite musicals, and driven her husband into a major funk, but they had obviously had the time of their lives. Every single one of them wore a radiant smile.

As they exited into the lobby, D. W. stood up and called out, "That's a wrap. Everybody back on stage, please!"

Cory reached out to give him one last, gentle pat on the wrist as he exited the row. She was startled to see him wince at her touch, flexing his left hand several times in response.

"What's the matter with your hand?"

"Oh, that, it's nothing. I must've strained it lifting sets or something." And he was off to deal with his players, who were all shuffling back on to the stage now to hear his critique.

Cory wasn't convinced, and decided to stick around awhile. She didn't know what was wrong, but she knew that D. W. definitely wasn't himself. As she watched him trudging down the aisle to the stage, she became even more concerned.

He seemed to be almost dragging himself along, as if he barely had the energy to make it down the small incline. He was also doing that odd hand-flexing thing again, over and over, as though he were trying to restore feeling to a numbed limb. She watched as he reached the front row and stood holding the back of the aisle seat for support.

She knew then that something was terribly wrong. He paused for a long moment before beginning to speak, and when he did open his mouth, he began to stammer.

"Well, that . . . well, that . . . was really . . . something," he said through labored breaths.

Cory rose and gripped the back of a chair for support herself, her hand at her throat, as a wave of panic swept over her. D. W. seemed to sense her movement, for he turned and gave her a long, piercing gaze. Cory wasn't quite sure what she saw on his face, but it looked like fear one moment, followed by love the next.

Still struggling to speak, he looked down at his left arm, now lying limp at his side, and then up at her again, squeezing out a tight smile.

"Well, isn't this . . . isn't this . . . one hell of a thing?" he said, and with that he collapsed.

CHAPTER 24

COMING IN FOR A
FINAL LANDING

D. W. didn't quite know where he was, and it didn't help matters that the setting kept changing. It bounced back and forth between some foggy, airborne, extraterrestrial domain, and a dark, heavy, earthbound landscape filled with disembodied voices and whirring, whooshing mechanical noises. No, he didn't know where he was, but he did find some comfort in knowing that he had been here before—that he had been to both places, actually, the otherworldly one, and the worldly one. Both were vaguely familiar to him and somehow strangely reassuring.

Then there was that other comforting, familiar feature of this middle-ground, nowhere-land where he found himself . . . those jade-green eyes. Every time he came to, they were looking down on him with love and concern. He couldn't make out the face around them; all he could see were the brilliant green orbs surrounded with thick auburn lashes. The eyes burned with an intense, almost manic energy, willing him back to health, refusing to let him go, driving the Reaper away. No, he couldn't see her face, but he knew who it was all the same . . . his Cory.

Other familiar faces gave him hope and reassurance, as well. Miss Triplett came to him frequently; it seemed, in fact, that

291

she was there almost constantly. Toby Schumann checked in frequently, telling him, "We've made it through worse times. We'll make it through this one too." Then there were the guys from his platoon, the ones who had perished in the firefight where he almost lost his legs in Vietnam. They were giving him a hard time, as usual, teasing him about "milking this thing to the hilt for sympathy." One of them even came to him one night, placed a mangled hand on his shoulder and said, "Not your time, yet, buddy, but we'll see you over here someday."

He came to one morning with a degree of consciousness and clarity that he hadn't experienced for days. He looked about him, saw the small, cluttered hospital room, and took in the various monitors and drips around his bed. There were tubes jutting from every limb of his body, it seemed, and despite the fact that he could see one of them was for a morphine drip, he felt an excruciating pain in his sternum. He didn't yet know that they had sawed his chest apart for open-heart surgery.

His eyes landed on the tiny figure curled up in a chair by his bed, Cory, fast asleep. He wanted to reach out and stroke her head, but when he tried to, he found that the tubes in his arms kept him from reaching her. So he lay there and watched her sleeping instead, thinking how incredibly beautiful and precious she was.

They were both in their early forties now, and he, especially, felt a little worse for wear. Looking down at his body, he saw how badly he had ballooned up, to a weight and size he would never have imagined possible when he was a slim, muscular kid. However, gazing over at Cory with love, he saw that she still seemed very much the smart, saucy gamin who had captured his eye, and soon afterward his heart, back when he was convalescing that other time, in the hospital at Camp Zama.

She seemed to feel his eyes on her, for soon after he tried to reach out for her, she awakened with a start and gave him an anxious look. She had probably been doing this for some time, he realized. She jumped up and came to his side.

"You're awake!" she cried.

"Well, uh, I think so anyway." He smiled back at her. "Not too sure of much of anything right now. I'm still pretty foggy."

She leaned over and kissed him. "D. W. Singer, as soon as I get you home, I'm going to kill you!"

He smiled. "Well, that's some bedside manner you have, young lady. Here I am, clinging to life by a thread, and you're planning to kill me as soon as I get home. Might as well go on, save you the trouble, and kick the bucket now."

A panicked look came into her eyes. "Don't even joke about such a thing. I'll make sure you go straight to hell if you do, leaving me and the kids alone like that."

They sat together for a few moments in silence. Despite enjoying engaging in this familiar verbal sparring with his wife and best friend, D. W. found that even the lightest conversation taxed his strength.

"I've been very sick, haven't I?" he asked.

She met his inquiring gaze with sober eyes. "We almost lost you several times. The cardiologist says it's a miracle you're alive at all, that you've been like a ticking time bomb for months, and that you must have been having warning signs all along the way. How could you have kept that to yourself, D. W.? Why couldn't you have shared it with me, so that we could get you some help?"

He tried to sidestep her. "Rugged individualism?" he joked, but she was having none of his attempts at humor.

"This isn't funny, D. W.," she said angrily. "You almost died, right there in front of me and a bunch of impressionable kids. Thank God Wilbur Strong knew CPR. The ambulance took forever, and if he hadn't kept your heart ticking until it came, I know you'd be gone now. I could see that you felt unwell the last little while, hon, but how could you keep how bad it was to yourself?"

"I don't know. I honestly don't know. One part was me not wanting to worry you. One part was male pride. Another part was just being damn scared and not wanting to admit what was happening to me . . . getting old and fat and infirm. What a comedown, after all."

She took his face in her hands. "Have I ever made you feel like that?"

"No, not you, babe. I know I do it to myself. But no matter where it comes from, there it is, and it isn't any fun, I can tell you that."

He lay back for a while, gathering his strength and drawing deep breaths. Then, he got the strength to talk a bit more.

"I guess the one bright side to this whole crazy thing is that it gave us the perfect reason to cancel that horrible play. What better excuse than 'the director is dying,' huh?"

Cory looked at him with a twinkle in her eyes. "I forgot. You couldn't have known. No, we didn't cancel the play. In fact, the play opened as scheduled, and it was a huge success."

He looked at her as if she had grown horns. "No way!"

"Yes, indeed," she replied. She turned and sorted through the items on his bedside table, and came up with what she was looking for, a crumpled section of newsprint.

"From the *Courier-Journal*, no less," she said, handing it to him with a proud smile.

He took it from her, nonplussed, not believing what he held in his hands. But there it was, the headline staring back at him: "Regional Theater Hits New Heights in Southern Indiana."

He stared at her, still unable to assimilate it. Finally, he blinked several times, brought the newsprint closer to his eyes and began to read:

> *Everyone in these parts is proud of the many small, community theater troupes that grace our region, but every now and then, one of them does such an outstanding job that it rises above the local norms. That's just the case with Singer Productions' Sound of Music, currently playing at the Hayswood Theater in Corydon, Indiana.*
>
> *The production is all the more remarkable because it is staged with an entirely amateur cast, most of them school children. What's more, it opened without its director and producer, D. W. Singer, who recently suffered a massive coronary, and still lies near death at the Veterans' Administration Hospital in Louisville.*

D. W. looked up at Cory. "Should I be given last rites?" he asked, tongue firmly in cheek.

"You've already had them," she replied with a grave face, and he shuddered, all attempts at humor gone. He went back to his reading.

> *Singer's eldest daughter, twenty-year-old Amy Singer, stood in for him on opening night, and what a marvelous job she and the whole troupe did.*
>
> *Cast member Wilbur Strong says he speaks for the whole*

ensemble: "We just couldn't let Mr. Singer down, not after he'd worked so hard to make all of us look good, and not with him being so sick and all. He always told us 'the show must go on,' and so that's what we did."

Indeed they did, and what a show. This critic has rarely seen a totally amateur production come off with such aplomb. Down to the youngest, most inexperienced player, everyone knew their lines to perfection, and delivered their musical numbers like true professionals.

Singer Productions' Sound of Music will be playing for the next two weekends, with matinees on Saturday and Sunday afternoons, and evening performances on Friday and Saturday nights, at Corydon's Hayswood Theater. But good luck getting tickets. Performances are sold out for the play's entire run.

D. W. let the paper drop from his hands, and sat staring at it for several moments. "It isn't possible. That was the worst dress rehearsal I've ever seen. It just isn't possible."

"I know," Cory agreed. "I know. But somehow they did it, somehow they pulled it off. I think maybe it was seeing you collapse right in front of them like you did. I think maybe it inspired them to make things better for you somehow. Oh, who cares how they did it? They just did! And you'd never believe how proud and pleased with themselves they all are."

"The little buggers," D. W. said with a chuckle. "I only wish they could have let me see some of all that magnificence while I was there directing them."

He found himself totally spent, and closed his eyes, lapsing soon into a deep sleep. He lay there for a long time, Cory still holding his hand, perched on the edge of his bed. Eventually she disengaged her hand from his and planted a gentle kiss on his lips.

"Got to go home and check on the kids, but I'll see you again in a bit," she whispered, exiting with a reluctant backward glance.

Alone and deeply asleep, he found that powerful dream images began coming to him. One after the other, they rolled forth in a rich, verdant tapestry, unreeling like a movie inside his closed eyes.

He saw a crowd of strangely hostile mourners, gazing at him over his father's grave, challenging him for challenging them.

He saw Breanna, playing Emily in their senior class production of *Our Town* so movingly that there wasn't a dry eye in the house when she was done.

He saw himself, hanging from the third floor banister of his father's house in Palmer's Ridge, contemplating jumping and impaling himself on the statue of Venus in the first-floor foyer below.

He saw Toby at the camp where he had been a counselor as a teen, and saw the boy go under the water when his canoe sank. Three big, blond boys jumped in, struggled to bring the boy to the surface, and pulled him back to the shore, where they pleaded for D. W. to revive him.

He saw men in uniform, his friends, falling all around him, ripped to pieces by a barrage of heavy artillery. He saw Jodie, his best male friend in Nam, writhing in pain on the ground, his brains oozing from a horrible hole in his skull, and wished he could somehow magically patch him up.

He saw Cory and their kids, in a thousand poses and situations—Easter egg hunts, Christmas pageants, and quiet Sunday mornings, nestled among the bedclothes, laughing and hugging and tickling each other.

More often, he saw Cory alone, gazing out their kitchen window at her flowerbeds, or a summer rain, with a special contented look in her eye, and he envied her that serenity.

Finally, he saw himself, tightrope walking among the limbs of a huge tree above his schoolyard, back in the far-smaller Palmer's Ridge of his childhood. The kids on the playground below were egging him on, some teasing and catcalling and telling him to come back down to the ground, others clapping and praising him and telling him what a wonderful, brave boy he was. Once again, exactly as he had then, he felt that their applause was the sweetest sound he had ever heard.

GOOD NIGHT, SWEETHEART, GOODNIGHT...

It was eleven p.m. and way past visiting hours, but Cory hurried down the darkened hospital hallway anyway. She knew from experience that the ICU nursing staff would let her in to see D. W., in spite of the late hour. She was his wife, after all.

It had been a long and difficult day for her. She had just returned to work, but her principal had given her grief about taking off so much time to be with D. W. Her cheeks still stung with indignation at the thought of it. This was a Catholic school, wasn't it? A school that was supposed to be dedicated to family values and Christian principles? So why was she being hassled for missing work for a few days when her husband had nearly died? She vowed to explore jobs in the public school system as soon as the current crisis cleared, and she had the time to look into other options.

She couldn't wait to see him again, even though it had been only a few hours since her last visit. He was doing well, the staff all told her, but somehow, she couldn't quite believe them. He had looked so awful, only days ago, collapsing at the theater, then gray-faced and drawn in the week after that. She had to check on his condition herself, as often as possible, in between her parenting and teaching duties.

She was almost at the doors of the intensive care unit, when something in the waiting room caught her attention. A solitary sleeping figure lay supine in a corner lounge chair, before a muted television playing footage of a developing hostage crisis somewhere. She stopped and approached the figure, and was startled by what she found.

It was Alexandra Singer, sound asleep and dead to the world. Cory was puzzled at first to find her there, but then it came to her. The strange conflicted woman with the strange conflicted relationship with her son was trying again to figure out some way to be mother to him. This was the only way that she knew how, by being present, albeit asleep, in front of a silent TV in an empty hospital waiting room. The more Cory thought about it, the more sense it made. What a wonderful metaphor it was, actually, for their bizarre relationship.

If Alexandra had been awake, Cory realized, she would be saying and doing all kinds of irritating things, questioning the doctors, dictating orders to the nurses, and generally making herself a total nuisance. But here she was, looking almost sweet in her slumber. She seemed the perfect picture of maternal love and devotion. At the same time, some old saying about letting sleeping dogs lie came to Cory's mind. Better, she decided, to let the old woman lay there looking uncharacteristically benign for the time being. Who knew what havoc she might create if anyone awakened her. Leaning down and giving her mother-in-law a swift peck on the forehead, Cory wished her a silent good night, and rushed into the ICU to check on her husband's condition.

Arriving at his bedside, she was pleased to see that he was awake and, more than that, happy to see her. She hoped that his eager smile meant his recent depression was lifting.

"I'm so glad you came back. I've been trying to stay awake, hoping you would."

She didn't say anything, but came to his side. She sat down in the chair by his bed, took his thick hand, and put it to her cheek. They sat there together for the longest time, watching the heart monitor by his bed, and smiling now and then, as they listened to the strong, steady beeps it made.

Finally Cory felt she needed to tell him. "Your mother is out in the waiting room . . . sound asleep, but there, nonetheless. It looks to me like she's probably been there all evening."

She saw again the familiar little crease between his eyebrows. She saw too his internal struggle as he tried to figure out how to respond to this news. Then, she was pleased to see, his face eventually cleared.

Drawing a long breath, he looked into her eyes. "Why don't you go wake her and tell her I'd like to see her?"

THE END

ABOUT THE AUTHOR

Fred Schloemer, Ed.D., LCSW is a career psychotherapist, educator, and award-winning author. He has published widely in professional journals and newspapers. His books include *Just One More Bird*, a self-help book for small children of alcoholics, and *From a Land in Between: Prose and Poem Tales of Alternative Lives*, an anthology dealing with sexual diversity. His last book, *Parenting Adult Children: Real Stories of Families Turning Challenges into Successes*, won the 2012 Nautilus Book Award Silver Certificate, a national honor given to books that promote positive social change. His first love, however, has always been fiction writing, and he returns to that venue here, in a fictional story inspired by real-life characters. He now lives in semi-retirement with his life partner, Ernie Schnell, on their small horse farm in southern Indiana. For more information, visit his website at www.schloemerservices.com, or write him at fredschloemer63@gmail.com.

Made in the USA
Charleston, SC
19 October 2014